Penguin Books
Summer Moonshine

D0036884

P. G. Wodehouse was born in Guildford in 1881 and
educated at Dulwich College. After working for the Hong
Kong and Shanghai Bank for two years, he left to earn his
living as a journalist and storywriter, writing the 'By the Way'
column in the old *Globe*. He also contributed a series of
school stories to a magazine for boys, the *Captain*, in one of
which Psmith made his first appearance. Going to America
before the First World War, he sold a serial to the *Saturday
Evening Post* and for the next twenty-five years almost all his
books appeared first in this magazine. He was part author
and writer of the lyrics of eighteen musical comedies
including *Kissing Time*; he married in 1914 and in 1955 took
American citizenship. He wrote over ninety books and his
work has won world-wide acclaim, being translated into many
languages. *The Times* hailed him as 'a comic genius
recognized in his lifetime as a classic and an old master of
farce.'

P. G. Wodehouse said 'I believe there are two ways of writing
novels. One is mine, making a sort of musical comedy
without music and ignoring real life altogether; the other is
going right deep down into life and not caring a damn . . .'
He was created a Knight of the British Empire in the New
Year's Honours List in 1975. In a BBC interview he said that
he had no ambitions left, now that he had been knighted and
there was a waxwork of him in Madame Tussaud's. He died on
St Valentine's Day in 1975 at the age of ninety-three.

P. G. Wodehouse

Summer Moonshine

Penguin Books

Penguin Books Ltd, Harmondsworth, Middlesex, England
Viking Penguin Inc., 40 West 23rd Street, New York, New York 10010, U.S.A.
Penguin Books Australia Ltd, Ringwood, Victoria, Australia
Penguin Books Canada Limited, 2801 John Street, Markham, Ontario, Canada L3R 1B4
Penguin Books (N.Z.) Ltd, 182–190 Wairau Road, Auckland 10, New Zealand

First published in the U.S.A. 1937
Published in Great Britain by Herbert Jenkins 1938
Published in Penguin Books 1966
Reprinted 1972, 1976, 1979, 1983, 1986

Printed and bound in Great Britain by
Cox & Wyman Ltd, Reading
Set in Linotype Times

1

It was a glorious morning of blue and gold, of fleecy clouds and insects droning in the sunshine. What the weather-bulletin announcer of the British Broadcasting Corporation, who can turn a phrase as well as the next man, had called the ridge of high pressure extending over the greater part of the United Kingdom south of the Shetland Isles still functioned unabated. Rabbits frisked in the hedgerows. Cows mused in the meadows. Water voles sported along the river-banks. And moving a step higher in the animal kingdom, the paying guests at Sir Buckstone Abbott's country seat, Walsingford Hall in the county of Berkshire, were all up and about, taking the air and enjoying themselves according to their various tastes and dispositions.

Mr Chinnery was playing croquet with Mrs Folsom. Colonel Tanner was telling Mr Waugh-Bonner about life in Poona, fortunate that he had started talking first and thus prevented Mr Waugh-Bonner telling him about life in the Malay States. Mrs Shepley was knitting a sock. Mr Profitt, whose backhand game needed polishing, was practising drives against a wall. Mr Billing was having a sun bath. And the stout young American, Tubby Vanringham, a towel about his neck, was crossing the terrace on his way down to the river.

Prudence Whittaker, Sir Buckstone's invaluable secretary, came out of the house, tall and slender and elegant. Directing an austere look at Tubby's receding back, she spoke in a cold crisp voice which sounded in the drowsy stillness like ice tinkling in a pitcher:

'Mistah Vanringham.'

The stout young man turned. He stopped, looked and stiffened, frigidly raising his eyebrows in a manner that indicated surprise and displeasure. After what had occurred a week ago, he had supposed that it was clearly understood between this girl and himself that they were no longer on speaking terms.

'Well?' he said distantly.

'Might I ask if you are going to bathe?'

'I am.'

'From the houseboat?'

'Yup. From the 'ouseboat.'

Miss Whittaker's nose quivered for a brief instant. Surprisingly, considering the classical regularity of the features in which it was set, it was a tiptilted, almost a perky nose. But her voice remained cold and level.

'I did not say "'ouseboat".'

'Yes, you did.'

'I did nothing of the kind. I would no more dream of saying "'ouseboat" than I would of employing a vulgarism like "Yup" when I meant "Yes," or saying "mustash" when I meant "moustarsh," or "tomayto" when I meant "tomarto," or –'

'Oh, all right, all right. What about it, anyway?'

'I merely wished to inform you – '

'I suppose,' said Tubby, with sudden *esprit de l'escalier* – the thrust was one which should have been delivered a week earlier – 'that when you go out to lunch with that boy friend who sends you jewellery, you say, "Oh, Percy, will you pass the potartoes!"'

Miss Whittaker's delicately modelled lips tightened, but she neither affirmed nor denied the charge.

'I merely wished to inform you that you cannot bathe from the houseboat.'

'Oh, no? Why not?'

'Because it is occupied. It has been let for the remainder of the summer.'

It had been Tubby Vanringham's intention to preserve throughout this distasteful scene an aloof hauteur, but this bit of bad news shook him from his proud detachment. The houseboat which lay moored at the foot of Sir Buckstone's water meadows was the only place for miles around where you could swim in the nude, and about the only place, unless you walked to the old bridge outside Walsingford Parva, where you could dive from a height into deep water.

'Oh, gee!' he said, dismayed. 'Has it?'

'Quate. And its tenant will naturally expect to enjoy privacy. He will not want to look out of his window and see strangers – fat strangers,' said Miss Whittaker, specifying more exactly – 'hurling themselves past it. So you must do your bathing elsewhere. That was all I wished to say. Good morning, Mr Vanringham.'

She withdrew into the house, gliding in that genteel way of hers, like a ladylike swan; and Tubby, after standing where he was for a moment, frowning darkly, walked on, kicking pebbles.

His soul, as he walked, was a black turmoil of conflicting emotions. This woman had treated him in a way which would have made even a man with so low an opinion of the sex as the late Schopenhauer whistle incredulously, but though he scorned and loathed her, he was annoyed to discover that he loved her still. He would have liked to bounce a brick on Prudence Whittaker's head, and yet, at the same time, he would have liked – rather better, as a matter of fact – to crush her to him and cover her face with burning kisses. The whole situation was very complex.

His aimless steps took him in the direction of the stable yard, and if any proof were required of the depths of sombre introspection into which he had been thrust, it is provided by the fact that he had passed the archway giving access to it before he became aware of the loud and booming voice which was speaking on the other side. A full quarter of a minute had elapsed before it penetrated to his consciousness and caused him, first, to halt, then to turn back and investigate. His soul might be in a turmoil, but he did not want to miss anything interesting.

The voice, which he had recognized by now as that of his host, Sir Buckstone Abbott, had dropped to a sullen rumble, but as he reached the archway, it rose again to its full strength.

He peeped in, and saw that Sir Buckstone was talking to his daughter Imogen, better known in the circles in which she moved as Jane.

Sir Buckstone Abbott seemed to be in the grip of something resembling frenzy. Sunshine and the fresh breezes which swept over the uplands on which he lived had imparted to his face a healthy red. This had now deepened to mauve, and even from a distance it was possible to see the glare in his eyes. The idea Tubby got was that the old boy was driving his daughter from his door for having erred – an impression which was heightened by the other's words.

'Ass!' he was saying, just as any father would to an erring daughter, towering over the girl as she crouched before him. 'Fool! Imbecile! Fathead!'

But it was not shame and remorse that had been causing Jane Abbott to crouch. One of those fascinating minor ailments, to which it was so subject, had developed in the interior organs of her Widgeon Seven two-seater, and she had been stooping over it with a spanner. She now rose, revealing herself as a small, slim, pretty girl of twenty, with fair hair and a boyish jauntiness of carriage. In her cornflower-blue eyes was the tender light which comes into the eyes of women when they are dealing with a refractory child or a misguided parent.

'Buck up, Buck,' she urged. 'Be a little soldier.'

'I can't.'

'Oh, come on. Where's your manly spirit?'

'Crushed. Utterly crushed.'

'Nonsense. I keep telling you that everything's going to be all right.'

'That's what your mother says,' said Sir Buckstone, impressed by the coincidence.

'And what mother thinks today, Manchester thinks tomorrow. I'll get it fixed. Leave it to me.'

'But these sharks have always got the law behind them. They're noted for it. You can bet that Busby – Oh, my God, there's Chinnery!' said Sir Buckstone, and disappeared nimbly. Though solidly built and of an age when the joints tend to lose their limber resilience, he was always very quick on his feet when he saw one of his paying guests approaching. Especially Mr Chinnery, to whom he owed money.

Tubby came into the stable yard, mystified. A thirst for knowledge had caused him momentarily to forget about his blighted life.

'What on earth was all that?' he asked.

'Buck's upset.'

'I thought he seemed a little upset. Why was he calling you a fathead?'

Jane laughed. She had an attractive laugh, and an attractive way of screwing up her eyes when she used it. Several men had noticed this. Tubby noticed it now, and for an instant the idea of falling in love with her flitted through his mind. Then he put the thought aside. He could have done it without difficulty, but he was through with women. Women had let him down once too often, and he was not going to put his battered heart within kicking distance of the foot of even so apparently trustworthy a girl as Jane. From now on, he proposed to model his sex relations on those of a Trappist monk.

'He wasn't calling me a fathead. He was talking to himself.'

'The old-fashioned soliloquy?'

'That's right.'

'Well, why was he calling himself a fathead?'

'Because he's been one. He's made an ass of himself, poor lamb. I'm furious about it, really, and if he hadn't been so crushed and miserable and gashing himself with knives like the priests of Baal, I'd have ticked him off properly. He should never have dreamed of doing such a thing, with money so tight. Imagine, Tubby! With overdrafts snapping at his heels and the wolf practically glued to the door, what do you think Buck goes and does? Publishes a book at his own expense.'

'Whose book?'

'His, of course, you idiot.'

Tubby was looking grave, like one who has discovered a hitherto-unsuspected blemish in an estimable character.

'I didn't know your father wrote books.'

'Just this one. About his big-game hunting binges in the old days.'

'Oh, not a novel?' said Tubby, relieved.

'No, not a novel. A book called "My Sporting Memories". And when the thing was finished, he started sending it to publishers, who one and all promptly gave it the bird.'

'Now, who was talking to me about publishers the other day?'

'After about the tenth rebuff, I told him that he had better reconcile himself to the idea that there wasn't a big popular demand and shove it away in a drawer. But Buck never knows when he's licked. He said he would have one more pop.'

'Atta-boy!'

'Oh, we Abbotts are like that. British.'

'And then what?'

'The next man he sent the manuscript to – a blighter named Busby – offered to publish it if Buck would put up the cash. And he couldn't resist the craving to see himself in print. He raised two hundred pounds – where he got it from is more than I can imagine – and that was that. The book duly appeared, all red and gold, with a frontispiece of Buck with a rifle in his hand standing with one foot on a lion.'

'That sounds to me like the happy ending. Came the dawn, is the way I should describe it.'

'It was not an end, but a beginning. Mark the sequel. This morning a totally unexpected extra bill comes in from this hound Busby for ninety-six pounds, three and eleven, for what he calls "incidental expenses connected with the office".'

'Not so hot.'

'It stunned poor old Buck like a blackjack. He came tottering to me with the document. He said he didn't know what the expression "incidental expenses connected with the office" meant, and I explained that it meant ninety-six pounds, three and eleven. He asked me if I could let him have the money as a loan out of my savings from my dress allowance, and I said, "What savings?" And then he said, well, what was he to do, and I said I was going up to London this morning, so give me the bill, I said, and I will go and see this Busby.'

'What can you do?'

'The idea is to try to get him to trim the thing a little.'

'How do you expect to swing that?'

'Oh, I shall plead and weep and clasp my hands. It might work. It does in the movies.'

Tubby was concerned. He had a brotherly protective affection for this girl.

'But, gosh, Jane, the guy's most likely a fat, double-chinned, pot-bellied son of Belial with pig's eyes and a licentious look. He'll probably try to kiss you.'

'Well, that ought to be good for the three and eleven.'

They started to stroll toward the archway. Tubby stopped short, in the manner of one who slaps his brow.

'Busby? Are you sure it's Busby?'

'Am I sure! The name is graven on my heart. J. Mortimer Busby, with a "Cr" after it. Why?'

'Well, it's rather an odd coincidence. I remember now who was talking to me about publishers. It was my brother Joe. I saw him about a year ago, and he said he was going to work for somebody in the publishing racket. And I'm pretty sure the name was Busby. Unless,' said Tubby, who liked to leave a margin for error, 'it was something else.'

'You seem a bit vague.'

'Well, you know how it is. You meet a guy and he tells you something, and you say, "Oh yes?" and then you go away and forget about it. Besides, I had had a late night. I was half asleep when I met my brother Joe.'

'I didn't know you had a brother Joe.'

'Oh, sure,' said Tubby, with a touch of the smugness of a man of property. 'I've got a brother Joe all right.'

'Why haven't I heard of him till now?'

'I guess he just hasn't happened to crop up.'

'Big brother or little brother?'

'Big.'

'Odd I've never heard your stepmother speak of him.'

'Not so odd,' said Tubby. 'She hates his gizzard. He cleared out and left home when he was twenty-one. I've always had the idea that she slung him out. I don't know. I was away when they had the big fight. When I came back, he'd gone.'

'Didn't you make inquiries?'

'Sure, I made inquiries. Until she told me that if I didn't keep my trap shut and mind my own business, I could leave, too, and start in as an office boy in the fish-glue business.'

'That sealed your lips?'

'You bet it sealed my lips. Sealed them good.'

'Well, I hope your brother Joe isn't working for Busby, because Busby would contaminate him.'

'Oh, I don't know,' said Tubby optimistically. 'Probably Joe would contaminate Busby. He's a great guy. As tough as they make 'em.'

They passed through the archway on to the terrace, and found it graced by the presence of Miss Prudence Whittaker. The secretary had come out of the house again to get a breath of air. Observing Tubby, she started to go in, plainly feeling that it was not much use getting breaths of air when that air was polluted. Tubby, on his side, clenched his fists and drew

11

in his breath with a sharp hiss, his face the while taking on a Byronic gloom.

Jane waved a hand.

'Good morning, Miss Whittaker.'

'Good morning, Miss Abbott.'

'I'm going up to London this morning. Anything you want me to do for you?'

'No, thank you, Miss Abbott.'

'No message for Percy?' asked Tubby unpleasantly.

The secretary glided away in disdainful silence. Jane, turning to Tubby to ask who Percy was, for this was the first time she had heard of any Percys in Prudence Whittaker's life, caught sight of his face.

'Golly, Tubby!' she exclaimed. 'What's the matter?'

'I'm all right.'

'Then you deceive the eye.'

'I'm fine,' said the sufferer moodily.

Jane was not to be put off like this:

'You're nothing of the kind. You look like one of those strong, soured men who have a row with the girl and go off and shoot lions in Africa. I expect Buck used to meet them in dozens when – Tubby! Have you and La Whittaker parted brass rags?'

Tubby reeled. This clairvoyant girl had taken his breath away. He had supposed his love a secret locked away behind a mask-like face.

'What do you know about me and La – I mean Miss Whittaker?'

'My poor child, it's been sticking out a mile for weeks. Your bulging eyes when you looked at her told their own story.'

'Is that so? Well, they've changed their act.'

'I'm awfully sorry. What happened?'

'Oh, nothing,' said Tubby. A man has his reserves.

'Who's Percy?'

'Nobody you know.'

Jane forbore to press the question. She was longing to hear all about that shadowy – one might say, mystic – figure, whose role seemed to be that of Serpent in the Vanringham-Whittaker Garden of Eden, but she was a tactful girl. Instead, she asked him what he was going to do about it. Tubby replied that he wasn't going to do anything about it. Jane screwed up her blue eyes and looked at the heat mist that flickered over the turf.

'Well, it's a shame,' she said. 'Have you thought of trying homoeopathic treatment?'

'Eh?'

'In cases like this, I always think that another girl should be applied immediately. What you need is plenty of gay feminine society. You're the sort of man who's lost if he hasn't a girl.'

'I can take them or leave them alone.'

'What girls have we? I'm lunching today with six from the old school, headed by Mabel Purvis, at one time president of the Debating Society. Would you care to join us?'

'No, thanks.'

'I thought you mightn't.' Jane paused. 'Of course, you know, Tubby darling,' she said, 'I don't want to seem callous and unsympathetic, but, however rotten it is quarrelling with someone you're fond of, there's a sort of bright spot to this particular bit of trouble.'

'What?' said Tubby, who had missed it.

'Well, but for this rift, you would have had to inform your stepmother, when she got back from America, that you were intending to marry a humble working girl. You know her better than I do, but I wouldn't have said offhand that she was a woman who was frightfully fond of humble working girls.'

This angle of the situation had presented itself to Tubby's notice independently once or twice since the severing of his relations with Miss Whittaker. The Princess von und zu Dwornitzchek – she had married and divorced the holder of this high-sounding title about two years after the death of the late Mr Franklin Vanringham – was, he knew, inclined to be finicky where his matrimonial plans were concerned, and she possessed, unfortunately, the power of the high, the middle and the low justice over him. That is to say, she could at will stop his allowance, and set him to work at the bottom of that fish-glue business of which he had already made mention; a prosperous concern in which she had inherited a large interest from her first husband, a Mr Spelvin. And though Tubby knew little or nothing of conditions at the bottom of fish-glue businesses, instinct told him that he would not like them.

'I wouldn't have cared about that,' he said sturdily, 'if Prue had been on the level.'

'Of course not,' said Jane, wondering what on earth it could be that the immaculate Miss Whittaker had done. 'Still, it's a point.'

'It is a point,' agreed Tubby. 'She's a tough egg.'

'She must be, if she slung your brother Joe out.'

'And with only ten dollars in his kick, mind you. Joe told me so.'

'Good gracious! What did he do?'

'Oh, all sorts of things. I know he was a sailor on a tramp steamer, and I believe he held down a job for a time as bouncer at some bar. He did a bit of prize-fighting too.'

Jane found herself liking this stalwart. The Princess Dwornitzchek was a woman for whom she had little esteem, and it saddened her at times that Tubby, such a dear in other respects, should allow himself to be so under her thumb. A man who could defy that overpowering millionairess was a man after her own heart.

'I could tell you all sorts of things about Joe.'

'I'd love to hear them, but I'm afraid I can't stop now. I've got to dress. What you had better do, it seems to me, is go and have your swim. That'll buck you up.'

Her words reminded Tubby of the other blow which he had sustained. Not such a wallop, of course, as having one's dreams and ideals knocked for a loop by a woman's treachery, but quite a sock in its way.

'Say, listen, Jane,' he said, 'what's all this I hear about the houseboat being rented?'

'Quite correct. Tenant clocks in today. Name of Peake.'

'Oh, shoot!'

'Why? You can still go on bathing from it.'

'Can I, do you think? Won't this fellow mind?'

'Of course not. Adrian's a great swimmer himself. He'll love to have a little playmate.'

The brightness which had come like a gleam of winter sunshine into Tubby's careworn face faded abruptly.

'Adrian?'

'That's his name.'

'Adrian Peake?'

'That's right. You seem to know him.'

Tubby gave a short, bitter snort. His air was that of a man who realizes that everything is against him.

'I'll say I know him. I haven't been able to move without treading on the fellow for a year and a half. Will I ever forget that time last August when he was on my stepmother's yacht at Cannes. Talk about getting in one's hair!'

Jane had become suddenly rigid, but Tubby did not observe this phenomenon. He continued, unheeding:

'Adrian Peake! My gosh! He's a sort of lapdog of my stepmother's. Trots after her wherever she goes. Marked her down the day she hit London, and has been sponging on her ever since. Adrian by golly Peake, is it? Then the thing's cold. I'm not going to put myself under an obligation to that twerp. Darned gigolo. I shall go and play croquet with Mrs Folsom.'

Jane Abbott's fists were now clenched and her small teeth set. She was looking at Tubby with an eye compared with which even that of Miss Prudence Whittaker had been kindly and sympathetic.

'It may interest you to know,' she said, in a steely voice, 'that Adrian and I are engaged.'

She was right. It interested him extremely. He jumped as if she had hit him.

'Engaged?'

'Yes.'

'You can't be!'

'I must go and dress.'

'But wait. Listen. There must be some mistake. You can't possibly be engaged to Adrian Peake. He's going to marry my stepmother.'

'Don't be an idiot.'

'He is, I tell you. Unless this is a different Adrian Peake. The one I mean is a slimy bird who looks like a consumptive tailor's dummy.'

He paused here, for Jane had begun to speak. For some moments she spoke with an incisive eloquence which made Tubby feel as if the top of his head had come off. Then she turned and walked away, leaving him to collect the wreckage.

Her father, whom she passed on the terrace, called to her, but she merely smiled a tight-lipped smile and hurried on. She was in no mood for conversation, even with a fondly loved parent.

2

Sir Buckstone Abbott was standing on the terrace because it was almost time for his daily conference with Prudence Whittaker, which always took place at this hour and, if the weather was fine, on this spot.

The Baronet was a man of routine. Every day he rose punctually at eight-thirty and, having shaved, bathed and gone through the complicated system of physical jerks which kept his stocky body in such excellent repair, breakfasted with his wife in her sitting-room. At ten-thirty he interviewed Miss Whittaker. The rest of the morning and the early afternoon he devoted to avoiding the paying guests. Between five and seven, he took the dogs for a run.

Unable to induce Jane to stop and chat with him, he resumed the scrutiny of his ancestral home which her passing had interrupted. He always took a look at Walsingford Hall at about this hour, and liked it less every time he saw it. Today's bright sunshine showed up the celebrated eyesore in all its revolting hideousness, and it was with a renewed sense of wonder at the mental processes of that remarkable woman that he remembered that the Princess von und zu Dwornitzchek had once said she thought it cute. Sir Buckstone had often dredged the dictionary for adjectives to describe the home of his fathers, but 'cute' was one which had not occurred to him.

Walsingford Hall had not always presented the stupefying spectacle which it did today. Built in the time of Queen Elizabeth on an eminence overlooking the silver Thames, it must, for two centuries and more, have been a lovely place. The fact that it now caused sensitive oarsmen, rounding the bend of the river and seeing it suddenly, to wince and catch crabs was due to the unfortunate circumstance of the big fire, which, sooner or later, seems to come to all English country houses, postponing its arrival until midway through the reign of Queen Victoria, thus giving the task of rebuilding it from the foundations up to Sir Wellington Abbott, at that time its proprietor.

Whatever may be said in favour of the Victorians, it is pretty generally admitted that few of them were to be trusted within reach of a trowel and a pile of bricks. Sir Wellington least of any. He was as virulent an amateur architect as ever grew a whisker. Watching the holocaust in his nightshirt, for he had had to nip rather smartly out of a burning bedroom, he forgot the cold wind blowing about his ankles in the thought that here was his chance to do a big job and do it well. He embarked upon it at the earliest possible moment, regardless of expense.

What Sir Buckstone was now looking at, accordingly, was a vast edifice constructed of glazed red brick, in some respects resembling a French château, but, on the whole, perhaps, having more the appearance of one of those model dwellings in which a certain number of working-class families are assured of a certain number of cubic feet of air. It had a huge leaden roof, tapering to a point and topped by a weathervane, and from one side of it, like some unpleasant growth, there protruded a large conservatory. There were also a dome and some minarets.

Victorian villagers gazing up at it, had named it Abbott's Folly, and they had been about right.

The clock over the stables struck the half-hour, and simultaneously, on time as usual, Miss Whittaker came out of the house, note-book in hand.

'Good morning, Sir Buckstone.'

'Morning, Miss Whittaker. Lovely day.'

'Oh, yay-ess, Sir Buckstone. Beautiful.'

'Well, everybody all right? Nobody complaining about anything?'

This, also, was routine. The Baronet's first question at these conferences always had to do with the welfare of his little flock.

Miss Whittaker consulted her note-book.

'Mrs Shepley has been annoyed by the pigeons.'

'What have they been doing to her?'

'They coo outside her window in the morning.'

'Well, I don't see what she expects me to do about that. Can't put silencers on them, what? Anything else?'

'Mr Waugh-Bonner thinks there is a mouse in his room.'

'Tell him to mew.'

'And Mr Chinnery has been asking for waffles again.'

'Oh, dash his waffles! What the dickens are these waffles he's always whining about?'

'They appear to be an American breakfast food.'

'Well, he's not in America now.'

'But he wants his waffles.'

Sir Buckstone, his brow furrowed, wrestled with his problem.

'Would my wife know how to make the damn things?'

'I have consulted Lady Abbott, Sir Buckstone, and she informs me that she can make a substance called fudge, but not waffles.'

'How about asking young Vanringham?'

The sweet Kensington music of Miss Whittaker's voice became marred by a touch of flatness:

'If you desi-ah that I inqui-ah of Mr Vanringham, I will do so, but – '

'You think he wouldn't know, either? Probably not. Well, old Chinnery will have to go without his waffles. Is that the lot?'

'Yes, Sir Buckstone.'

'Good.'

'There have been two telephone messages. The first was from the secretary of the Princess Dwornitzchek. The Princess is in mid-ocean and will be arriving almost immediately.'

'Good,' said Sir Buckstone again. He welcomed the return of one who could not only look at Walsingford Hall without shuddering but was actually contemplating buying it. 'She's made a quick trip. What was the other telephone message?'

'It was for Lady Abbott, Sir Buckstone. From her brother.'

Sir Buckstone stared.

'From her brother?'

'Yes, Sir Buckstone.'

'But she hasn't got a brother.'

Miss Whittaker was polite but firm.

'I only know what the gentleman said on the telephone, Sir Buckstone. He asked me to inform Lady Abbott that her brother Sam was in London and would be coming to see her as soon as possible.'

'God bless my soul! Well, all right. Thank you, Miss Whittaker.'

For some moments after his secretary had left him, Sir Buckstone Abbott stood in thoughtful mood, digesting this piece of information. It is always disconcerting for a man of regular habits to find his wife unexpectedly presenting him with a bouncing brother-in-law. But it was not long before he shelved this subject for meditation in favour of that other, more urgent one from which his mind had been temporarily diverted. Once more in front of his eyes, seeming to be written in letters of flame across the summer sky, appeared those sinister figures £96 3s. 11d. He was contemplating them and wondering moodily if there was any possible chance of his daughter Jane weaving so magic a spell about this Busby that he would consent to a fairly substantial reduction, when his reverie was interrupted by a voice which called his name. At the same time the scent of a powerful cigar floated to his nostrils. He turned, and was shocked to find Mr Chinnery at his side. Only the most intense preoccupation could have caused him to be caught standing like this.

Although Sir Buckstone liked Americans, was a member of the Overseas Club and had married an American wife, Elmer Chinnery was the one of his paying guests of whom he was least fond. Where he merely accelerated his pace to avoid a Waugh-Bonner or a Shepley, he seemed almost to possess the wings of a dove when he sighted Elmer Chinnery.

The reason for this was the fact, which has already been revealed, that he owed Mr Chinnery money. And in addition to that, the unfortunate loan appeared to be the only subject, except waffles, on which the other was prepared to converse. And your English aristocrat hates talking about money.

Mr Chinnery was a large, spreading man with a smooth face and very big horn-rimmed spectacles. He had come to reside at the Hall some time back, being indeed one of the earliest of the current generation of squatters. He had been a partner in the fish-glue business from which the Princess Dwornitzchek's first husband had drawn his fortune, and was enormously rich in spite of the inroads made on his income by the platoon of ex-wives to whom he was paying alimony. For, like so many substantial citizens of his native country, he had married young and kept on marrying, springing from blonde to blonde like the chamois of the Alps leaping from crag to crag.

'Say, Abbott,' said Mr Chinnery.

To a casual auditor, there would have seemed nothing in these words to disturb and dismay, but we who know the facts are able to understand why, as he heard them, Sir Buckstone flung out his hands in a wide, despairing gesture like the Lady of Shalott when the curse had come upon her. We may not sympathize, but we can understand.

'It's no use, my dear chap. Honestly, it isn't.'

'If you could manage something on account – '

'Well, I can't. I'm sorry.'

An uncomfortable silence fell. Sir Buckstone was thinking how monstrous it was that a man whose income, even after his wives had had their whack at it, must be very nearly in six figures should keep making this ridiculous fuss about a mere few hundred pounds. Mr Chinnery was saying to himself what a lesson it all was to a fellow not to drink old port. It had been under the influence of his third glass of this beverage that he had allowed himself to yield to his host's suggestion of a small loan.

'If I sell the house – ' said Sir Buckstone.

'M'm,' said Mr Chinnery.

They both looked at the house, and that uncomfortable silence fell once more. The same thought was in both their minds. A house like that would take some selling.

'Even twenty pounds – ' said Mr Chinnery suddenly.

'Ah!' said Sir Buckstone, simultaneously and with infinite relief. 'Here's Jane.'

His daughter, never more welcome to a father's eyes than at this moment, was coming out of the house and making her way toward them to receive any last parental message before starting for London.

The process of dressing had done Jane good. She was no

longer the tight-lipped, stony-eyed, fermenting girl who had left Tubby lying in fragments all over the terrace. She had ceased to feel as if small boys had been chalking up rude words on the wall of her soul, and was her gay, cheerful self again.

Tubby, she reminded herself, was just a half-wit, if that, and no girl of intelligence would allow herself to regard any observations which he might make as anything but the crackling of thorns beneath the pot. She did not intend to give another thought to his idiotic droolings. Her conversation with him was just an unpleasant incident of the past, to be buried away and forgotten, like mumps and the time when she had been sick at the children's party.

'Just off, Buck,' she said. 'Any little toy or anything you want me to bring you back?'

'You're going to London?' said Mr Chinnery. 'You'll find it warm there.'

'I suppose I shall, but I've got to go. I've a luncheon party. Besides, father's been having a spot of trouble with a bloodsucker, and he wants me to attend to it for him.'

'Bloodsucker?'

'A human vampire bat of the name of Busby,' said Jane.

Addressing Mr Chinnery, she had turned away from Sir Buckstone, and so did not observe the sudden look of agony and apprehension which now shot into his weatherbeaten face. She did hear him cough in a strangled sort of way, but attributed this to his having swallowed some gnat or other summer insect. She went on brightly. She was always bright with the paying guests.

'You see, he wrote a book about his sporting memories and had it published at his own expense – paid this man two hundred pounds down like an officer and a gentleman – and now the ghoul has sent in a whacking bill for extras. I'm going to call and reason with him.'

There was a long pause. Mr Chinnery was breathing heavily. Sir Buckstone again made that odd, bronchial sound. But neither spoke. Then Mr Chinnery, having fixed the Baronet with what, even when filtered through horn-rimmed glasses, was easily recognizable as the stare of a man who has been wounded to the quick, gave a low gulp and shuffled off.

The sense of strain in the atmosphere did not escape Jane.

'What on earth's the matter?' she asked.

Sir Buckstone looked at her as King Lear might have looked at Cordelia – rather, in fact, as Mr Chinnery had just looked at him.

'You only said the one thing you shouldn't have said,' he replied bleakly. 'You merely put your foot in it right up to the knee. Some months ago I borrowed five hundred pounds from Chinnery, and there hasn't been a day since when he hasn't asked me for it back and I haven't told him I haven't got the cash. And then you come along and talk about me publishing books at my own expense.'

Jane whistled.

'Golly, Buck, I'm sorry.'

'Too late to be sorry now.'

'I must have shaken his faith in Baronets a bit.'

'I should think you have wrecked it for ever. I look forward,' said Sir Buckstone in a flat voice, 'to some very stimulating chats with Chinnery in the near future.'

Jane was remorseful, but she felt that she was being blamed unfairly. Fathers, she considered, should be more frank with their daughters about these facts of life. Then the daughters would know where they were.

'Well, never mind,' she said. 'When I get back, I'll go and prattle to him and soothe him. But why did you want five hundred pounds?'

'Who doesn't?' said Sir Buckstone, rather reasonably.

'I mean, what did you do with it?'

'I published my sporting memories.'

'That didn't come to five hundred quid. What happened to the rest of it?'

Sir Buckstone gestured sombrely, like a pessimistic semaphore.

'It went. This place eats money. And I hadn't so many lodgers then.'

'Paying guests.'

'Lodgers. Lodgers they are, and lodgers they always will be.' Sir Buckstone sighed. 'I little thought, when I succeeded to the title, that the time would shortly come when I should find myself running a blanked boarding establishment.'

'You mustn't be so morbid about it, precious. There's nothing to be ashamed of. Half the landed nibs in England take in paying guests nowadays. Ask anybody.'

Sir Buckstone declined to be comforted. When embarked on this particular topic, it was his custom to wallow in self-pity.

'When I was a boy,' he said heavily, 'my ambition was to become an engine driver. As a young man, I had dreams of ambassadorships. Arrived at middle age and grown reconciled to the fact that I hadn't brains enough for the Diplomatic Service, I thought that I could at least be a simple country gentleman. But Fate decided otherwise. "No, Buckstone," said Fate, "I have other views for you. You shall be the greasy proprietor of a blasted rural doss-house."'

'Oh, Buck!'

'It's no use saying, "Oh, Buck!"'

'Not greasy.'

'Greasy,' insisted Sir Buckstone firmly.

'Why don't you try to look on yourself as a sort of jolly innkeeper? You know – shirt sleeves and joviality. Entrance number in Act One just after the Opening Chorus of Villagers.'

'Because I'm not a jolly innkeeper,' said Sir Buckstone, who was quite clear-eyed about his status. 'I wish you would marry a rich man, Jane.'

Where are they all? What's become of the old-fashioned millionaire who used to buy girls with his gold? There's Mr Chinnery, of course. But hasn't he still got the one he bought last?'

'Ever considered this young Vanringham?'

'Oh, I'm not Tubby's type. He likes them tall and willowy. Besides, where did you get the idea that Tubby's a millionaire? All he's got is what his stepmother allows him, and I don't think she likes me.'

'Good God, Jane! What makes you think that?'

'Intuition,'

'You must make her like you,' said Sir Buckstone earnestly. 'You must cultivate the woman assiduously. Do you realize that she is the only person on earth who might conceivably buy this ghastly house? Miss Whittaker tells me she's on the ocean now, so she will be coming here in the next few days, I imagine. Make yourself pleasant to her. Spare no effort.

Heavens! Just to think of somebody taking this monstrosity off our hands!'

'Tubby told me he believed the deal would go through.'

'He did?'

'He said the Princess admires Walsingford Hall.'

'She once told me she thought it cute.'

'Well, there you are.'

'But she's an erratic woman. Liable to change her mind at any moment.'

'I don't believe a taste for glazed salmon-coloured bricks can ever be eradicated. If it's there, it's there.'

'Well, let us hope for the best.'

'That's the spirit.'

'And now, I suppose, you ought to be off,' said Sir Buckstone. 'I've got to go and see your mother. A rather strange thing has occurred. Miss Whittaker tells me that a telephone message has arrived from her brother.'

'Miss Whittaker's brother?'

'Your mother's brother.'

'But mother hasn't got a brother.'

'Exactly. That is why I feel it's so odd that he should be ringing up on the telephone. I put that point to Miss Whittaker, but she stuck to her story. It's all most peculiar, and I shall be glad to get to the bottom of it.'

'I wish I could come too. But I want to catch Busby before lunch. That's psychology, Buck. Some people would say wait till he's mellowed with food, but I think publishers are like pythons. They hate to be disturbed while they are digesting. I prefer to deal with a snappy, alert Busby.'

'Get back as early as you can.'

'I will. I want to go down to the houseboat and see how Mr Peake is getting on.'

'Is that the name of the fellow who's taken the *Mignonette*?'

'Yes. Adrian Peake. I met him when I was at the Willoughbys' that week-end.'

'Nice chap?'

'Charming.'

'Then we'd better have him up here as soon as possible. It's about time,' said Sir Buckstone, thinking of Mr Chinnery, Mr Waugh-Bonner, Colonel Tanner and others, 'that I saw someone charming. I'll send Miss Whittaker down with a note. But you can't go and see the fellow today. I want you here, the instant you get back, to soothe old Chinnery. A full afternoon's work it will be .'

'Oh, Buck! Must I?'

'Certainly you must. It was your own suggestion. You said you would prattle to him. Play clock golf with him, too, and ask him to tell you all about his wives and waffles. Otherwise, I shall have him on my neck till bedtime. Extraordinarily pertinacious that man is. Like a horsefly.'

'What a pity you ever bit his ear.'

'A great pity. But no good regretting it now. What's done is done. "The Moving Finger writes; and, having writ, moves on; nor all your Piety nor Wit – '

'Yes, I know. I was given that to write out a hundred times at school too.'

'" – shall lure it back to cancel half a Line, nor all your Tears wash out a Word of it,"' said Sir Buckstone, who was a hard man to stop. 'The thing about it all that I find so bitter is that the fellow hasn't the slightest earthly need for the money. He must have millions. No ordinary purse could stand the drain of what he pays out to ex-wives.'

'Not to mention ex-waffles, I expect. All right, I'll soothe him.'

'Good girl,' said Sir Buckstone paternally. Then he was struck by another thought. 'I say, Jane, this brother of your mother's. When he shows up, I'll have to ask him to stay, won't I?'

'Of course.'

'For an indefinite visit.'

'Yes.'

'And,' said Sir Buckstone, making his point, 'I don't suppose I can very well charge him anything, dash it. Crawling in, upsetting my home life, swigging my port – and not so much as five pounds a week out of it. Hell!' said Sir Buckstone, with old-fashioned English hospitality.

Jane said that he must not be a Shylock. Sir Buckstone replied that it was impossible for a man situated as he was not to be a Shylock and that, anyway, Shylock's was a character which he had come greatly to admire. He then moved heavily

25

toward the house; and Jane, going to the stables, started up her Widgeon Seven for the drive to London and Mr Busby.

3

Mr Mortimer Busby, the enterprising publisher with whom the Society of Authors has for so many years waged a spirited but always fruitless warfare, leaned forward to his desk telephone and took off the receiver.

The movement caused him to wince and utter a stifled yelp, for his skin was sensitive this morning to sudden movements. The brilliance of the weather had led him on the previous day to stay away from the office, and like Mr Billing, of Walsingford Hall, to indulge in a sun bath. But, unlike Mr Billing, who always cannily smeared himself with oil, he had adopted no precautions against blisters and was suffering the consequences.

'Send Mr Vanringham to me,' he said.

The Outer Office replied that Mr Vanringham had not yet returned.

'Eh?' said Mr Busby dangerously. He did not approve of his employees wandering from the fold during business hours. 'Returned? Where's he gone?'

'If you remember, sir,' the Outer Office reminded him, 'you left instructions that Mr Vanringham was to go to Waterloo this morning to see Miss Gray off on the boat train.'

Mr Busby's severity softened. He recalled now that Miss Gwenda Gray, star author on his list, was sailing for America today to add one more to the long roll of English lecturers who have done so much to keep the depression going in that unfortunate country; and that Joe Vanringham, in his capacity of odd-job man and hey-you to the firm, had been dispatched to the train with fruit and flowers.

'All right,' he said. 'Send him in when he comes back.'

He had hardly replaced the receiver when the telephone rang again. More cautiously this time, he stretched out a hand to it.

'Hullo?'

'Hello, chief.'

'Who's that?'

'Vanringham, chief.'

'Don't call me "chief."'

'Okay, chief. Well, here I am at St Pancras.'

Mr Busby quivered from the top of his round head to the soles of his number ten shoes.

'What in the name of – What on earth are you doing at St Pancras?'

'Waiting for Miss Gray. You told me to see her off to Scotland this morning.'

A slight bubbling noise was all that Mr Busby was able to achieve for some moments. Then he recovered speech.

'You infernal idiot! America! She's going to America.'

'America? Are you sure?'

'Of all the – '

There came from the other end of the wire the sound of a remorsefully clicked tongue.

'You're absolutely right. It all comes back to me. It was America.'

'The boat train leaves from Waterloo.'

'By golly, you're right again. That explains why she hasn't shown up. But why did you tell me St Pancras?'

'I did not tell you St Pancras. I said Waterloo. Waterloo!'

'Then that's how I came to get confused. I don't know if you are aware of it, but when you say "Waterloo", it sounds just like "St Pancras". Some slight defect of speech, no doubt, which a good elocution teacher could soon put right. Well, what I called up to ask was, shall I eat the fruit?'

'Listen,' said Mr Busby, in a strangled voice. Miss Gray was a novelist who sold her steady twenty thousand copies a year and was inclined, if proper attention was not paid to her, to become touchy. 'There may be just time. Get in a taxi – '

An odious chuckle floated over the wire.

'Cheer up, chief. I've only been indulging in a little persiflage. You know how you come over all whimsy sometimes. I'm at Waterloo, all right, and everything has gone like a breeze. I gave her the fruit and flowers, and she was tickled to death. The train has just pulled out, and the last I saw of her, she was leaning out of the window, sucking an orange and crying, "God bless Mr Busby!"'

Mr Busby hung up the receiver. His face was a pretty purple, and his lips moved soundlessly. He was telling himself for the hundredth time that this was the end and that today he really would strike the name of Vanringham from his pay roll. But for the hundredth time there came to him the disconcerting thought that he would have to seek far to find another slave as good at his job as Joe.

A considerable proportion of Mr Busby's clients were women who paid for the publication of their books and were apt, when their bills came in, to call at the office in a rather emotional spirit. Whatever Joe's faults, he had a magic touch with these. They were as wax in his hands. So Mortimer Busby, groaning inwardly, forced himself to suffer him. He did not like Joe. He resented his sardonic smile and that look of his of amused astonishment, as if he could never get used to the idea that anything like Mr Busby was sharing the same planet with him. And he objected to the things he said. But he did approve of that amazing way he had of intercepting raging female novelists, paying them a couple of compliments, telling them a couple of funny stories and sending them away beaming and giggling, all animosity forgotten.

He endeavoured to restore his composure by plunging himself into his work, and, after a quarter of an hour, was beginning to feel reasonably tranquil once more, when there was a breezy smack on the door, which only one member of his office force would have had the effrontery to deliver, and Joe Vanringham ambled in.

'You sent for me, chief?' he cried heartily. 'Well, here I am. Old Faithful reporting for duty. What can I do for you?'

There was a certain family resemblance between the brothers Vanringham, and if anyone had seen Joe and Tubby together, he might have guessed that they were related, but this resemblance was a purely superficial one. There was between them the fundamental difference which exists between a tough cat which has had to fend for itself among the alleys and ash-cans of the world and its softer kinsman who has for long been the well-nourished pet in a good home. Tubby was sleek, Joe lean and hard. He had that indefinable air which comes to young men who have had to make their way up from a ten-dollar start.

Mr Busby eyed him sourly, for the memory of that tele-phone conversation still rankled. The Busbys did not lightly forget. He found, moreover, in his young assistant's manner this morning a more than ordinarily offensive exuberance. Always lacking in reverence and possessed of a strong bias to-ward freshness, Joe Vanringham seemed to him today rather less reverent and slightly fresher than usual. The word 'effervescent' was one which would have covered his deport-ment.

'There's a woman in the waiting-room, come about a bill,' he said. 'Go and attend to her.'

Joe nodded sympathetically.

'I get you, chief. The old, old story, eh?'

'What do you mean, the old, old story?'

'Well, it's happened before, hasn't it? But don't you worry. I'm in rare shape this morning. I could tackle ten women, come about ten bills. Leave it to me.'

'Look out!' cried Mr Busby.

Joe lowered the hand with which he had been about to administer a reassuring pat to his employer's shoulder, and looked at him with a mild surprise.

'Eh?'

'I'm all skinned.'

'Somebody skinned *you*?'

'Shoulders. Sun bathing.'

'Oh, I see. You should have used oil, chief.'

'I know I should have used oil. And how many times have I told you not to call me "chief"?'

'But I must employ some little term of respect on these occasions when you give me audience. Boss? Magnate? Do you like "magnate"? Or how about "tycoon"?'

'You just call me "sir".'

'"Sir"? Yes, that's good. That's neat. Snappy. Slips off the tongue. How did you come to think of that?'

Mr Busby flushed. He was wondering, as he had so often wondered before, whether even the admirable service which this young man rendered him in his capacity of watchdog was sufficient compensation for this sort of thing. The words 'You're fired!' trembled on his lips, but he choked them down.

'Go and attend to that woman,' he said.

'In one moment,' said Joe. 'First, I have a more painful task to perform.'

He moved to the cupboard under the bookshelf and began to rummage in it.

'What the devil are you doing?'

'Looking for your smelling salts. I'm afraid,' said Joe, returning and regarding his employer with a compassionate eye, 'there is a nasty jolt coming to you, tycoon, and I think we should have restoratives handy. Did you read the papers this morning?'

'What are you talking about?'

'I repeat: Did you read the papers this morning?'

Mr Busby said that he had seen *The Times*. Joe winced.

'A low rag,' he said. 'But even *The Times* had to admit that the thing had got over.'

'Eh?'

'My play. It opened last night.'

'Have you written a play?'

'And in what manner! A socko! It has everything.'

'Oh?'

'"Oh?" is not much of a comment. However, let it go. Yes, the old masterpiece opened last night and smacked London right in the eyeball. Extraordinary scenes. Fair women and brave men tied up in convulsions. Even the stage hands laughing, while thousands cheered. A big, vital production. Shall I read you the notices?'

A sudden suspicion came to Mr Busby.

'When did you write this play?'

'Out of office hours, I assure you. Abandon all hope, my Busby, that by claiming that it was written in your time, you can ease yourself in on the proceeds. And I wouldn't have put it past you,' said Joe with frank admiration. 'I've always maintained, and I always shall maintain, that you stand alone. Those contracts of yours! I always picture the author, having signed on the dotted line, leaping back as a couple of sub-clauses in black masks suddenly jump out of a jungle of "whereases" and "hereinafters" and start ganging on him with knuckledusters. But this time, as I say, no hope, buzzard.'

Mr Busby said that he did not want any of Joe's impertinence, and criticized in particular his mode of address. Joe explained that in calling Mr Busby 'buzzard' he had merely been endeavouring to create a pleasant, genial, informal atmosphere.

'For this morning,' he said, 'I am the little friend of all the world. I have had no sleep, but I love everybody. I am walking on air with my hat on the side of my head, and a child could play with me. Do let me read you the notices.'

Mr Busby betrayed no interest in the notices. The compassionate look in Joe's eyes deepened.

'They affect you,' he said. 'They affect you vitally. That is why I wanted the smelling salts. You see, owing to the stupendous success of this colossal play, unhappy Busby, I have decided to leave you.... Brace up, man! Put your head between your legs, and the faint feeling will pass off.... Yes, Busby, my poor dear old chap, we are about to part. I have been happy here. I shall be sorry to tear myself away, but we must part. I am too rich to work.'

Mr Busby grunted. Oddly enough, considering that the latter had never seen him, he did rather resemble the picture Tubby had drawn of him. He was noticeably porcine, and grunting came easily to him.

'If you leave now, you forfeit half a month's salary.'

'Tchah! Feed it to the birds.'

Mr Busby grunted again.

'It's a success, is it?'

'Haven't you been listening?'

'You can't go by a first night.'

'You can by one like that.'

'Notices don't mean a thing.'

'These do.'

'The heat'll kill it,' said Mr Busby, struggling to be optimistic. 'Crazy, opening in August.'

'Not at all. An August opening gives you a flying start. And the heat won't kill it, because the libraries have made a ten weeks' deal.'

Mr Busby gave up. Optimism cannot live in conditions like these. He made the only possible point left to him.

'Your next one will be a flop, and a year from now you'll be running back here with your tail between your legs. And you'll find your place filled.'

'If the place of a man like me can ever be filled. I wouldn't count on it,' said Joe dubiously. 'But you haven't heard the notices yet. I think I had better just skim through them for you. Let me see. "Sparkling satire." – *Daily Mail*. "Mordant and satirical." – *Daily Telegraph*. "Trenchant satire." – *Morning Post*. "Somewhat – " Oh, no that's *The Times*. You won't want to hear that one. Well, you see what I mean about leaving you. A man who can elicit eulogies like those can hardly be expected to go on working for a crook publisher.'

'A what?' said Mr Busby, starting.

'Book publisher. Fellow who publishes books. He owes a duty to his public. But I mustn't stand here talking to you all the morning. I've got to go and see that lurking female of yours. The last little service I shall be able to do for you. My swan song. And then I must go and buy the evening papers. I suppose they will all strike much the same note. One grows a little weary of this incessant praise. It makes one feel like some Oriental monarch when the court poet is in good voice.'

'What did *The Times* say?' asked Mr Busby.

'Never mind what *The Times* said,' replied Joe austerely. 'Suffice it that its office boy took entirely the wrong tone. Let me tell you rather about the scenes of unrestrained enthusiasm at the end of the second act.'

Mr Busby said that he did not wish to be told about the scenes of unrestrained enthusiasm at the end of the second act.

'You would prefer to hear about the furore at the final curtain?'

'Nor that, either,' said Mr Busby. Joe sighed.

'A strange mentality, yours,' he said. 'Personally, I cannot imagine a more delightful way of passing a summer morning than to sit and listen to the whole story over and over again. Still, please yourself. Just so long as you have grasped the salient point, that I am leaving you, I will go. Good-bye, Busby. God bless and keep you, and when the Society of Authors jumps out at you from behind a bush, may you always have your fingers crossed.'

With a kindly smile, he turned and left the presence. He would have preferred to make straight for the street, where voices were now calling the midday editions of the evening papers, but the word of a Vanringham was his bond. Mindful of his promise to Mr Busby, he directed his steps to the waiting-room, and arriving at its glass door and looking in, paused spellbound.

Then, having straightened his tie and brushed a speck of dust from his sleeve, he opened the door and walked in.

4

There were few more tastefully appointed waiting-rooms in all London than that provided for the use of his clients by Mortimer Busby. So much of his business was conducted with women of the leisured class that he had aimed at creating the Mayfair-boudoir atmosphere which would make them feel at home, sparing no expense on chintz and prints, on walnut tables and soft settees, on jade ornaments and flowers in their season. Many writers had said hard things about Mr Busby from time to time, but all had had to admit that they had been extremely comfortable in his waiting-room.

Jane Abbott, seated on one of the settees, did nothing, in Joe Vanringham's opinion, to lower the room's tone, but, rather, raised it to an entirely new level. Preparing for the interview before her, she had hesitated whether to put on all she had got and, as it were, give Mr Busby the sartorial works, in order to charm and fascinate, or to don something dowdy in order to excite commiseration. She had decided on the former course, and felt that she had acted wisely. She was feeling full of confidence, that confidence which comes to girls only when they know that their frocks are right and their hats are right and their stockings are right and their shoes are right.

Joe, too, felt that she had acted with wisdom. Through the glass door he had stared at her like a bear at a bun, and though his breeding restrained him from doing so now, there was a stunned goggle implicit in his manner. You could see that he approved.

'Good morning,' he said. 'What can I do for you?'

He spoke gently, kindly, almost tenderly, and a feeling of relief swept over Jane. Tubby's words had led her to expect that she would have to deal with a gross person rather on the order of a stage moneylender, and only now did she realize that, despite the moral support of the hat, the frock, the shoes and the stockings, she had been extremely nervous. All nervousness left her as she gazed upon this gentle, kind, almost tender young man. His face, though not strictly handsome, was extraordinarily pleasant; there was a hard, attractive leanness about him; and she liked his eyes.

'Well, to begin with, Mr Busby,' she said, smiling at him as he seated himself opposite her and leaned forward with deferential cordiality in every lineament of his not strictly handsome, but very nice face, 'I must apologize for bursting in on you like this.'

'Floating in like some lovely spirit of the summer day,' he corrected.

'Well, bursting or floating, I hope I haven't interrupted you when you were busy.'

'Not at all.'

'I ought to have made an appointment.'

'No, no, please. Any time you're passing.'

'That's very nice of you. Well, this is why I've come. I have just left my father – '

'Only a temporary rift, let us trust.'

' – frothing at the mouth about this bill of yours.'

She ceased to smile. The moment had come for gravity – even, if it proved necessary, for sternness. She saw that he, too, had become serious, and hoped that this did not mean obduracy.

'Ah, yes, the bill. Let me see, what bill was that?'

'The one you sent him for incidental expenses connected with the office. That book of his, you know, which you published for him.'

'What was it called?'

'"My Sporting Memories." It was about his big-game hunting experiences.'

'I see. Far-flung stuff. Outposts of the Empire. How I saved my native bearer, 'Mbongo, from the wounded puma. The villagers seemed friendly, so we decided to stay the night.'

'That sort of thing, yes.'

'I like your hat,' said Joe. 'How wise you are to wear black hats with your lovely fair hair.'

This seemed to Jane evasive.

'It doesn't matter whether you like my hat or not, Mr Busby. The point is that my father – '

'Who is your father?'

'Sir Buckstone Abbott.'

'Plain or Bart?'

'He is a Baronet. But does that matter, either?'

'It doesn't much, does it?' said Joe, struck by her reasoning.

'Than shall we stick to what does. The point is that my father is – '

'At a loss to comprehend?'

'Yes. He quite understood that the money he paid you at the beginning would be all, and now along comes this other bill.'

'May I see it?'

'Here it is.'

'H'm. Yes.'

'What does that mean? That you think it is a bit steep?'

'I think it's precipitous.'

'Well, then?'

'The thing is absurd. It shall be adjusted at once.'

'Thank you.'

'Not at all.'

'And when you say "adjusted" – '

'I mean cancelled. Expunged. Struck off the register. Razed to its foundations and sown with salt.'

Even though her companion's face was pleasant; even though his manner, at first gentle, kind and almost tender, had now become gentle, kind and quite definitely tender, Jane had never hoped for anything as good as this. She gave a little squeak.

'Oh, Mr Busby!'

The young man seemed puzzled.

'May I ask you something?' he said. 'You keep calling me "Mr Busby". I dare say you've noticed it yourself. Why is that?'

Jane stared.

'But you are Mr Busby, aren't you?'

'When you say that, smile. No, I am not Mr Busby.'

'What are you, then? His partner?'

'Not even his friend. I am just a passer-by. Simply a chip drifting down the river of Life.'

He studied the bill, a soft smile playing about his lips.

'Masterly!' he murmured. 'A genuine work of Art. Do you know how Busby estimates these incidental expenses connected with the office? Broadly speaking, they represent the sum which he thinks he can chisel out of the unfortunate sap of the second part without having the police piling in on him. What happens is this: Busby goes out to lunch. The waiter hands him the bill of fare. "Caviar," he reads, and his heart leaps up within him. And then his eye lights on the figure in the right-hand column and there comes the chilling thought: Can he afford it? And he is just about to answer with a rueful negative and put in his order for a chop and French-fried, when he suddenly remembers – '

Jane had been bubbling inarticulately, like her Widgeon Seven when it took a steep hill.

'You – you – you mean,' she cried, at last achieving coherence, 'that you have nothing to do with the firm; that you have just been playing the fool with me; raising my hopes – '

'Not at all.'

'Then what did you mean by saying that you would have the bill cancelled?'

'I meant precisely that.'

The quiet confidence with which he spoke impressed Jane in spite of herself. She looked at him pleadingly.

'You aren't just being funny?'

'Certainly not. When I said that I wasn't a friend of Mr Busby's, I did not intend to imply that we were not acquainted. I know him very well. And my bet is that I shall be able to sway him like a reed.'

'But how?'

'I shall appeal to his better feelings.'

'Do you think that will do any good?'

'Who knows? Quite possibly, though I have never actually spotted it yet, he has a heart of gold.'

'And if he hasn't?'

'Why, then we must try something else. But I fancy everything will be all right.'

Jane laughed.

'That's what my mother always says. Whatever happens, all she says is "I guess everything's going to be all right".'

'A very sensible woman,' said Joe approvingly. 'I look forward to meeting her. Well, I'm sure we shall be able to achieve the happy ending in this case. Have no further anxiety.'

'I'm afraid I don't feel so confident as you.'

'That is because you don't know your man.'

'Busby?'

'Me. When you come to know me better, you will be amazed at my gifts. And now the only thing we have not decided is: Will you wait here, or will you go on?'

'Go on?'

'And book a table. I think we might lunch at the Savoy, don't you? It's handy.'

'But I've a luncheon engagement.'

'Then perhaps you had better go on. That will give you time to telephone and break it.'

Jane reflected. If this extraordinary young man really was in a position to persuade Mortimer Busby to see the light, the least she could do in return was to lunch with him.

'It will do me good,' he pointed out, 'to be seen in public with a girl in a hat like that. My social prestige will be enhanced.'

'I was only lunching with some friends,' said Jane, wavering.

'Then trot along and telephone. I will be with you in a few minutes. The Grill, I think, not the restaurant. It is quieter, and I shall have much to say to you.'

It was some quarter of an hour later that Jane, sitting in the lobby of the Savoy Grill, was informed that she was wanted on the telephone. She went to the box reluctantly. Mabel Purvis, who had arranged the old school friends' reunion from which, a few moments before, she had excused herself, had been plaintive and expostulatory on the wire, and she feared that this was Mabel, about to be plaintive again.

'Hullo,' she said. 'This is Imogen.'

But it was a male voice that spoke:

'Oh, there you are. Well, it's all fixed.'

'What?'

'Yes. Busby has receipted the bill.'

'Not the whole bill.'

'In full.'

'Ooh!'

'I thought you would be pleased.'

'But you're a perfect marvel. However did you manage it?'

'Full details will be supplied when we meet.'

'When will that be?'

'In a trice.'

'Good. Do hurry.'

'I will. Oh, and one other thing.'

'Yes?'

'Will you marry me?'

'What?'

'Marry me.'

'Did you say, would I marry you?'

'That's right. Marry. *M* for mayonnaise – '

Jane began to giggle feebly.

'Are you sobbing?' said the voice.

'I'm laughing.'

'Not so good. I don't like the sound of that. Mocking laughter, eh? No, rather sinister. You won't marry me?'

'No.'

'Then will you order me a medium dry Martini? I'll be right along.'

5

'Why not?' asked Joe.

Jane was inspecting her plate of hors d'œuvres, conscious, when it was too late, as everybody is, that she had made the wrong choice.

'Don't you always feel,' she said, 'that what you really want is just sardines?'

'I thought I had made it abundantly clear that I wanted you.'

'I mean, instead of a lot of potato salad and pickled cabbage.'

'Don't let us wander off on to the subject of potato salad,' he said gently. 'You don't seem to realize that I have paid you the greatest compliment a man can pay a woman – or so I read somewhere.'

'Oh, I do.'

'Then stick to the point and let us have none of this light talk about pickled cabbage. I asked you to marry me. You said you wouldn't. I now come right back at you by asking: Why not?'

'I promised mother I would never marry a man I had only known five minutes.'

'More like twenty, surely.'

'Well, even twenty.'

'You're upsetting all my plans.'

'I'm sorry. But you do realize, don't you, that we are practically strangers?'

'Girls often employ that apparently specious argument on a man. Only to discover later that he was a tadpole and they were a fish in the Palaeozoic Age. Then they look silly.'

'Do you think you and I were?'

'Of course. I remember it distinctly. Bless my soul, those were the days. Never a dull moment.'

'I don't think I like tadpoles.'

'Ah, but I've come on a lot since then. I'm a pretty brilliant figure these days. For one thing, I've written a play.'

'So has everybody.'

'True. But where I get the bulge is that mine has been produced, and with stupendous success. I'll tell you all about it, shall I? Or I might read you the notices. I have them here.'

'Later on, I think, don't you?'

'Any time that suits you.'

'I mean, I'm very glad you have had a stupendous success, and I'm simply dying to hear all about it, but you haven't told me yet about Mr Busby.'

'Oh, that?'

'Yes.'

'A bagatelle. You really want to hear what happened?'

'Start at the beginning and don't leave out anything. So far, it seems like a miracle to me.'

Joe took a sip of hock cup.

'Well, it's scarcely worth talking about, and I shall always regard it as one of my purely minor triumphs, but here is the scenario. When I left you, I went to his room. "Ha, Busby!"

I said. And he said, "Oh, it's you, is it?" And I said yes, it was, and told him that I had come about your bill.'

'And then –'

'Well, then, I admit, I began by taking the wrong line. The one I sketched out for you, if you recall.'

'You appealed to his better feelings?'

'Exactly. I said here was a lovely girl, the loveliest girl I had ever seen, with the most wonderful eyes and a sort of how-shall-I-describe-it about her, looking like a Fournier picture in *La Vie Parisienne* come to life, asking a favour of him, and was he going to refuse it? Was he going to send her away with those wonderful eyes swimming in tears? Was he going to compel her to break it to her white-haired father – '

'He's only grizzled.'

' – her grizzled father that the ramp was still on and that he had got to dig down into his jeans for ninety-six pounds, three and eleven? Was he, from sheer sordid greed, going to cast a blight on a once-happy home and make a deserving big-game hunter wish that he had never seen a charging rhinoceros in his life? Well, to cut a long story short, he was. He was quite definite about it. I begged him to think again. I said that this was not the real Mortimer Busby speaking. I implored him to make a gesture. I'll tell you something about your eyes,' said Joe. 'Most people would say they were blue – the deep, soft, unearthly blue of a Southern California summer twilight, and, in a sense, they would be right. They are blue. But at certain moments there comes into them a sort of green, like the sea at – '

'Never mind my eyes. I expect they're all right – '

'They're super-colossal.'

' – but in any case, it's too late to do anything about them now. You were saying you asked him to make a gesture. Upon which – '

'Upon which, he curtly refused to make a gesture. So I did. I raised my hand and allowed it to hover over his back like a butterfly about to settle on some lovely flower.'

'Why was that so good?'

'Because he had already informed me that he had been sitting in the sun and got his shoulders skinned. Well, after that everything went as smooth as the oil he should have used, but didn't. I told him that, unless he let Conscience be his guide, I proposed to slap him on the back and keep right along slapping; and that, though he would no doubt yell for assistance, before that assistance could arrive I should have been able to administer fully fifty sloshes – thirteen, as he was a publisher, of course, counting as twelve. Was not this, I said, a heavy price to pay for the satisfaction of gypping a retired hippopotamus shooter out of a mere ninety-six, three, eleven? He saw my point, and with pretty eagerness reached for his fountain pen and started signing. The receipted bill is on the table before you. Or, rather,' said Joe, retrieving it and cleaning it with his napkin, 'in the butter dish. Here you are.'

Jane took it devoutly.

'You really are the most wonderful man on earth,' she said.

'I'm pretty good,' admitted Joe. 'But surely, if you feel that way – '

'No. My admiration stops short of marrying you.'

'Ah, come on. Make an effort.'

'I'm sorry.'

'You'll be sorrier. When it is too late, you will realize what you have missed, and will suffer from what is called remorse. Let's get this thing threshed out. What seems to be the difficulty?'

'For one thing, I'm already engaged.'

'Well, you were engaged for lunch.'

'That's true.'

Joe mused.

'You're engaged, are you?'

'Yes.'

'Engaged, eh?'

'Yes, Mr Bones, engaged.'

'Who is this insect?'

'Nobody you know.'

'Well, tell me the whole sordid story. Is he worthy of you?'

'Quite.'

'That's what you think. Rich?'

'Poor.'

'As I supposed. Just after you for your money.'

'What money?'

'Isn't your father rolling in the stuff?'

'He hasn't a bean. We live on a handful of rice, like the coolies. That's why I'm eating so much now. I don't often taste meat.'

'But I thought Barts had it in sackfuls.'

'Not my Bart.'

'Odd. They always have in the manuscripts submitted to my late employer. And in those manuscripts, I may mention, they don't stand for any nonsense from penniless suitors. They reach for the horsewhip and get after them. Has your father shown any activity in that direction?'

'No.'

'I don't believe the man's a Bart at all. A knight at the most.'

'You see, he hasn't heard yet that I've got a penniless suitor.'

'You haven't told him of this ghastly entanglement of yours?'

'No.'

'Cowardy custard.'

'It isn't cowardy custard, at all. I want them to get to know and learn to love each other before I break the news. When they do, I shall announce the engagement. And never will the wedding bells have rung out more merrily in the little village church –'

'Don't go on. You're making me sick.'

'I'm sorry. Will you send us a fish slice?'

'Certainly not. I disapprove of the whole thing. Most unsuitable. You must get out of it at once. Write him a letter, telling him it's all off, and then come along with me to the nearest registrar's.'

'You think that would be fun?'

'I should enjoy it.'

'I shouldn't.'

'You won't write him a letter, telling him it's all off?'

'I will not.'

'Just as you say. I don't want to rush you, of course.'

'No, I can see that.'

'My wooing must be conducted in a slow, formal, orderly manner. There must be nothing of which Emily Post would disapprove. First of all, we must tell each other all about ourselves.'

'Why is that?'

'So that we can discover mutual friends, mutual tastes, and so on. On that foundation we can build. At present, I can see that the mere fact that we went around together a lot in the Palaeozoic Age isn't enough. We shall have to start from scratch, just as if we had never met before. I must face the fact that you don't even know my name. Oh, by the way, you said one rather disturbing thing on the telephone. Unless I am mistaken, your opening words were "This is Imogen".'

'I was christened Imogen.'

'But what a perfectly ghastly name. How did you get it?'

'It was my mother's doing, I believe.'

'Well, I wouldn't say a word against your mother, of course –'

'You'd better not.'

'But I can't possibly call you Imogen.'

'Have you considered the idea of calling me Miss Abbott?'

'What, an old buddy like me?'

'As a matter of fact, most people call me Jane.'

'Well, that's not so bad. I like Jane. Or I might call you Ginger. Because of your hair.'

'My hair is not ginger.'

'It is. It's a lovely golden ginger. However, Jane will do. Jane? Jane? Yes, Jane's all right. And now let us go into this matter of mutual friends. Nothing creates a pleasanter bond than the discovery of a flock of mutual friends. Do you know a man named Faraday?'

'No. Do you know a girl named Purvis?'

'No. Do you know men named Thompson, Butterworth, Allenby, Jukes and Desborough-Smith?'

'No. Do you know girls named Merridew, Cleghorn, Foster, Wentworth and Bates?'

'I do not. We don't seem to move in the same circles at all. Do you live in London?'

'No. I live at a place called Walsingford Hall, in Berkshire.'

'Ah, that explains it. Buried in the country, eh? No wonder you don't know Faraday, Thompson, Butterworth, Allenby, Jukes and Desborough-Smith. Nice place, is it?'

'No.'

'You surprise me. It sounds fine. Why not?'

'Because my great-great-uncle rebuilt it in the Victorian era. It's awful. We're trying to sell it.'

'I would, if I were you. Then you could come to London and meet Faraday, Thompson, Butterworth, Allenby and the rest of the boys.'

'The trouble is that it's so hideous that our only hope is somebody astigmatic.'

'Have you any cockeyed prospect in view?'

'Well – touch wood – yes. There's an American woman, the Princess Dwornitzchek – What's the matter?'

'There!' said Joe, speaking a little thickly, for the fist which he had banged upon the table had struck the prongs of a fork, and he was sucking it. 'I knew, if we went on long enough, we should scare up some mutual – I won't say "friend" – acquaintance.'

'Do you know the Princess?'

'My stepmother.'

'She isn't!'

'She is too. I have documents to prove it.'

Jane looked at him, open-mouthed.

'You aren't Tubby's brother Joe?'

'I certainly am Tubby's brother Joe. Though, taking into consideration my eminence, it might be better to put it that he is my brother Tubby. Fancy you knowing him. Go on. You say it.'

'Say what?'

'About it being a small world.'

'Well, it is extraordinary that you should be Tubby's brother Joe the very morning he was talking about you.'

'It isn't the only morning I've been Tubby's brother Joe, by any manner of means. No, indeed. Many and many's the morning, rain and shine, fair weather and foul – ' An idea struck Joe. 'He's not this fellow you're engaged to?'

'No,' said Jane shortly. She had remembered that she had not yet forgiven Tubby.

'Good. I should have hated to blight a brother's life. So he was talking about me, was he? He could have no nobler subject. What was he saying?'

'He said he thought you were in Mr Busby's publishing business.'

'So did Busby, poor devil. I had to break it to him that I wasn't. Painful. What else?'

'He told me that you and your stepmother had not got on very well together.'

'A conservative way of putting it. Did he go into details?'

'He said she had – "slung you out" was the expression he used.'

'So that's the story going the round of the clubs, is it? Let me tell you that I left home of my own volition and under my own steam. Shall I tell you all about it. It will make you think even more highly of me, for it shows me up in a very attractive light. One morning, out of a blue sky, what do you think? She sprang it on me that she wanted me to marry a certain wench of means, a girl I particularly disliked. I said I wouldn't. Heated words ensued. I will not give you the whole of the discussion, just the gist. And remember that when I employ a shrill, mean, squeaky voice, it's my stepmother speaking, and when I use a firm, manly, resonant voice, it's me. "You will marry this girl on pain of my signal displeasure."'

'Did she really talk like that?'

'Just like that. It was one of the things I disliked in her. Well, I drew myself up and said "No! No!" I said. "There are some matters on which a man is not to be dictated to. Besides, I'm going to wait for young Ginger."'

'Jane, if you don't mind.'

'I beg your pardon. "I'm going to wait for young Jane," I said. "She'll be along at any moment, and a fine sap I should look if I was married to someone else when she arrived." She glared at me through her lorgnette. "Is this your final word?" I lit a cigarette. "It is," I said. "You fully realize the consequences?" "I do," I said, and off I went, scorning her gold. Pretty creditable, don't you think?'

'Only what any man would have done.'

'Tubby wouldn't have done it in a hundred years. Nor, or I am vastly mistaken, would Faraday, Thompson, Butterworth, Allenby, Jukes or Desborough-Smith. Especially Desborough-Smith. Only a man of the most sterling nature would have done it. You're sure you don't want to marry a fellow capable of a thing like that?'

45

'No, really, thanks. I don't believe it, either.'

'Well, on the whole, I don't blame you.'

'Isn't it true?'

'Not in the least. I just made it up. But why did you think it wasn't?'

'Tubby told me that you left your stepmother when you were twenty-one. Even she wouldn't have expected you to get married at twenty-one.'

'You have a very keen, incisive mind,' said Joe admiringly. 'Lovely eyes, beautiful hair, perfect teeth and a keen, incisive mind. What you might call a full hand. Can you wonder that you have been selected for the position of Mrs J. J. Vanringham?'

'Why did you really leave home?'

The smile suddenly faded out of his eyes. There was a short silence.

'Oh, there were reasons.'

'What reasons?'

'Suppose we talk about something else.'

Jane gave a little gasp, and the colour flamed into her face. She was a girl whom men had always rather gone out of their way to treat with a deferential respect, and to be snubbed was a new experience for her.

'Perhaps you will suggest a few subjects which you consider inoffensive,' she said. 'That will save a lot of trouble.'

Even to herself it sounded fatuous. And it was plain that he thought so, too, for the curious hard look vanished from his face, and his mouth widened into the familiar grin.

'I'm sorry,' he said.

'Not at all,' said Jane distantly.

It was the injustice of it that stung her. She felt that she had been lured on and made a fool of. If a man as good as says to you: 'I am just a cheerful idiot. Let us talk nonsense for a while. It may amuse you till you feel you have had enough of it,' you accept him on those terms. You are naturally aggrieved when he suddenly changes the rules of the game and draws himself up with a cold, 'Madam, you strangely forget yourself'.

'I'm afraid I was abrupt.'

'You were abominably rude.'

'A much better way of putting it. You have a very happy gift of phrase.'

'Snubbing me for asking a perfectly natural – '

'I know, I know. My head is in the dust. I spoke without thinking. Your question brought up a picture which I don't like looking at, and I snapped automatically, like a dog with a sore paw. Of course I'll tell you why I left home.'

'I haven't the slightest desire to know.'

'Of course you have. You're all agog. You mustn't be pompous.'

'I'm sorry you find me pompous.'

'Quite all right. Faults on both sides.'

Jane got up.

'I must be going.'

'Don't be silly. You can't go yet. You haven't had your fruit salad.'

'I don't want any.'

'Then you shouldn't have ordered it,' said Joe severely. 'Three shillings! Do you think I'm made of money? Heaven knows I do not grudge you fruit salad, whatever the expense – '

'Good-bye.'

'You're really going?'

'Yes.'

'Very good. Then I shall sit here and howl like a wolf.'

Jane started to move to the door. A long, low, eerie howl broke from his lips. She came back.

'Are you going to sit down? Or will you have the second verse?'

Jane sat down, conscious as she did so of a feeling which, when she analysed it, she was disgusted to recognize as uneasiness. For the first time, she began to appreciate in this young man a something that was menacing to her peace of mind. She was not, perhaps, actually as the dust beneath his chariot wheels, but he had undeniably made her sit down when she did not want to, and it was disturbing to become aware that in one on whom she had been looking as a genial clown she had found a personality stronger than her own. He stood revealed as a young man who got what he wanted.

'If you like to make an exhibition of yourself – '

'I love it. Ah, here's your fruit salad. Eat it reverently.

Three bobs' worth. And now about my reasons for parting company with the Princess Dwornitzchek. I left because I have a constitutional dislike for watching murder done – especially slow, cold-blooded murder.'

'What do you mean?'

'My father. He was alive then – just. She didn't actually succeed in killing him till about a year later.'

Jane stared at him. He appeared to be serious.

'Killing him?'

'Oh, I don't mean little-known Asiatic poisons. A resourceful woman with a sensitive subject to work on can make out quite well without the help of strychnine in the soup. Her method was just to make life hell for him.'

Jane said nothing. He went on. There was a brooding look in his eyes, and his voice had taken on an edge.

'How well do you know her?'

'Not very well.'

He laughed.

'If you want to know her better, go and see that play of mine. I've put her in it, hide, heels and hair, with every pet phrase and mannerism she's got and all her gigolos and everything, and it's a scream. Thank goodness she is – or was when I knew her – a regular theatregoer, and she's sure to see it when she comes back. It'll take the skin off her.'

Jane was feeling cold and unhappy.

'You're very bitter,' she said.

'I am a little bitter. I was fond of my father. Yes, she's going to get a shock when she sees that play. I'm counting on it to have much the same effect as the one in *Hamlet*. There was a good dramatist, too, by the way – Shakespeare. But I'm afraid that's all it will do – give her a jolt. It won't cure her. She's past curing. The time I'm speaking of was years ago, but she's still at it.'

'At it?'

'Making a fool of herself with boys half her age. She was doing it when father was alive, and she's doing it now. I suppose if we looked up the recent Von und zu Dwornitzchek, we should find he was a lad in the twenties with lavender spats and a permanent wave. She's undefeatable. She'll be just the same when she's eighty. Or maybe she'll decide to settle down before that, and I shall find myself with a step-stepfather half a dozen years younger than myself who looks like a Shubert chorus boy. When I saw Tubby a year ago, he seemed to think that everything pointed to a man named Peake, who apparently never leaves her side. I trust not. I have met this Peake once or twice, at parties and so on, and he appeared to me a most kickworthy young heel. But I'm afraid he's the next in line. He's just her type. But I mustn't bore you with this family gossip. Will you have a cigarette?'

He held out his case, and was surprised to see that his guest had risen and appeared to be making preparations for departure.

'Hello!' he said. 'The party isn't over?'

Jane was seething internally with an electric fury that made her want to scream and claw and scratch, but because girls of her class are taught to discipline their emotions, she forced a wintry smile.

'I must go.'

'Oh, don't go yet.'

'I must. I hadn't realized it was so late.'

'It isn't late. Three o'clock. The shank of the afternoon.'

'I promised I would be home early.'

'But coffee? How about coffee?'

'No, thanks.'

'Only one-and-six.'

'I don't want any coffee.'

'Well, it's all most upsetting. I had been looking forward to another couple of hours of this.'

'I'm sorry.'

'Still, if you must go, you must. And now to make plans.'

'Plans?'

'For our next meeting. When do we meet again?'

'I don't know. I'm never in London. Good-bye.'

'But listen – '

'I'm sorry,' said Jane. 'I can't wait. Thank you very much for everything. Good-bye.'

She was out of the room before he could push his chair back and get up. Reaching the courtyard a few moments later, he found no signs of her. He stood, looking this way and that, feeling a little bewildered. It might be his imagination, but it seemed to him that in her departure there had been something almost abrupt.

Remembering that there was a bill to be paid and that his absence might be occasioning the grillroom authorities anxiety and concern, he returned to his table, where he ordered coffee for one and an A.B.C. Railway Guide.

Sipping thoughtfully, he began to turn the pages till he came to the W's.

6

Jane Abbott did not loiter on her homeward journey. She pushed her two-seater along at a rare pace. It ruffles a girl of sensibility, who shortly after breakfast has heard the man she loves called a twerp and a gigolo, to hear him, a few hours later, at luncheon, described as a kickworthy heel; and when a girl of sensibility is ruffled, she finds a certain release of spirit in ignoring the speed laws and keeping the needle up to the fifty-five mark. Teeth clenched and eyes smouldering, she sent her Widgeon Seven shooting through the quiet English countryside like a lambent flame.

The results of this whirlwind drive were twofold. It unquestionably relieved her feelings, and it brought her to Walsingford Parva, the little village that stood on the river-bank some half a mile from the gates of Walsingford Hall, so expeditiously that, glancing at her watch, she saw that she would have time to pay a brief visit to the houseboat *Mignonette* before going on to prattle and play clock golf with Mr Chinnery.

Halting the car at the gate which gave entrance to the water meadows, she hurried along the towpath, and was presently in sight of her objective.

The *Mignonette*, attached to the mainland by a narrow and rickety plank, lay off a willow-bordered field dappled with buttercups and daisies at a point where the stream widened out into a sort of miniature lagoon. It was a small squat craft; in its early youth a snowy white, but now, owing to never having received the lick of paint which it had been wanting for years, a rather repellent grey. This dinginess of exterior, taken in conjunction with the fact that the low rail which ran round its roof was broken in places, gave it a dishevelled, dissipated appearance, as of a houseboat which has been out with the boys.

At the moment of Jane's arrival Adrian Peake was in the little saloon which was to serve him for the next six weeks as a combined living and sleeping apartment. He was prodding the bunk with a dubious forefinger, and there was on his beautiful face the unmistakable look of a man who has been let in for something unpleasant by a woman and has just begun to realize the magnitude of the unpleasantness of what he has been let in for. Passionately fond of his creature comforts, he was finding out that the houseboat *Mignonette* was no luxury hotel.

Adrian Peake was an extraordinarily good-looking youth, slender of build and rather fragile of appearance, with wistful expressive eyes which somehow seemed to emphasize and underline his fragility. Women thought him delicate, and often told him to sit quiet while they rubbed his forehead with eau-de-Cologne. The Princess Dwornitzchek thought he needed feeding up, and had been doing it for months with caviar and *truite bleue* and minced chicken and pêche Melba at the more expensive class of restaurant. But though he must have absorbed very nearly his weight in these delicacies, he went on looking wistful and fragile.

Tubby Vanringham, as we have seen, thought him a twerp. And though Jane Abbott had denied this hotly, the charge is one which should, perhaps, be weighed and inquired into.

Much would seem to turn on what a twerp really is. Adrian Peake was one of those young men, with whom London nowadays is so bountifully supplied, who live, like locusts, on what they can pick up. Sometimes they sell cars on commission, dabble in gossip writing, do a bit of interior decorating, make film tests which never come to anything and, if they can find somebody to put up the money, run bottle-party night clubs. But mostly they prefer to exist beautifully on free lunches, free dinners, free suppers and free cocktails with little sausages on sticks.

If 'twerp' is the correct word to describe one who acts thus, then unquestionably Adrian Peake was a twerp in good standing. It is significant, in this connexion, to recall that Tubby's brother Joe had spoken of him as a heel, for, as all students of humanity are aware, a heel and a twerp are practically indistinguishable.

He had ceased to prod the bunk and was looking about him at the furnishings of the saloon, which were of a simple austerity which sent a chill down his spine, when Jane's voice brought him out on to the roof.

The sight of him, standing there gleaming in white flannel and the blazer of the dining club to which he had belonged at Oxford, completed the restoration of Jane's peace of mind. Joe was forgotten, and the poisoned dart which Tubby had planted in her bosom ceased to smart. Whatever slight defects of character Adrian Peake may have possessed, he was undeniably ornamental and, gazing at him, she was herself again. She marvelled how anyone, even a Theodore or a Joseph Vanringham, could possibly think him anything but perfect, and attributed their attitude to a sort of mental kink. It was a kink which she had noticed in some of the male guests at the Willoughbys' during that weekend which had brought him into her life. Men, it appeared, did not much like Adrian, and it showed, she considered, how crass and blind men as a sex were.

'Darling!' she cried.

'Oh, hullo,' said Adrian.

A slight sensation of flatness and disappointment came momentarily to mar Jane's mood of ecstasy. At a reunion like this, she had expected something warmer. It occurred to her that it might be pique at her belated arrival that was causing this lack of effusiveness. Adrian, she knew, was inclined to sulk a little on occasion. He was a ready pouter when things did not go just as he could have wished them to go.

'I'm terribly sorry I couldn't get here earlier, angel,' she said. 'I had to go to London. I've only just got back.'

'Oh, yes?'

'I had a luncheon engagement, and Buck wanted me to see a man for him who had sent him a hundred-pound bill he didn't think he ought to pay.'

This struck Adrian as a little odd. From the houseboat

52

Mignonette an excellent view of Walsingford Hall was to be obtained, and he had been looking at it quite a good deal, thinking how rich its owner must be. The vast, salmon-hued pile offended every artistic instinct in him, and looking at it made him feel as if he were listening to an out-of-tune piano, but it suggested large sums of money in the bank. And he would have supposed that a man of Sir Buckstone Abbott's opulence would simply have tossed a trifling account like that to his secretary and told her to make out a cheque.

Then he reflected that it is always these very rich people who make the greatest fuss over small amounts. He could remember the Princess Dwornitzchek questioning a two-shilling cover charge with a passionate vehemence which had nearly wrecked one of London's newer night clubs.

'It must have been warm in London,' he said. 'Where did you have lunch?'

'At the Savoy Grill.'

Adrian winced.

'I had mine,' he said with gloom, 'at the Goose and Gander. Gosh!'

'Wasn't it good?'

'Garbage. Have you ever had lunch at the Goose and Gander?'

'No.'

'They give you ham and eggs. And what they do to the ham, to get it that extraordinary blackish-purple colour,' said Adrian, brooding coldly in the past, 'I can't imagine.'

Once more, Jane was conscious of that sensation of flatness. She had been looking forward to this moment for weeks, dreaming of it, counting the minutes to it, and now that it was here, something seemed to have gone wrong with it. She had pictured their conversation, after these weeks of separation, having something of a lyrical quality. This note had not yet been struck.

She fought the insidious feeling of depression gallantly.

'Oh, well, what does all that matter? You're here. That's the great thing. Come on down.'

'All right. Stand clear.'

He jumped with a lissom grace, floating down to her side like something out of the Russian ballet. They walked away, and came through buttercups and daisies and the meadow-sweet that lay in their path like snow to a small spinney fragrant with the warm scent of ferns and blackberries.

'I say,' said Adrian, who had been wrapped in thought, 'are there mice on that boat?'

Jane was gallant, but she could not fight against this. Depression had its way with her.

'I don't know. Why? Would you like some?'

'I thought I heard a scratching noise.'

'Probably just rats.'

'Rats!'

'Water rats. I believe they use the *Mignonette* as a sort of club.'

Adrian turned and subjected the *Mignonette* to an anxious scrutiny. His sensitive features were a little twisted, and his wistful eyes sadder than ever. He was telling himself that he might have expected this sort of thing from that raffish, out-at-elbows pleasure craft.

'Rats?' he said thoughtfully. 'I wonder if any of them have died on board.'

'Do you want to send a wreath?'

'I noticed a smell in the saloon.'

'What sort of smell?'

'A funny smell?'

'Well, we all like a good laugh, don't we?'

'I believe those sheets are damp.'

'They're not.'

'They felt damp. And the bunk's very hard.'

Jane's hair was not red, but she had a red-haired girl's quick temper.

'The *Mignonette* isn't the Princess Dwornitzchek's yacht.'

Adrian stared.

'Eh?'

'I hear that's one of your favourite haunts.'

'Who told you that?'

'Her stepson. Tubby. He's staying at the Hall.'

'What?'

'Didn't she tell you?'

'She did say he was staying down in the country somewhere, but I wasn't paying much attention.'

'Odd. I thought you hung on her lips, eager to catch her lightest word.'

Jane gave a little shiver of shame. Before her eyes there had risen a vision of Joe Vanringham, looking at her with an eyebrow cocked and a mocking smile on his lips. A remark like that was just the sort of remark which would have excited his derision. And though she had blotted out Joe Vanringham from her life for ever, she did not like to see visions of him grinning at her. It is not pleasant for a girl to be grinned at by wraiths from the underworld.

Her words excited in Adrian Peake, not derision but concern. He became plaintive:

'Jane, darling! What's the matter?'

'Oh, nothing.'

'But there is. You're funny.'

'Like the smell in the saloon.'

'Jane, my sweet, what is it? Do tell me.'

All the brightness had gone out of Jane's afternoon. Long after she had supposed its venom impotent, that poisoned dart of Tubby's had stabbed again, like a dying snake taking a last bite.

'Oh, it's nothing. Just an idiotic thing Tubby said to me.'

'What?'

'Oh, nothing. He was just drivelling. Are you very fond of the Princess?'

'Not so very.'

'Then why do you spend weeks on her yacht?'

'Oh, well. She invited me.'

'Her invitations aren't royal commands, are they?'

'No, no, of course not. But I couldn't very well get out of it. These rich women so easily take offence. One has to be diplomatic.'

'Oh, Adrian!'

'I didn't want to hurt her feelings. She's a well-meaning old thing.'

'Not so very old. And not so very well-meaning. And I shouldn't think you could hurt her feelings with an axe.'

'Jane, darling, what's all this about?'

Jane melted. Her little gusts of temper were always like summer storms that quickly blow themselves out and leave the sky blue again. She perceived that she had been allowing her baser nature to come to the surface.

'I'm sorry,' she said. 'We're having what's technically known as a lovers' tiff, aren't we? It's my fault. I'm being a pig. I don't know why I'm talking like this. Original sin, or something, I expect. But it's your fault, too, really, my poppet. You're spoiling all the fun. It's a bit hard on a woman when she comes wailing for her demon lover, and finds that all he can talk about is mice and smells and damp sheets. Why not tell me you're glad to see me again?'

'But of course I am.'

'And it doesn't matter if the *Mignonette* is a bit uncomfortable? Can't you put up with a little discomfort for the sake of being near me?'

'But I'm not near you. I'm stuck away in a beastly boat, and you're up at the house. I should have thought it would have been so simple to have got your father to invite me to the Hall.'

'Not so simple as you think.'

They had sat down in the warm quiet of the spinney. Jane plucked a fern and twisted in round her finger.

'Hold your nose still. I want to tickle it. How brown you are.'

'When I was at Cannes last summer,' said Adrian proudly, 'I got brown all over.'

'Were you at Cannes last summer?'

'Oh, yes. All August and most of July.'

'I'd love to have seen you paddling, with your little spade and bucket.' Jane paused. 'But of course, I remember, you were on the yacht.'

'Er – yes.'

'You and your yachts! You and your Princess! I wish you wouldn't see so much of that woman, Adrian. It gives idiots like Tubby a chance to be idiotic.'

Adrian sat up.

'What was it Tubby said?'

'Well, if you really want to know, he's got the impression that you're engaged to her.'

'Engaged to her!'

'I told you he was just drivelling.'

'It's an absurd lie!'

'Well, naturally. You don't think I imagined that you were training to become a bigamist. But it wasn't a pleasant thing to get shot at you all of a sudden.'

'I should say not. It was abominable. I don't wonder you were upset. I'd like a word with Tubby.'

'Oh, that's all right. I ticked young Tubby off like a sergeant-major, curse him. It must have taken him hours to pick up the pieces. But you do see how people talk, don't you?'

'Of course, of course, of course. It just shows – But all that happened really was that I was sorry for her. She's a lonely old woman.'

'You keep calling her old. She looks about thirty.'

'And she seemed to like having me around.'

'Well, tell her that in future she can't.'

'She's quite nice, really.'

'Oh, I've nothing against her, except that she's a hard, arrogant, vindictive, domineering harridan, if harridan's the word I want. And now I simply must rush.'

'No, don't go.'

'I must. I promised Buck I would be back early, to make a fuss of Mr Chinnery.'

'Who's Mr Chinnery?'

'One of the lodgers.'

Adrian laughed. The word struck him as quaint and whimsical.

'But I want to talk to you.'

'What about? Mice?'

'No. I'm serious. I'm worried, Jane.'

'I can tell you what to do about that. I was reading an article in the paper this morning. You stand in front of the glass and smile and say fifty times, "I am bright and happy! I am bright and – "'

'No, really, I mean it. I'm worried about all this hole and corner business.'

'Are you referring to our romantic secret engagement?'

'But why has it got to be secret? Why have I got to lurk on this infernal boat? I know you think it amusing and exciting, and all that – '

'I don't, at all. You haven't grasped the idea.'

'It's underhand, Jane; it really is. And I hate doing anything underhand. Why not tell your father we're engaged?'

'And have him coming down to interview you with a horse-whip?'

'What!'

'Well, Barts do, you know, to the penniless suitor. I want you to get to know each other before we say anything. That's why you're on the *Mignonette* – not because I think it exciting and amusing. You must be patient, my wonder man. You must brave the mice and smells, and wait for the happy ending. And now I simply must rush. I ought to have been home ages ago.'

Because she had lost her temper and said unpleasant things and was thoroughly penitent and ashamed of herself, Jane threw herself into their parting embrace with a warmth that she did not often show, and which she would not have shown now, had she been aware that it was being observed.

Sauntering past the spinney and pausing, as he saw what was in progress, like some worthy citizen taking a front place at a dog-fight, there had come, silently and without any heralding of his approach, a small, round, rosy man in a loose sack suit and square-toed shoes of a vivid yellow. He was chewing gum. On his head was one of those hats designed primarily for the younger type of Western American college student; and on his face a look of tender and sentimental approval, as of one who likes to see the young folks happy.

Jane had been happier just before she caught sight of this person than immediately after becoming aware of his presence. With a little cry, she disengaged herself from Adrian's arms and hurried away across the meadow to where she had left the car.

As for the little man in the sack suit, he smiled a genial smile, revealing in the process a set of teeth of that perfect whiteness and regularity which Nature can never produce and only the hand of the artist is able to achieve, and resumed his walk.

7

The morning following Jane Abbott's visit to London dawned bright and fair. The ridge of high pressure extending over the whole of the British Isles was still in operation, and a sun as genial as that of yesterday shone down on Walsingford Parva, lighting up its thatched cottages, its picturesque church, its Jubilee watering-trough and the Goose and Gander, its only inn. And farther along the river-bank it shone down on Joe Vanringham, walking pensively along the towpath.

The reason Joe was pensive was that he had just eaten his first breakfast at the Goose and Gander, and was viewing the future with concern.

When, on the previous afternoon, he had taken the earliest possible train to the market town of Walsingford and thence had proceeded in a hired cab to Walsingford Parva, which was not on the railway, he had acted in ignorance of local conditions. At Walsingford Parva, he had assumed, he would be sure to find some snug, cosy, rustic hostelry from which he could conduct his operations in comfort. And all that Walsingford Parva had had to offer him was the Goose and Gander.

The Goose and Gander – J. B. Attwater, propr, licensed to sell ales and spirits – was all right for what it set out to be, but all it set out to be was a modest ale-house where thirsty sons of the soil could drop in and take their pint before going off to their homes at closing time. It did not expect resident guests. Resident guests flustered it. The arrival of Joe, scarcely an hour after that of the little man in the sack suit, had given the Goose and Gander something very like what an earlier age used to call the vapours.

It had pulled itself together and done its best, but its best had been terrible, and it was becoming increasingly clear to Joe, as he walked along, that an extended sojourn under the roof of J. B. Attwater was going to be a testing experience and one that would call for all a man had of fortitude and determination.

He was just wondering why J. B. Attwater, in purchasing

mattresses for his beds, had preferred to select the kind that are stuffed with clinkers, when he passed the clump of willows which had been impeding his view and saw that the vague white object beyond them was a houseboat.

Houseboats are always interesting. This one appeared to be deserted, and a far less inquisitive man than Joe would have felt urged to go aboard and explore. He mounted the narrow plank and stood on the deck, thus placing himself in the perfect position for seeing Walsingford Hall. He had seen the Hall before, for one got a glimpse of it from the garden of the Goose and Gander, but not so comprehensively as now. And he looked at it long and steadily, taking his time over it. There was repulsion in that look, because the place reminded him of a pickle factory, but also a sort of devotional ecstasy. Whatever its architectural short-comings, it housed the girl he loved.

He had been gazing some little while, like a fastidious pilgrim at a rococo shrine, when there was a dull bumping sound, and Adrian Peake, who had been in the saloon looking for his cigarette-case, came out, rubbing his head. The low doors of houseboat saloons are tricky till you get used to them.

There was a momentary silence. Both were unpleasantly surprised. As he had indicated in his conversation with Jane at the Savoy Grill, Adrian Peake was not a man for whom Joe cared. To Adrian, Joe was a fellow he knew slightly in London and had had no desire to meet again in the country.

'Oh, hullo!' he said.

'Good morning,' said Joe. 'I'm afraid I'm trespassing.'

'Oh, not at all.'

'I didn't know there was anybody here. Do you own this craft? I thought it was a derelict.'

'I'm not surprised,' said Adrian, with a morose look at his little home. 'No, I don't own it. I've taken it for a few weeks.'

'I'm at a pesthouse called the Goose and Gander.'

'I have my meals there,' said Adrian dejectedly.

He was no more dejected than Joe. In his darkest thoughts about the Goose and Gander, he had never supposed that life there involved Adrian Peake as a table companion.

'I'm just going off to breakfast there now,' said Adrian. 'Did you have breakfast there?'

'Yes. Ham and eggs.'

'That seems to be the only food they've ever heard of. They gave me ham and eggs yesterday. How do you suppose they get the ham that extraordinary blackish-purple colour?'

'Will power?' hazarded Joe.

'And have you ever tasted such filthy coffee?'

'Never,' said Joe, though he had lived in French hotels.

Something almost of cordiality came into Adrian Peake's eyes. As has been said, he had always disliked Joe, but he found him now sympathetic and a kindred spirit.

'The bread's not any too good, either,' he said.

'No,' said Joe. 'But what are you doing down here, living on a houseboat? Writing a novel?'

'No, just camping out.'

'Well, sooner you than me.'

There was a pause.

'Well,' said Adrian, 'may as well be getting along, I suppose. You coming my way?'

'I thought, if you don't mind, I'd stay on here for a while.'

'Do.'

'I might have a swim, if you've really no objection to me making myself at home.'

'You'll find a towel in the saloon,' said Adrian. He checked the impulse to warn his companion against bumping his head. That brief feeling of camaraderie had already waned. Soberer thought told him that he wanted Joe to bump his head.

Joe, alone once more, started to give himself up again to tender contemplation of Walsingford Hall. But he had scarcely settled down to it, when he saw that his meditations were about to be interrupted. A tall sender figure was coming across the water meadows.

Sir Buckstone Abbott was a man of his word. He had promised that he would send Miss Whittaker down to the houseboat with a note inviting its tenant to come up and see him some time, and here was Miss Whittaker bearing that note. She halted at the foot of the plank and looked up. Joe came to the broken rail and looked down. He did not know who this vision might be, but in the absence of the *Mignonette*'s proprietor, it was plainly for him to do the honours.

'Good morning,' he said.

'Good morning,' said Miss Whittaker.

'Nice day.'

'Very nace. Mr Peake?'

Joe remained tranquil. Only yesterday he had been accused of being J. Mortimer Busby, and a man to whom this happens learns to take it. Without heat, he replied that he was not Mr Peake.

'He has gone off to the inn to have breakfast, and at this moment is probably standing with reluctant feet where the eggs and bacon meet. My name is Vanringham.'

This statement seemed to surprise and, oddly, to displease his visitor. Her tiptilted nose quivered, and she repeated the word with a rising inflexion which betrayed unmistakable distaste.

'Vanringham?'

'You seem startled and revolted.'

'I know a Mr Vanringham,' said Miss Whittaker, as if that explained it. Then, dismissing the nauseous subject: 'Sir Buckstone Abbott desired me to call and leave a note for Mr Peake. I will put it in the saloon, so that he will find it when he returns.'

She spoke, however, with a diffident note in her voice, and Joe saw that she was standing with reluctant feet where the gangplank and river-bank met, eyeing the former dubiously. It was plain that it did not enjoy her full confidence. He came to the rescue of beauty in distress.

'No, please. I'll come down and get it,' he said, and made a courtly spring.

We have seen Adrian Peake performing this feat with lissom grace and complete success. Joe was not so adroit. Arriving ashore, he tripped and staggered and, clutching the air, was embarrassed to find his arms full of unexpected Whittaker. He released her immediately, but it had been disconcerting.

'I beg your pardon!' he said.

'Not at all.'

'I lost my balance.'

'Quate,' said Miss Whittaker.

Joe took the note from her, and stood looking meditatively at it. The sight of that 'A. Peake, Esq.' on the envelope saddened him. He was thinking how much better 'J. J. Vanringham, Esq.' would have looked.

For it was, he had no difficulty in divining, a note of invitation. Some revelry was afoot up at the soap works, and Adrian Peake, purely because he was the tenant of the *Mignonette*, had been asked to come along and sit in. Obviously, by taking the houseboat, he had fallen within the scope of Sir Buckstone Abbott's feudal benevolence.

No such hospitality would be extended to the lessee of a back bedroom at the Goose and Gander. When it came to mixing with the merrymakers of Walsingford Hall, poor devils who mouldered at the Goose and Gander hadn't a hope. They weren't even considered. In short, for all practical purposes, by coming to Walsingford Parva and establishing himself at the Goose and Gander, he had not advanced his ends in the slightest degree. He was as far removed from the girl he loved as if he had remained in his flat in London.

Adrian Peake, skipper of the *Mignonette*, was plainly going to be given the run of the Hall. He would be popping in and out there all the time, like a rabbit. He would be in a position to see Jane daily. The best Joseph Vanringham could expect to see was J. B. Attwater, licensed to sell ales and spirits, and that extraordinary girl with the adenoids who had brought him his breakfast.

It was bitter, and he recognized it as such. But he did not allow himself to remain brooding long over life's little ironies. A man alone with a woman has his social obligations.

'So you know somebody of my name?' he said, making light conversation. 'Not a very common name. In fact, the only other Vanringham I know is my brother Tubby. Is he the one you've met?'

'The name of the Mr Vanringham with whom I am acquainted,' said Miss Whittaker, speaking as if the admission soiled and degraded her, 'is Theodore.'

'That's Tubby, all right. Where did you happen to run into him?'

'Mr Theodore Vanringham is one of the guests of my employer, Sir Buckstone Abbott.'

'What? Good heavens! Do you mean to say Tubby's up there at the pickle factory?'

'I beg your pardon?'

'Is my brother staying at Walsingford Hall?'

'Quate. Then if you will be so kind as to see that Mr Peake receives the note – Thank you. Good morning.'

She glided away, leaving him staring after her, stunned. But it was only for a moment that he stood thus inactive. Recovering swiftly, he darted off along the towpath toward the Goose and Gander. J. B. Attwater, he knew, possessed a telephone, and it was his aim to get to it as quickly as possible.

It had shaken Joe to his foundations – this discovery that Tubby was a guest at the Hall. The news changed the whole aspect of affairs. He ceased to look on himself as an outcast. He had a friend at court, possibly a powerful friend at court. 'Young Vanringham's brother?' they would say. 'My dear! We must ask him up immediately!' Or would they? It was this point that he wished to have made clear to him without delay, and his fingers trembled so much that he could hardly lift the receiver. But eventually he managed it and found himself in communication with somebody who appeared to be Sir Buckstone's butler. A brief intermission, and Tubby's voice came over the wire.

It was a hollow, toneless voice, for the butler's summons had reached Theodore Vanringham at a moment when he was deeper than usual in gloomy thoughts on Woman's perfidy. Watching Miss Whittaker's movements with a pair of field-glasses, he had seen her cross the meadow to the houseboat, where a male figure, whose features he had been unable to discern, had leaped from the roof and clasped her in his embrace. Not even the news that a brother whom he had not seen for a year wished to speak to him on the telephone could rouse him to any real animation after that.

'Hello, Joe,' he said sombrely.

Joe, to whom recent events had given animation enough for two, barked like a seal.

'Hey, Tubby!'

'Where are you talking from?'

'The local inn. I'm staying there. Say, Tubby – '

'Why?'

'Never mind why. Listen, Tubby; this is urgent. What is your standing in that joint?'

'Eh?'

'At Walsingford Hall.'

'What is my standing at Walsingford Hall?'

'Yes. How do you rate? If you suggested ringing in an only brother, would they say "Fine! Any brother of yours," or would there be angry mutters of "Oh, my God, not two of them"?'

'You mean you want to come here?'

'That's right.'

'Well, come on, then.'

'Can you work me in?'

'You don't have to be worked in.'

'I can't just walk in.'

'Sure you can, if you've got the money. Step up to the front door and press the bell.'

'How do you mean, money?'

'The price of admission. You can't be a paying guest if you don't pay.'

'Paying guest?'

'You know what a paying guest is.'

'But Sir Buckstone Abbott doesn't take in paying guests?'

'He certainly does.'

'You mean the place is a sort of residential hotel?'

'That's about it. Do you want to join the troupe?'

'You bet I do.'

'Then come on up, and I'll introduce you to the boss.'

8

The road that led to Walsingford Hall from the village of Walsingford Parva was steep and dusty, but Joe, though the sun was now shining more strongly than ever, skimmed up it like the god Mercury on winged feet, too busy with golden thoughts to notice what might have discouraged a less eager pedestrian. Where his brother Tubby would have puffed, he sang.

Only the author of a thesauras could have done justice to his emotions as he walked. Roget, for instance, would have described him as glad, happy, pleased, elated, entranced, ecstatic and overjoyed, and he would have been right. He saw now how silly he had been in not realizing from the start that providence was bound to look after a man as good as himself. It was just good men like himself for whom it reserved its special efforts. In uplifted mood he reached the top of the hill, and came upon Tubby sitting on a stile by the roadside.

'Hello, Joe,' said Tubby. 'Fancy you bobbing up.'

'Yes,' said Joe.

No further word was spoken on the subject of this unlooked-for reunion after weary months of separation. Each seemed to think that this about covered it. The Vanringhams were not a family who made much of a fuss about long-lost brothers.

'Listen, Tubby,' said Joe, 'are you certain?'

'You'd better come and sit down and cool off,' said Tubby, eyeing him critically. 'You look as if you had been chasing an electric hare. Am I certain about what?'

'This paying-guest thing.'

'Sure.'

'Are you a paying guest?'

'Sure.'

'Can anyone be a paying guest?'

'Sure.'

'Well, this is the most amazing thing I ever heard. How long has this been going on?'

'I don't know. Quite a time, I guess. There were already six souls in captivity when I arrived. Half these folks with big houses take in paying guests nowadays. They have to, or they don't eat.'

'So I can just walk in and ask for a reservation?'

'If you've got what it takes. You pay as you enter. Can you ante up?'

'Of course.'

'Prices run kind of high.'

'That's all right. I've plenty of money.'

'Been robbing a bank?'

'Been knocking the drama-loving public's eye out with the biggest comedy hit there's been in years. Don't you ever read the papers? My play opened the night before last. A smacko.'

'Then you're just the sort of bird they need up here. They'll put out the red carpet.'

Joe regarded his brother affectionately.

'Gosh!' he said. 'It was a bit of luck finding you on the premises.'

'Who told you I was here?'

'A female with an Oxford accent. I don't know her name. She came to that houseboat down there when I happened to be on it just now.'

Tubby started. His face darkened. He was eyeing Joe in a cold and unbrotherly manner.

'Was it you,' he said gratingly, 'that I saw hugging Miss Whittaker?'

'Is her name Whittaker? No, of course, I didn't hug her.'

'You did.'

'I didn't, blast you. Do you think a busy man like me has got time to go about hugging girls. Apart from being too spiritual anyway.'

'I distinctly saw you leap from the boat and clasp her in your embrace.'

'Ah, that's different. Yes, I did that. But purely because I lost my equilibrium and had to clutch at a straw. She was the straw. But how did you see us? You weren't there.'

'Field-glasses,' said Tubby briefly.

The significance of the statement was not lost on Joe.

'You were snooping after her with field-glasses? Tubby, this means something. You had better tell me all about it, my lad. Is this love?'

Tubby shuffled his feet.

'Well, it is and it isn't.'

'Make up your mind.'

'Well, it's this way, Joe: I – '

A sudden urge to confide his tragedy to a sympathetic ear overcame Tubby. He was not a man who found it easy to keep his troubles to himself.

'Listen, Joe, I'll tell you the whole thing. I love her. Yes, I'll admit that I love her.'

'Of course.'

'What do you mean, of course?'

'Well, don't you always love every girl you meet?'

Tubby began to wonder whether, in classing his brother's ear as sympathetic, he had not made an incorrect diagnosis. But he persevered.

'Oh, I know I've played around in the past – '

'I'll say you have. You started telephoning girls as soon as your childish voice had learned to lisp in numbers.'

'I know, I know. But this was the real thing.'

'I see.'

'Quite different from those boyish flirtations.'

'I see.'

'I worshipped the very ground she walked on.'

'I see.'

Joe looked at his brother commiseratingly. He felt that it was his duty to speak out. The impression he had gathered from Miss Whittaker's manner was that Tubby had added one more to his long list of lemons in the garden of love, and it seemed to him that he ought to be given some inkling of the state of affairs. No use letting the poor clam go on living in a fool's paradise.

'Say, Tubby,' he said, 'I don't want to shatter your dreams and all that, but are you sure you've clicked in that direction quite so solidly as you imagine? I ought to tell you that, when we were discussing you, the girl's manner struck me as odd. It seemed to be lacking in warmth. I don't want to alarm you, but if you haven't already started getting measured for the wedding trousers, I think I'd put it off for a while, if I were you. I believe you've picked another loser.'

'Oh, sure.' A hacking, mirthless laugh broke from Tubby's lips as if he had been a fiend in hell listening to another fiend telling a good one. 'All is over between us, if that's what you mean. Everything completely washed up.'

'Why, what happened?'

'Oh, we had a fight.'

'What about?'

'Well, it started because she didn't like the way I talked.'

'What did you say that shocked her so much?'

'I said I liked tomayto ketchup.'

Joe considered this, and found himself perplexed. He could see nothing so very licentious in the words, nothing calculated to give offence to a broad-minded modern girl.

'She said I ought to say "tomarto ketchup."'

'Oh, I get you. Well, why didn't you point out that a girl who says "Quate" and "desi-ah" has a nerve criticizing other people's "tomaytoes"?'

'I did. And it got her a good deal steamed up. One word led to another, and in about a couple of minutes we were going at it hot and heavy. And just as I was saying she dropped her aitches and she was calling me an obstinate, pig-headed vulgarian, guess what.'

'What?'

'What do you think?'

'What?'

'The afternoon mail came in.'

He paused dramatically. Joe shook his head.

'I'm sorry, Tubby. I want to be a ministering angel, but I can't follow the plot. Why was that such a terrific second-act curtain?'

Tubby's voice shook, growing shrill with the anguish of remembered wrongs:

'Because there was a package for her. A smallish brown-paper package. Registered! And I could feel there was a cardboard box inside it.'

'You felt it?'

'Sure. I said, "Hello, what's this?" and picked it up.'

'Inquisitive young hound.'

'Nothing of the kind. I was simply changing the subject. And I had taken out my knife and was starting to cut the string for her, purely with the idea of doing the civil thing and saving her trouble, when she let out a kind of screech and snatched the package from me. At the same time blushing. Blushing! Get that. Her whole map flooded by a crimson blush.'

'Strange.'

'Nothing strange about it. I saw the reason in a flash. Inside that package she knew there was jewellery. She had been two-timing me, and this was a present from the other fellow.'

'Why on earth should you think that?'

'What else could I think, when she wouldn't show it to me?'

'It might have been something she just didn't want you to see.'

'You're darned right, it was something she didn't want me to see. It was a brooch or a sunburst from this city slicker in the background. Her behaviour, when I taxed her with it, was enough to tell me that. I said, "If you won't let me look, I shall know what to think." She said, "Think what you please." I said "Very good. Then this is the end." She said, "Quate." And there the matter rests.'

Joe, softened by his own great love, was much too tender-hearted not to be moved by this unbaring of a strong man's soul. He gave his brother's shoulder a kindly slap. It would have made Mortimer Busby leap like a jumping bean, but it seemed to please Tubby. He snorted rather gratefully.

'Chin up!' said Joe.

'Oh, I'm all right,' said Tubby with another of those hacking laughs. 'You don't suppose I care, do you? Come on, let's go.'

He rose and started toward the gates of the Hall. Joe followed him, pondering over this revelation. They turned in and made for the terrace.

'So everything's off?'

'Right off.'

'Any idea who the other fellow is?'

'I'll tell you who I thought it might be, for a time. A guy named Peake.'

'Peake?'

'I told you about him last time we met. The twerp that's always hanging around Heloise. It struck me as darned suspicious when Prudence told me that he had turned up here and was living on the houseboat. And then I asked myself: Was Peake the sort of man who would spend his cash buying jewellery for girls? And I felt, no, he wasn't. I could see him sending poisoned chocolates to someone – cheap ones, of course – but not jewellery. And then it turned out that the reason he was down here was because he was engaged to Sir Buckstone's daughter Jane. That cleared him. I saw that I had wronged the bird. Peake was innocent. . . . Wait here,' said Tubby, 'and I'll go and find the old boy and tell him you've arrived.'

He went into the house, leaving Joe standing rooted to the spot, trying to cope with this shocking piece of news, so much harder to digest than even a Goose and Gander breakfast. His brother's words had stunned him.

From time to time, since Jane had left him, Joe Vanringham had given a certain amount of fugitive thought to the unknown to whom she was betrothed, but never in his most gloomy moments had he imagined that this shadowy figure would turn out to be anyone like Adrian Peake. The mental picture he had drawn had been of some red-faced young squire of the neighbourhood, hunting foxes and massacring pheasants with a hearty, 'Eh, what?' Girls, he knew, were notoriously odd in matters of the heart – goddesses had mated with shepherds, and princesses with tenders of swine – but it seemed incredible that any girl could have been so odd as to get engaged to Adrian Peake.

Adrian Peake! He was able to understand now his guest's abrupt departure from the luncheon table.

Adrian Peake! His gratitude to providence waned. It had not turned in so grand a job as he had supposed. Far, very far from it. It was all very well for providence to introduce him into Walsingford Hall and then sit back smiling and rubbing its hands as if that had fixed everything nicely. What did it profit him to be at the Hall if Adrian Peake was to be there too? The one essential for a Young Lochinvar is a clear field with the other fellow out of the way.

What was really required, he perceived, was some master-stroke that would eliminate Adrian Peake from the Walsing-ford scene and keep him eliminated.

He awoke from his thoughts to see Tubby returning.

'His Nibs will be out in a minute,' said Tubby. 'He's just washing the dog. He's tickled pink, as I anticipated.'

'Tubby,' said Joe, 'I've been thinking.'

'What about?'

'This business of yours. Wondering if you are right in dismissing Peake so lightly. I believe he's your man.'

'But I told you he was engaged to Jane Abbott.'

'Where did you hear that?'

'From Jane in person.'

'Does Sir Buckstone know about it?'

'I guess not. I seem to remember Jane saying something about it being a secret. I don't blame her for not wanting to spring it on him. Peake hasn't a bean in the world, except what he can cadge from people. I should imagine Sir Buckstone would hit the ceiling. Still, they seem to be definitely engaged.'

'But even so – '

'If Peake's tied up with Jane, what would he be doing fooling around with –'

'Just the sort of thing he would do, if you ask me. Being engaged to one girl wouldn't stop Peake making passes at another girl. The more the merrier with A. Peake. He's that sort of fellow.'

A dark flush came into Tubby's face.

'Oh,' he said. 'Trying to turn this joint into an abode of love, is he? Well, first thing after lunch, I step along to that houseboat and paste him right on the smush.'

A thrill of quiet happiness pervaded Joe Vanringham. It was clear to him that the houseboat *Mignonette*, with all its claims on Sir Buckstone Abbott's hospitality, would shortly be vacant. He thought he had read Adrian Peake's character well enough to be convinced that to remain in a spot where people were scheming to paste him in the smush would be totally foreign to his policy.

'Peake,' he said, with virtuous distaste, 'is obviously a heartless philanderer. Look at this note. Miss Whittaker left it for him.'

Tubby leaped.

'A note?'

'Here it is. What do you make of that? What does that suggest to you?'

'She wouldn't leave a note for him if he wasn't the fellow.'

'Precisely. A sound piece of reasoning. Gosh, Tubby, you're shrewd.'

'Gimme,' said Tubby.

This, Joe felt, was not so good. That his brother should see the contents of the envelope which he was holding was the last thing he desired. He knew only too well how sedative they would be. Thinking to peruse words of guilty passion from the girl who had deceived him and finding only an innocent invitation to buns and croquet from a blameless Baronet, he would be discouraged in his crusade. He would waver, hesitate, possibly abandon altogether that excellent plan of his of pasting Peake in the smush.

He set himself to squash the idea.

'You can't read another man's letters!'

'Watch me,' said Tubby, and flicked it from his grasp.

It was just as Joe had feared. Before his eyes, his incandescent brother was visibly cooling off. He had come in like a lion. Reading this note had made him a lamb.

'No,' he said. 'You're wrong. Peake isn't the fellow. This is just a note from Sir Buckstone, asking him to come up and mix.'

Joe did his best: 'Still – '

'No, it can't be Peake.'

Joe continued to do his best, though he was feeling baffled and despondent, like a cinquecento Italian prince who, after engaging a hired assassin to do a job of work, is informed that the fellow has got religion and retired from business.

'Still, just to be on the safe side, don't you think it would be as well to see him and tell him that if he's around these parts tomorrow, you will twist his neck and drop him in the river? It can't do any harm.'

'Yes, it can. And I'll tell you why. What about Jane biting a piece out of my leg for talking tough to her boy friend. And here's another thought: Suppose Peake went and told Heloise. She's pretty sold on him. No, I'm well out of it, I guess. It would never have done, anyway. . . . Hey!' said Tubby, driving a finger into Joe's ribs. He indicated a stocky figure approaching across the terrace. 'Here comes Sir Buckstone. I'll leave you to it.'

9

Sir Buckstone Abbott's weather-beaten face seemed to be wavering between a hospitable smile and the rigidity of embarrassment. In the manner in which he smacked his gaitered leg with his hunting crop there was something almost coy. Joe gathered that he did not, as a rule, conduct these business conferences in person.

'Mr Vanringham?'

'How do you do?'

'How do you do?'

'I have been admiring your view,' said Joe agreeably.

Sir Buckstone took a look at it and delivered another on-slaught on his leg.

'Eh? Oh, yes, capital view. The river and all that.'

'Yes.'

'On a clear day you can see to – I forget where, but quite a distance.'

'It's pretty clear this morning.'

'Oh, very. Yes, nice and clear. Er – your brother tells me, Mr Vanringham – I hear that you – ah – '

'Yes.'

'Delighted. We are all very fond of your brother. Tubby, eh? Ha-ha! Tubby.'

'I hope you will have room for me at the Hall.'

'Oh, yes, lots of room. Big place. Costs the deuce of a lot to keep up. Er – ha – hr'rmph,' said Sir Buckstone, catching himself a nasty one with the hunting crop.

Joe felt that the time had come to help him out.

'When I was chatting with my brother, Sir Buckstone, I rather got the impression that before a fellow entered into residence at Walsingford Hall, there were certain formalities to be observed. Putting it briefly, he hinted that one had got to come across.'

A look of relief came into the Baronet's face. As Joe had surmised, he seldom appeared at these business chats in person. He eyed Joe with affection, approving of his tact.

'Well, as a matter of fact,' he said, 'yes. One or two of my guests do pay a sort of – er – nominal sum. Helps to keep things going and all that sort of thing. But I usually leave – That is to say, my secretary, Miss Whittaker, generally attends – In short, I am not quite sure – '

Once more Joe felt impelled to help out:

'Perhaps if I had a talk with Miss Whittaker – '

'Yes, that is what I should suggest.'

'I shall enjoy meeting Miss Whittaker again.'

'You've met her?'

'We have had one short but very agreeable interview.

Almost a romp it became at one time. Shall we go and find her, then?'

'Certainly. By all means.' Sir Buckstone coughed. He had taken a great liking to this young man, and benevolence was struggling with the business sense. 'You – er – you mustn't let her overcharge you.'

'Oh, that's all right.'

'She sometimes allows her anxiety to help to – er – colour her views on – '

'That's quite all right.' It occurred to Joe that this was an excellent opportunity to give the father of the girl he loved some idea of his financial condition. Fathers like to know these things. 'Money means nothing to me.'

'It doesn't?' said Sir Buckstone, startled. They had been strolling along the terrace, but he now halted in order to get a better view of this *lusus naturæ*.

'Not a thing. You see, I've so much of it. And pouring in all the time. Take this play of mine that's running in London now.'

'You're a dramatist, are you?'

'Yes. Well, as I say, take this play of mine. An enormous success. Suppose we put my royalties for the London run at ten thousand pounds.'

'Ten thousand?'

'We want to be conservative.'

'Of course. Conservative, yes.'

'Then, on top of that there are the provincial rights, the American rights, the Australian rights, the picture rights, radio rights, amateur rights, future musical-comedy rights, future picture rights on those, translation into the French, the German, the Italian, the Czechoslovakian – Shall we say fifty thousand pounds in all?'

'Fifty thousand!'

'We are being conservative,' Joe reminded him.

'That's a great deal of money.'

'Oh, no. Just a beginning. Merely scratching the surface, you might say. We now come to my next one.'

'You have written another?'

'Not yet. But when I do. Suppose we pencil in a hundred thousand for that, because, of course, one will make one's price for the picture rights stiffer. We must take that into consideration.'

'Of course.'

'Yes, I think we may safely say a hundred thousand pounds. And then – this is where it begins to mount up – there comes the one after that. Try to imagine what that will make!'

'A fortune!'

'Positively.'

Sir Buckstone's head was swimming, but a possible flaw in his companion's reasoning occurred to him. Far-fetched, perhaps, but worth pointing out.

'Suppose your next ones aren't successful?'

Joe raised his eyebrows with a short, amused laugh.

'Of course, of course,' said Sir Buckstone, feeling foolish. 'Of course. Don't know why I said it.'

He was conscious of a slight giddiness. A sudden roseate thought had crossed his mind. Here was this chap – well-knit, clean-cut, quite passably good-looking – with more money than he knew what to do with – Might it not possibly happen that Jane –

'Bless my soul!' he said.

His affection for this sterling young fellow was growing momently.

'Well, I congratulate you. It is a splendid position for you to have reached at your age – er – your brother did not tell me your name?'

'Joe.'

'Joe, eh? Well, my dear Joe, you are certainly entitled to be proud of yourself.'

'Very kind of you to say so, Sir Buckstone.'

'Call me Buck. Why, you're a millionaire!'

'More or less, Buck, I suppose.'

'Bless my soul!' said Sir Buckstone.

He fell into a thoughtful silence. They moved along the terrace and became aware of an elegant figure, standing there in maiden meditation. Sir Buckstone nudged Joe gently.

'Oh, Miss Whittaker,' he called.

'Yes, Sir Buckstone?'

'I believe you know Mr Vanringham? Mr Joe Vanringham. Brother of the other one. He is coming to join us here.'

'Oh, yay-ess?'

'Yes. And I thought – he thought – we both thought he might have a word with you.... Good-bye, then, for the present, Joe.'

'See you later, Buck.'

The Baronet disappeared, glad to be removed from contact with the sordid, and Joe turned to Miss Whittaker, to whom it was his intention to talk like a Dutch uncle. His heart ached with an elder brother's pity for Tubby, severed from this girl by what he was sure was only a temporary misunderstanding; and all that was needed, he felt, to clear up this annoying little spot of trouble was a word or two in season from a level-headed man of the world.

These plans, however, which level-headed men of the world form in careless ignorance of what they are up against often fail to reach fruition. There is a type of girl, born in Kensington and trained in business colleges, to whom it is not easy to talk like a Dutch uncle. To this class Prudence Whittaker belonged.

'For about how long,' she asked, 'would it be your intention to remain at the Hall, Mr Vanringham?'

'Miss Whittaker,' said Joe, 'can you look me in the eye?'

She could, and proved it by doing so.

'Miss Whittaker,' said Joe, 'you have treated my brother shamefully. Shamefully! My brother, Miss Whittaker.'

'I would prefer to confine our conversation entirely to business, Mr Vanringham.'

'He loves you passionately, madly, Miss Whittaker.'

'I would prefer – '

'And all you have to do in order to place matters once more on their former hotsy-totsy footing is to come clean about that brown-paper package.'

'I would prefer – '

'If it was, as he supposes, jewellery from a city slicker, then there is no more to be said. But if – '

'I would prefer, Mr Vanringham, not to discuss the matter.'

There had come over her classically modelled face an almost visible glaze of ice, and so intimidating was this that Joe decided to humour her wishes. Already his lower slopes were beginning to freeze.

'All right,' he said resignedly. 'Well, what's the tariff?'

'Thirty pounds a week.'

'Including use of bath?'

'There is a bathroom attached to the room which you would occupy.'

'What, in an English country house?'

'Walsingford Hall was thoroughly modernized by Sir Buckstone's predecessah. I can assure you that you would be quite comfortable.'

'But are bathrooms everything?'

'Sir Buckstone has an excellent chef.'

'Is food everything, Miss Whittaker?'

'If you are thinking of your fellow guests – '

'Frankly, I am. I saw a film the other day, the action of which took place on Devil's Island, and the society there struck me as being very mixed. Nothing of that sort here, I trust?'

'Sir Buckstone's guests are all socially impeccable.'

'Are what?'

'Socially impeccable.'

'I'll bet you can't say that ten times, quick.'

Prudence Whittaker maintained a proud silence.

'And now,' said Joe, 'the most important thing of all. What about the treatment of the inmates? I will be quite frank with you, Miss Whittaker. I have just come from the village, and there are ugly stories going about down there. People are talking. They say that as the ploughman homeward plods his weary way of an evening, he sometimes hears screams coming from Walsingford Hall.'

A shapely foot began to tap the terraced turf.

'Of course,' said Joe, 'I quite realize that in an institution like this you must have discipline. Please don't think me a foolish sentimentalist. If the order has gone out that the gang is to play croquet, and Number 6408, let us say, wants to play hopscotch, naturally, you have to be firm. I understand that. It is as if somebody on a Continental tour tried to sneak off to Beautiful Naples when Mr Cook had said they were to go to Lovely Lucerne. But discipline is one thing, harshness another. There is a difference between firmness and brutality.'

'Mr Vanringham – '

'I am told that when one of the paying guests tried to escape last week he was chased across the ice with bloodhounds. Was that right, Miss Whittaker? Was that humane? There are limits, surely?'

'Mr Vanringham, do you desi-ah a room, or do you not? I am a little busy this morning.'

'You aren't in the least busy this morning. When I came up, all you were doing was just standing there with blinding tears of wild regret in your eyes, thinking of Tubby.'

'Mr Vanringham!'

'Miss Whittaker?'

'Do you or do you not – '

'Yes, ma'am.'

'Very good. I will go and see to it.'

She walked away, a dignified, disdainful figure. And Joe, though there were a number of things he would have liked to ask her – whether, for example, the American honour system was in operation at Walsingford Hall and what she thought of his chances of becoming a trusty – did not seek to detain her.

He had other work to do. That thrumming hunting crop of Sir Buckstone's had given him the inspiration which he had been seeking ever since Tubby had failed him, and it was his desire at the earliest possible moment to establish connexion with Adrian Peake.

He crossed the terrace and started off down the steep dusty road that led to the Goose and Gander.

Adrian Peake had finished his breakfast and was smoking a cigarette on the rustic bench outside the inn's parlour. He was gazing up at Walsingford Hall.

Much had happened to disturb Adrian Peake this morning. He had not liked meeting Joe. The ham had been as bad as yesterday's, and the coffee worse. And he had started the day badly by having a broken night, due partly to the eerie lapping of the water against the side of the boat, partly to the scratching noise which had brought back to his mind Jane's unfortunate remark about the water rats' club, and partly to the unknown bird, which, rising at five sharp, had begun going 'Kwah, kawh' like a rusty hinge.

Nevertheless, the eye which he was directing at Walsingford Hall was a happy, contented eye. The house seemed to him to breathe opulence from every brick; and to one who from boyhood up had been consistently on the make, the thought that he had won the heart of its heiress was very pleasant on this lovely morning. Architecturally, Walsingford Hall offended his cultured taste, but it had the same charm for him which a millionaire uncle from Australia exerts in spite of wearing a loud check suit and a fancy waistcoat. Wealth is entitled to its eccentricities of exterior, and, in return for what lies beneath, we are prepared to condone the outer crust.

With a happy little sigh, he threw away his cigarette, and was lighting another when Joe arrived. Having no desire for further conversation, he rose and started to move to the gate.

There was tenseness in Joe's manner.

'Where are you going?'

'Back to the boat.'

'Don't!' said Joe.

He thrust Adrian gently back on to the rustic bench, then sat down himself and placed a kindly hand on the other's shoulder. Adrian removed the shoulder and hitched himself farther along the bench.

'What do you mean?'

'I wouldn't if I were you.'

'Why not?'

'Somebody is there whom I don't think you will want to meet.'

'Eh?'

'At least, he's on his way there. My brother Tubby hurried down ahead of him to warn you.'

'Warn me?'

'Rather considerate of him, I thought.'

'What are you talking about?'

'I'm telling you. Just after you left me, my brother Tubby, who, it appears, is staying at the Hall, arrived, very hot and breathless. "Where's Peake?" he asked. "Gone to the inn," I said. "Tell him to stay there," said Tubby. "Sir Buckstone Abbott is after him with a hunting crop. He says he intends to rip the stuffing out of him."'

'What!'

'That's what I said. But Tubby explained. He tells me you have become engaged to Sir Buckstone's daughter. Is it true?'

'Yes.'

'Secretly?'

'Yes.'

'And your means are somewhat straitened?'

'Yes.'

'Then that's the trouble. That's what he resents. I don't know how well you know Sir Buckstone. I mean, have you ever studied his psychology?'

'I've never met him.'

'I know him intimately. A delightful man if you don't rub him the wrong way, but, if you do, subject to fits of ungovernable fury. You can't blame him, of course. It's that sunstroke he had when he was big-game hunting in Africa. He's never really been the same since. Sometimes I think he's not altogether sane.'

Adrian Peake's face had taken on a pallor which would have brought any member of his circle of female acquaintances, could she have seen it, rallying round solicitously with eau-de-Cologne and champagne. He was wondering what madness had led him to urge Jane to tell her father about their engagement, and wishing that girls did not take a fellow so literally.

'His attitude in the present case certainly suggests it,' said Joe. 'Tubby tells me the man seemed absolutely berserk. All he would talk about was this idea he'd got of taking you apart. Tubby tried to reason with him. "Oh, I wouldn't." Tubby said. "I will," replied Sir Buckstone testily. "I want to see what's inside him." And then a lot of stuff about your liver. He's like that when he gets into these lunatic furies of his. Nothing can stop him working them off. In this case, for instance, any ordinary man would have paused and said to himself: "I simply mustn't disembowel this fellow. He will bring an action against me for assault and battery and win it hands down. I will curb myself. I will exercise self-control." But not Sir Buckstone. He doesn't think of the jam it may get him into. All he cares about is the passing gratification of beating you to a jelly. Just so long as he can feel that you will spend the next few months in hospital – '

Adrian Peake rose abruptly.

'I'm going to get out of here! '

'I would. Right away. It was what I was about to suggest.

I'll take the boat off your hands. How much did you pay for it?'

'Twenty pounds.'

'I'll mail you a cheque. And now I'd be off, if I were you. Don't stop to pack. I'll send your things on. What's the address?'

'It's in the telephone book. I wonder when there's a train.'

'I wouldn't wait for trains. Hire a car.'

Adrian's thrifty soul writhed a little at the thought, but he saw that the advice was good.

'I will.' He paused. He did not like Joe, but he supposed that he ought to display at least a formal gratitude for what he had done. 'Thank you, Vanringham.'

'Not at all. Good-bye.'

'Good-bye.'

Joe leaned back on the rustic bench, gazing contentedly up at the sky through the branches of the tree that shaded it. A voice spoke behind him, and he turned.

Framed in the open window of the parlour was a small, round, rosy man in a loose sack suit. He was also wearing, though Joe could not see these, square-toed shoes of a vivid yellow. On his head was a hat of the kind designed primarily for the younger type of Western American college student. He was chewing gum.

'Nice day,' he said.

'Very,' said Joe.

'Say, did I hear that young fellow call you Vanringham?'

'Yes.'

'T. P.?'

'J. J.'

'Oh,' said the little man. One would have supposed that he was disappointed. 'Well, pleased to have met you.'

'Quate,' said Joe.

10

Jane had been having her usual busy morning. Owing to the fact that her father, shirking his responsibilities in a way that ought to have brought the blush of shame mantling to his cheek, deliberately avoided their society, and that her mother had, up to the present, given no sign that she was aware of their existence, the task of entertaining the paying guests devolved almost entirely upon her.

Sometimes a keen-eyed croquet player would espy and intercept Sir Buckstone before he could dive into the nearest shrubbery, but as a rule it was left for Jane to play the jolly innkeeper. Her mornings, in consequence, were always full.

Today she had played clock golf with Mr Chinnery, listened to Colonel Tanner on life in Poona and heard what Mr Waugh-Bonner had to say about mice in bedrooms. She had admired Mrs Shepley's knitting, discussed the news in the paper with Mrs Folsom, advised Mr Profitt on his backhand drive, and would no doubt have got together with and encouraged Mr Billing in his activities, had he not been, as on the previous day, taking a sun bath. She was now in the dining-room doing the flowers.

For some moments, tense and concentrated, a small white tooth pressed against her lower lip and her small nose twitching, she stood arranging pansies in a shallow bowl. There was not the slightest chance that a horde of gorging paying guests, absorbed in food, would notice her handiwork one way or the other, but this did not prevent her striving for perfection. She was an artist, and liked to get things right. Satisfied at length, she stepped back; and, as she did so, a voice behind her said, 'Hello'.

The dining-room at Walsingford Hall opened on to the terrace. It had French windows, flung wide on this beautiful morning, and through these there had come a figure which, only vaguely familiar at first glance, she recognized immediately as she came forward. It was the little man in the sack suit who had intruded upon her farewells to Adrian down in the water meadows.

'Hullo!' she said, taken aback. The apparition had startled her.

He advanced into the room. His eyes were kindly and his jaws rose and fell in a rhythmic motion.

'Saw you in here, so I came in.'

'Oh?'

'Bulpitt's my name. Sam Bulpitt.'

In the county of Berkshire there were girls, many of them, who long ere this would have raised haughty eyebrows and pointed the way to the back door. But Jane was far too friendly a little soul to come the Baronet's daughter over anyone, even a man wearing shoes as gamboge as those. She supposed that he represented some commercial firm – one, possibly, that dealt in cheap jewellery or imitation silk stockings – and had arrived in pursuance of his professional duties to try to drum up trade, but she smiled at him amiably.

'How do you do, Mr Bulpitt?'

'I'm fine. How are you?'

'I'm fine.'

'Nice place you've got here.'

'You like it?'

'I think it's swell.'

'Good. Er – is there anything I can do for you, Mr Bulpitt?'

'I guess not. Just go right along looking like a lovely radiant woodland nymph surrounded by her flowers.'

'Very well,' said Jane. She crossed to the sideboard and began to busy herself with the big vase that stood on it. 'And presently, no doubt, you will tell me what the idea is.'

'Pardon?'

'I was just wondering why you were here.'

For the first time, it seemed to strike the little man that he had been remiss. He chuckled amusedly, showing those gleaming teeth of his like one who realizes that the joke is on him.

'Why, sure. Ought to have told you that at the start, shouldn't I? You must be thinking I'm loco. I've come to see Alice. You'll be her little girl, of course.'

'I beg your pardon?'

'I'll bet a dollar on it. You're the living spit of what she was twenty-five years ago. Smaller, of course. You're perteet, and she was always kind of buxom. But I'd known you anywheres.'

A possible solution occurred to Jane.

'When you say Alice, do you mean my mother?'

'Sure.'

'I never knew her name was Alice. Buck always calls her Toots. Do you know her, then?'

'Sure. Matter of fact, she's my sister.'

The vase rocked in Jane's hands.

'You're not my mysterious uncle?'

'That's right.'

Jane laughed happily. She was always fond of watching her father's reaction to the unforeseen. She anticipated great pleasure from the spectacle of his first meeting with the new relative.

'Well, well, well!'

'Sure,' said Mr Bulpitt, who had been intending to say that himself.

Here he made an unexpected exit on to the terrace, busied himself delicately there for a moment and returned. His jaws were no longer moving, but it was plain that this was only a temporary phase, for he took a package of gum from his pocket and began stripping a piece of it. He inserted it in his mouth, once more setting the machinery in motion.

'You can buy gum anywhere in England now, they tell me,' he said, in passing.

'Can you?'

'Yessir. March of Civilization. Surprised me when I found it out.'

'Have you just arrived in England?'

'That's right. In France before that. Down South. Nice, Cannes, Monte Carlo. Came the southern route on one of those Italian boats. Get gum in France, too. Amazing. Well, how is the old-timer?'

'The old-timer?'

'Alice. Grand girl. Wish I'd seen more of her these last twenty-five years. How's she doing?'

'Oh, she's splendid.'

'That's good. Say, to think of her being mistress of a great place like this. How did that come about?'

'You mean how did mother come to marry Buck?'

'Yeah. Last I saw of her her station was humble. She'd gotten a job demonstrating underclothes.'

'When Buck met her, she was in the chorus of a musical comedy.'

'I see. Same thing. So she went on the stage, did she?'

'In a piece called *The Pink Lady*.'

Mr Bulpitt was interested.

'Say, was she in that? Some show, that was. Never saw the

New York production myself, because I was out on the road with a patent floor sweeper all the time it was running. Saw the Western company, though. Twice. Once in Kansas City and once in St Louis. Boy, that was music. Don't get any like it nowadays.' He put back his head and closed his eyes. 'To – ah – you – ah – beryootiful lady, I – Pardon me,' he said, recovering, 'you were saying – '

'They brought the New York company over to London and Buck went to see it and fell in love with mother at first sight and sent a note round asking her to supper – he was a great dasher in those days – and mother went, and about a week later they got married.'

The story seemed to affect Mr Bulpitt deeply. In the formative years of his life he had been a singing waiter, and the nightly rendering of mushy ballads to an audience inclined on the slightest provocation to cry into its beer made him susceptible to sentiment.

'A real romance! '

'Oh, rather.'

'The great English lord and the little American Cinderella.'

'Well, Buck's not a lord, and I'm bound to say I've never looked on mother as a little Cinderella, but it was very sweet, wasn't it?'

'You betcher. There's nothing like romance.'

'No.'

'It's love that makes the world go round.'

'Well put.'

Mr Bulpitt paused. He coughed. His eyes had taken on a meaning glint. His hand stirred slightly, as if he were about to drive home his remarks by prodding her in the ribs. And though he allowed it to fall without making this physical demonstration, Jane had no difficulty in divining what was to come. It was her companion's intention, she perceived, dismissing the amours of the older generation, to touch upon those of the younger.

'And say, talking of love and romance – '

'Yes, I know.'

'Down by the river yesterday evening.'

'Yes.'

'Who was he? '

'A friend of mine.'

'Well, I sort of guessed he wasn't somebody you couldn't stand the sight of. What's his name?'

'Adrian Peake.'

'Quite a smacker you were giving him.'

'Quite.'

'Reminded me of a painting by that fellow, you see his stuff everywhere, that does pitchers of guys in three-cornered hats and short pants.'

'Marcus Stone.'

'That's right. You're pretty fond of him, I guess?'

'Very. And now,' said Jane, 'I'm sure you must be wanting to see mother.'

She moved to the bell and pressed it. But in supposing that this action would cause her companion to change the subject, she had vastly mistaken her Bulpitt. He was not a man who changed subjects.

'Good-looking young fellow.'

'Yes.'

'Known him long?'

'Not very.'

'What does he work at?'

Jane flushed. The question was a simple one – even a less-probing person than Samuel Bulpitt would probably have asked it – but she found it disturbing. Hearing it, she experienced a quite definite twinge of regret that she was unable to reply that Adrian was a rising young barrister or even an earnest toiler in an office, and it made her feel disloyal.

'I don't quite know what he does. He was a gossip writer at one time. He's got a sort of income. Quite small.'

'I see,' said Mr Bulpitt, nodding. 'Lowly suitor.'

The door opened. Pollen, the butler, appeared. Mr Bulpitt wiped his hand on his trouser leg and extended it reverently.

'Lord Abbott?'

'No, sir,' said Pollen, ignoring the hand. 'You rang, miss?'

'Yes. Will you tell my mother that Mr Bulpitt is here.'

'Very good, miss.'

The butler withdrew, and Mr Bulpitt returned to his cross-examination, as fresh as ever.

'Any prospects?'

'I beg your pardon?'

'This boy. Does he show any sign of getting places?'

'No.'

'Oh? And what does his lordship think about it?'

'He doesn't know.'

'You haven't wised him up?'

'Not yet.'

'I see. Well, it's too bad he's quitting. You'll miss him.'

'Quitting?'

'Leaving. This boy Peake. Didn't you know?'

'But he can't be. He only came yesterday.'

'Well, that's what he was saying to that young J. J. Vanringham down at the inn.'

Jane started.

'Vanringham!'

'That's what he told me his name was. Hard-looking guy with a pair of shoulders on him. I heard them talking. I only came in at the tail end of the conversation, but Peake was saying he was hiring a car and lighting out.'

Samuel Bulpitt was a solid little man, but he was flickering before Jane's eyes as if he had been a picture in the smoke. The discovery that Joe Vanringham had had the nerve, the audacity, the crust to follow her to her home filled her with a fury which for the moment took her mind completely off the astonishing fact that Adrian Peake had decided to curtail his visit. She was conscious of an overwhelming desire to be alone and out in the open. Like someone recovering from a swoon she wanted air.

'Do you mind if I leave you?' she said. 'Mother will be here in a minute.'

'Go right along,' said Mr Bulpitt agreeably.

She flashed out through the French windows, and he started to potter about the room, sniffing the flowers. And a few moments later the door opened again and Lady Abbott came in.

At the moment when Pollen arrived with his message, Lady Abbott had been reclining upon a settee in her boudoir, thinking of her Buck and how much she loved him and what a pity it was that he allowed himself to get fussed about trifles like owing Mr Chinnery five hundred pounds. She herself never fussed about anything. She was large and blonde and of a monumental calmness which not even earthquakes on the terrace or the falling in of the roof would have been able to disturb.

And if this placidity should seem strange in one who had once earned her living in the chorus of musical comedy, it must be remembered that it is only in these restless modern days that the term 'chorus girl' has come to connote a small, wiry person with india-rubber legs and flexible joints, suffering, to all appearances, from an advanced form of St Vitus's dance.

In the era of Lady Abbott's professional career, the personnel of the ensemble were tall, stately creatures, shaped like hour-glasses, who stood gazing dreamily at the audience, supporting themselves on long parasols. Sometimes they would emerge from the coma for an instant to bow slightly to a friend in the front row, but not often. As a rule, they just stood statuesquely. And of all these statueque standers none had ever stood with a more completely statuesque immobility than the then Alice (Toots) Bulpitt.

She was looking rather like a statue now, as she paused in the doorway and surveyed this brother who had been absent from her life for a quarter of a century. It was Mr Bulpitt who supplied the animation fitting to so dramatic a reunion.

'Well, well, well!' said Mr Bulpitt. 'Well, well, well, well, well!'

A flicker of interest disturbed the marmoreal calm of Lady Abbott's face.

'Gosh, Sam,' she said, 'have you been chewing that bit of gum ever since I saw you last?'

Mr Bulpitt performed another of his delicate withdrawals to the terrace.

'Different piece,' he explained, returning and speaking more clearly. 'Well, well, well, well, well!'

Lady Abbott permitted herself to be drawn into a brotherly embrace.

'It's great seeing you again, Alice.'

'Great seeing you, Sam.'

'Gave you a surprise, eh?'

'You could have knocked me down with a feather,' said Lady Abbott, quite untruly. The feather had not been grown by bird that could have disturbed her balance for an instant. 'What are you doing on this side? Business?'

'And pleasure.'

'You still travelling with those floor sweepers of yours?'

'Gee, no. I quit peddling them fifteen years ago.'

'What are you doing now?'

'Well, you might say I'd retired. I thought I had. But you know how it is. You get with a bunch of the boys and they talk you into things. Say, you look just the same, Alice.'

'You're kind of fatter.'

'I guess I have put on a pound or two.'

'Those teeth are new, aren't they?'

'This year's,' said Mr Bulpitt rather proudly. 'Say, this is a great place you've got here, Alice.'

'I like it.'

'And that's a great girl you've got.'

'Imogen?'

'Is that her name? Just been talking to her. She was telling me about your romance.'

'Oh, yes?'

'Some romance. Like a fairy story.'

'Yes. I'm glad you liked Imogen.'

'She's swell. So, if the old man's all right, too, seems to me you've got a full hand.'

A tender look came into Lady Abbott's beautiful eyes as it always did when she thought of her husband.

'Buck's great. You'll like Buck. Come along and I'll take you to him. He's in his study.'

'Sure. What do I call him. Your lordship?'

'I've never heard of anyone calling him anything except "Buck".'

'Regular fellow, eh?'

'One of the gang,' said Lady Abbott.

She led the way along passages and round corners, until they came to a door from behind which proceeded the sound of voices. She pushed it open and went in.

The voices which had proceeded from behind the study door

were those of Sir Buckstone Abbott and Mr Chinnery. But at the time of Mr Bulpitt's intrusion upon Jane in the dining-room only the former had been present. He was working on some papers connected with the estate.

It was a task which he never enjoyed and it might have been supposed that, finding it so irksome, he would have welcomed any interruption that took his mind off it. This, however, was not the case. When, after he had been occupied for some little while, the door suddenly burst open and Mr Chinnery came charging in, he was not pleased but annoyed; and more than annoyed, outraged. It was an understood thing that, when in his study, he was supposed to enjoy those privileges of sanctury which outlaws of old were allowed to claim at the altar.

His first impression, however, that his guest had invaded his privacy in order to take up once more the matter of that five-hundred-pound loan was not correct. Mr Chinnery's moonlike face was pallid and his eyes, peering through their glasses, had a hunted look. It was plain that he had more serious things on his mind than frozen assets.

'Abbott,' said Mr Chinnery, 'I've had a shock.'

It was on the tip of Sir Buckstone's tongue to tell him to go and work off its effects elsewhere, but he refrained – not so much because he shrank from being brusque as because he had no time to speak.

His visitor continued:

'That fellow's here!'

'What fellow?'

'I'd gone down to the village to buy some stamps, and I was passing the inn, and out he came.'

'Who?'

'This fellow.'

'What fellow?'

'This fellow I'm telling you about. He came out of the inn. Yes, sir, right plump spang in the middle of an Old World English village where who in God's name would ever have thought he'd have been without a thousand miles of Goosh!'

Mr Chinnery sank into a chair and passed his tongue over his lips. His manner was that of a stag at bay. Imagine a stag in horn-rimmed spectacles, and you have Elmer Chinnery at this moment. Landseer would have liked to paint him.

'Listen, Abbott,' he said. 'You know, I guess, that I've not been altogether too fortunate in my matrimonial ventures. I'm easily led, that's what's the trouble with me, and I'm too soft-hearted to say no, and the result is I don't seem to pick 'em right. So, what with one thing and another, I'm paying out alimony three ways now, and a fourth pending. That's why I skipped out of New York, because I heard my fourth wife was trying to have me served with the papers. And now this fellow arrives. Here! In this Old World English village. Can you beat it?'

'What fellow?'

'I can't do it!' cried Mr Chinnery feverishly. 'I can't afford to pay out any more alimony. No fortune can stand the strain. And it isn't as if I'd got all the money in the world. People think I have, but I haven't. And I've had some extra expenses lately,' he added, collecting himself sufficiently to give his companion a meaning glance. 'Some heavy extra expenses. And now this fellow pops up right plumb spang in the middle of –'

Sir Buckstone's voice took on the timbre of that of one of those lions roaring outside the camp fire, of which he had written so feelingly in his recently published volume, 'My Sporting Memories' (Mortimer Busby Co., 15s.). He was a sensitive man, and the meaning look had stirred him up.

'What fellow?'

'This fellow I'm telling you about that I was down in the village buying stamps and saw him coming out of the inn. You know who he is? America's champion plasterer. Claims he always gets his man, and he does too. He's like a blood-hound.'

'Plasterer?' said Sir Buckstone, puzzled. He had had plasterers in the house only two weeks ago, but he had discerned nothing in their bearing to inspire alarm. They had made the deuce of a mess, slopping stuff all over the place, but they had appeared to him stolid and, except for their tendency to whistle 'Body and Soul' off the key, quiet men. He could not see a plasterer in the role of bloodhound.

'Process server,' interpreted Mr Chinnery, realizing that he was talking to an unenlightened foreigner.

'Oh?' said Sir Buckstone. 'Ah? You mean the man who serves the papers on you?'

Mr Chinnery quivered.

'Serves the papers,' he said emotionally, 'is right. He never misses. He's like a stoat and a rabbit. Listen while I tell you how he got me, the time my first wife – no, it was my second – was chasing me with that inhuman mental cruelty suit of hers. I was lying up at an hotel in Stamford, Connecticut, reckoning he'd never be able to trail me down there, and I'm sitting at the open window after breakfast, smoking a cigar and thinking I'd got him fooled at last, when all of a sudden there he is, on top of a ladder with the papers in his hand, and he threw them in my lap, saying: "Ahoy there, Mr Chinnery!" Threw them at me, y'understand! I claimed it was not fair and didn't count, but the courts said it did, and there it was. And I'm walking through this Old World English village just now, buying stamps, and out of the inn he comes. How did he find me? That's what gets clear past me, Abbott. How in all get-out did he ever come to know that I was living in these parts? I tell you, the fellow's like one of those Indian temple priests in the stories, where the guy steals the jewel that's the idol's eye and lights out and thinks he'd hid himself away perfectly safe, and suddenly he looks over his shoulder and here come all these sinister Indian priests around the corner.'

Mr Chinnery paused for breath. Sir Buckstone was smiling dreamily. All this reminded him of the old happy days of his youth.

'The great man in London in my time,' he said, 'was a fellow named Bunyan. Ferret Bunyan, we used to call him. He once served me for two pounds seven and six, I remember, for a knee-length-hosiery bill. I thought it rather a compliment, and so did all my friends. I mean to say, he being such a big pot and me just a young chap about town. It was long before I came into the title.'

Mr Chinnery was in no mood for Edwardian reminiscences.

'Never mind about that. It isn't any Bunyans I'm talking about; it's this man Bulpitt.'

Sir Buckstone started.

'Bulpitt? Is his name Bulpitt?'

He gave a little moan. It signified that hope was dead. Questioning his Toots on the previous day, he had learned that this brother of hers had started his career as a singing waiter and continued it as a traveller in patent floor sweepers, but even then he had not quite despaired. These walks in life might not seem an auspicious beginning to the climb up the ladder of wealth, but with Americans, he had told himself, you never knew. Half the American millionaires you met had started out in a small way. Mr Chinnery himself had once sold hot dogs. In spite of everything, he had clung hopefully to his dream of an affectionate brother-in-law with a large balance at the bank.

But not any longer. If, in these last twenty-five years, Toots's brother Sam had raised himself from the modest position of a singing waiter to that of America's foremost process server, the fact did him credit, of course, and showed what could be accomplished by a man of grit and enterprise, but it was no longer possible to entertain any illusion that he might have the stuff in any appreciable quantity. Even the most gifted of plasterers does not pay super-tax.

He sat among the ruins of his shattered hopes, chewing his pen and thinking how different it all would have been had his wife been the sister of Henry Ford. And as he sat, the door opened and Lady Abbott came in, escorting Mr Bulpitt.

Their arrival was greeted by a loud crash, as of some heavy body falling on something hard. It was caused by Mr Chinnery. Springing from his chair like the hunted stag he so much resembled, he had had the misfortune to slip on a loose rug. When the moment for introduction came, he was sitting on the floor.

His behaviour, the eccentricity of which might have caused hostesses to show surprise, had no effect whatever on Lady Abbott's impregnable calm. She did not even raise her eyebrows. She might have been watching big fish-glue men take tosses out of chairs all her life.

'Here's Sam, Buck,' she said.

Sir Buckstone, still brooding on what might have been, stared dully at the little man. Mr Bulpitt bustled forward, hand outstretched.

'Pleased to meet you, Lord Abbott.'

'Haryer?' said Sir Buckstone, still moody.

'I'm fine,' said Mr Bulpitt.

At this point, he appeared to observe that there were foreign substances on the carpet. He peered down at Mr Chinnery, and gave a glad cry of recognition.

'Well, well, well, well, well!' he said, beaming. 'If here isn't an old friend!'

Disaster often brings out the best in a man. In this extremity Elmer Chinnery bore himself well. He had been looking like some trapped creature of the wild. His manner now took on an almost Roman dignity.

'All right,' he said. 'Gimme.'

'Eh?'

'Let's have 'em,' said Mr Chinnery.

His word and the mute appeal of his extended hand clarified the situation for Mr Bulpitt. He saw that a misunderstanding had arisen, and laughed heartily.

'Did you think I was after you again? Nothing for you today, brother.'

Mr Chinnery rose. He stood rubbing the seat of his trousers, for the fall had caused him some pain, an incredulous hope dawning in his eyes.

'What?'

'Not a thing.'

'Aren't you acting for my wife?'

Lady Abbott intervened.

'This is my brother Sam, Mr Chinnery.'

Elmer Chinnery gaped.

'Your brother?'

'Sure,' said Mr Bulpitt.

'He's visiting us.'

Comprehension was coming slowly to Mr Chinnery.

'Are you over here just on a vacation?'

'Yes,' said Lady Abbott.

'No,' said Mr Bulpitt.

'No?' said Lady Abbott. 'I thought you told me you had retired from business.'

'Well, I have and I haven't. It's this way,' said Mr Bulpitt: 'I'd been planning to quit and settle down, but when I hit London I happened to get together with some of the boys, and the long and the short of it is I let myself be talked into taking on one more job. The reason I'm in these parts is I'm sort of killing two birds with one stone. I was coming, anyway, to visit you and his lordship, but I'm here in my professional capacity, too, what I mean. It's where this Miss Prudence Whittaker is suing this T. P. Vanringham for breach of promise and heart balm, and I've come to slip the plaster on him.'

11

Joe Vanringham, having seen Adrian Peake off on his journey to London, had wandered into the front garden of the Goose and Gander and was sitting there, waiting for the vehicle which J. B. Attwater had promised should soon be on hand to take him and his belongings up to the Hall.

The morning had now reached the very height of its perfection, and the quiet, sun-bathed garden was hushed and warm and heavy with the fragrant scent of J. B. Attwater's roses and wallflowers. Winged things hummed and flitted. From somewhere out of sight came the liquid murmurings of fowls. A dog of nondescript breed snored gently in the shade of the hollyhocks. It was an environment that made for dreamy contentment, and nobody could have been more dreamily contented than Joe. He was in the frame of mind when a weaker man would have started writing poetry.

He found the sudden irruption of the outer world upon his peace, accordingly, when it occurred, particularly jarring. There was a sound of hurrying footsteps. Somebody banged the gate. A snort smote his ears. He peered resentfully round the bush behind which he was sitting, and saw that the intruder was Sir Buckstone Abbott. The Baronet was striding up the path to the inn's front door, looking neither to right nor left.

Joe's resentment vanished. He had taken an immediate liking to Sir Buckstone, and anything the other cared to do was all right with him. If Sir Buckstone wished to snort and race about on this beautiful morning, let him, felt Joe.

'Hello, there, Buck,' he cried. 'Getting into training for the village sports?'

The sound of his voice had a remarkable effect on the athlete. Sir Buckstone stopped in mid-stride as if he had been hit by a bullet, then bounced toward him with consternation written on his every feature.

'Joe! What are you doing here?'

'I've been paying my bill, and am now waiting for a cab to take me up the mountainside. One of these days, Buck, you ought to have a funicular railway built.'

'Your brother's not here?'

'I think he's up at the house.'

'Thank God!' Sir Buckstone wiped his forehead with a spacious handkerchief. 'I was afraid he might have come down with you. Yes, of course, he's up at the house.'

Joe had begun to be concerned. It was clear to him now that trouble of some kind must have broken out in this Eden. Your level-headed British Baronet does not behave like a cat on hot bricks without good reason.

'Is something the matter?' he asked.

Sir Buckstone's momentary relief gave way to the old horror and alarm. His manner became portentous. He looked like Hamlet's father's ghost about to impart a fearful tale.

'My dear fellow, the most terrible thing has happened. Haven't you heard?'

'No.'

'No, of course you haven't. How could you?'

'Heard what?'

'About this man being after your brother with the papers.'

'Papers?'

'Yes, papers, papers. Good heavens, you know what papers are. To serve on him. In this breach-of-promise and heart-balm case of his.'

'I don't understand.'

'Of course you don't, of course, you don't. I keep forgetting you haven't heard. My secretary, Miss Whittaker, is suing your brother for breach of promise, and a man has come down to serve the papers on him. It gave me the most ghastly shock when I saw you here. I thought your brother must be with you, right out in the open where this fellow might descend upon him at any moment.'

He became active again with the handkerchief, and now Joe was able to understand his emotion.

'Gosh!' he said.

'Exactly. It is a frightful position of affairs. What is the Princess going to say if this fellow succeeds in serving those papers and your brother is taken into court? You've never met the Princess Dwornitzchek, of course. . . . Yes, you have, though. What am I thinking of? If that boy's your brother, she's your stepmother.'

'No getting away from that.'

'Then you know what a perfectly ghastly woman – I beg your pardon. Shouldn't have said that.'

'On the contrary,' Joe assured him warmly, 'your words are music to my ears.'

'You don't like the Princess?'

'I regard her as the sand in Civilization's spinach.'

'A very happy way of putting it. I thoroughly agree with you. But the devil of it is that she was on the verge of buying my house, and if she finds out that her stepson is being sued by my secretary for breach of promise and heart balm, there's not a chance of her going through with it. She will break off the negotiations immediately. You see, I'm practically *in loco parentis* to the boy. When this Dwornitzchek woman – '

'This Dwornitzchek disease.'

'Exactly. Thank you. When this Dwornitzchek disease dumped your brother on me, she told me in so many words that she would hold me responsible for him. I was to keep a sharp eye on him, she said, because he was a damned fool with women – '

'Tubby has always been a little susceptible. Where other young men's fancies lightly turn to thoughts of love only in the springtime, he is an all-the-year-rounder. You don't catch Tubby waiting until a livelier iris has begun to gleam upon the burnished dove.'

'That's what I mean. She said she relied on me to see that he didn't get into any entanglements. I laughed at the idea. Scoffed at it. He can't get into any trouble of that kind here, I said. And now this happens.'

'Bad.'

'Couldn't be worse. My wife keeps saying that she guesses everything is going to be all right, but what she bases that assumption on is more than I can imagine. As far as I can see, the girl has a cast-iron case.'

'Would you say that?'

'Certainly. Your brother was unquestionably engaged to marry her.'

'Yes, but – '

'And broke it off.'

'Yes, but – '

'And, what's more, she has letters to prove it. Any jury would give her damages without leaving the box.'

'But, listen – '

'I haven't time to listen. I've got to see Attwater.'

'What I'm trying to say is that I don't think she can get away with it. I've heard the whole story from Tubby. It's quite true that he broke off the engagement, but his motives – '

'Blast his motives! I beg your pardon, my dear fellow,' said Sir Buckstone penitently. 'You must forgive me, please. I'm upset. I don't know what I'm saying. This thing has come as a thunderbolt.'

'I'll bet it has.'

'My head's in a whirl. If you knew how I had been looking forward to selling that infernal house – By the way, not a word of this to a soul.'

'Of course not.'

'You will be meeting my daughter Jane shortly. There are reasons why I wish it to be kept from her, above all. Don't say a word.'

'Not a syllable.'

'Thank you, Joe. And now excuse me. I mustn't waste any more time. I ought not to have stayed talking like this, with every moment precious. I've got to see Attwater immediately.'

'J. B. Attwater?'

'Yes.'

'Licensed to sell ales and spirits?'

'Yes, yes, yes, yes, yes,' said Sir Buckstone, and made the portal of the Goose and Gander in two jumps.

Joe remained where he was, musing. All this stark tragedy, coming out of a blue sky, had left him saddened. He looked about him and sighed. The garden was still quiet and sun-bathed. It still smelt of roses and wallflowers. The winged things were still humming and flitting, the fowls were still murmuring, and the nondescript dog had not moved a muscle.

That warring passions should be aflame in this Paradise seemed to him a very melancholy thing, and he would doubtless have indulged in quite a good deal of wistful philosophizing, had he not been interrupted just as he had begun by saying to himself that that was how things went in this life. The gate clicked again, and he saw that here was more company.

The little man in the sack suit with whom he had had that brief exchange of civilities through the parlour window was making his way toward him. He had evidently been walking briskly, for there was perspiration on his rosy face. He was still chewing gum.

Joe eyed him askance. He had nothing against this round little man, as round little men went, but he was occupied with his thoughts and resented intrusion upon them by any man, little or big, rosy or pallid, round or oblong. He blew a reserved smoke ring to indicate this.

It had no deterrent effect on the little man. He had come to talk, and he began talking immediately.

'Nice day.'

'You told me that,' Joe reminded him.

'Kind of warm, though. I been hurrying.'

'Oh, yes?'

'Yes, sir. And I'm all in a lather. Sweating like a nigger at election,' said the little man, with poetic imagery.

Joe privately considered that he was stressing the purely physical more than was in the least necessary, but he did not say so. He did not say anything, hoping that silence would discourage.

'I was looking for you,' said the little man. 'Wanted to see you. About that boat. That houseboat. The one you took off that young fellow that was going away. I happened to hear you when I was in the parlour. You wouldn't consider parting with that boat, would you?'

For the first time, this conversation began to grip Joe. It had already occurred to him that it would be nice if he could pass on the *Mignonette* to somebody, thus relieving himself of a liability.

'Do you want it?'

'Yes, sir, I'd be glad to have it. I've a notion it would be

kind of fun, living on a houseboat. Just scribble me a line –
Bulpitt's the name – here's a fountain pen and a piece of paper
– and I'll slip you the money. What shall we say?'

'I told the owner I would pay him twenty pounds.'

'Then we'll call it twenty-five?'

'No, no, only twenty. I don't want to make a profit.'

'You're not a business-man,' said his companion rebukingly.

'I'm a dreamy artist,' said Joe.

'Well, if that suits you, it suits me. Give me the memo.
Here's the twenty. Thanks. I'll go pack my grip,' said the little
man, showing himself plainly to be one of those who think
on their feet and do it now.

He toddled briskly into the inn, and a few minutes later Sir
Buckstone came out.

There was a marked change for the better in the Baronet's
aspect since Joe had last seen him. He was not precisely
radiant, but a great deal of his agitation had gone, and in its
place had come something that bordered on the contented and
the complacent.

'Dished him!' he said.

'I beg your pardon?'

'That plasterer. I've outmanoeuvred him. You know what
suddenly occurred to me, Joe, thinking the thing over up at
the house? It came to me all in a flash. What does an army
need?'

The question puzzled Joe a little. It seemed to him that they
had got off the subject. However, he gave it his attention.

'A stomach,' he said. 'To march on.'

'A base,' said Sir Buckstone. 'A base from which to operate.
And what base of operations has a plasterer in Walsingford
Parva except the Goose and Gander? This isn't a popular
resort, with people letting rooms on every side. Nobody's got
any rooms, except what they need themselves. No. Bar the
Goose and Gander to this chap Bulpitt – his name's Bulpitt –
and he becomes helpless. He's nonplussed. So I've just been
seeing Attwater about it. Used to be my butler before he
retired and took over the inn, and is devoted to the interests
of the family. So, to cut a long story short, my dear Joe, I told
Attwater he'd got to kick this fellow out – tell him his room's
wanted, or something. And he's going to do it. So there the

101

little blighter will be, bereft of his base. He'll be helpless. Won't know what the dickens to do. I'd like to see his face,' said Sir Buckstone chuckling quite heartily.

Joe did not join in his merriment. A certain uneasiness had stolen upon him. His companion's wish would, he felt, only too shortly be gratified. And the face which he would see would be one not twisted in baffled fury but wreathed in happy smiles.

His surmise was correct. At this very moment, Sam Bulpitt came out of the inn, carrying a bag very nearly as big as himself. Its weight was making him puff, but his contentment was manifest.

Sir Buckstone, however, did not perceive it. He called to the little man. It was plain that it was his intention to exult, to gloat, to sneer and jeer in ungenerous triumph.

'Hey, you! Bulpitt!'

'Your lordship?'

'Don't call me "your lordship," blast you. So you're leaving, eh? Ha?'

'Yessir. Going off to my houseboat. Have a nice time. I always did kind of like camping out,' said Mr Bulpitt. 'It's the gypsy in me.'

12

It was not immediately that Sir Buckstone broke the silence that followed his brother-in-law's departure. For fully half a minute he remained wrestling with emotions which appeared to preclude speech.

Then he said, in a low, grating voice:

'Houseboat?'

It was becoming increasingly clear to Joe that a situation had arisen which would call for somewhat delicate handling, and he set himself to pick his words carefully. There had begun to burgeon within him a warm feeling of gratitude to Mr Bulpitt. There, he told himself, was the sort of man he liked – one of few words and with the dramatic sense to exit on the telling line, instead of sticking around and going into a lot of explanations which could not but have proved a source of embarrassment.

'Houseboat?' said Sir Buckstone. 'Did he say "houseboat"?'

Joe coughed.

'I think "houseboat" was the word he mentioned.'

'What houseboat?'

'Could it possibly,' suggested Joe deferentially, 'be that one of yours?'

'But there's somebody living on that. Man named Peake.'

Joe coughed again.

'I was meaning to tell you about that. I was chatting with Peake a short while ago, and the impression I got from something he let fall was that he was thinking of leaving. I'm very much afraid that what must have happened is that Peake has sublet the boat to this man Bulpitt.'

'Gor!'

'I fear so. As a matter of fact, I didn't like to damp you by suggesting it just now, when you were sketching out your plan – your extraordinarily ingenious plan – for having Bulpitt kicked out of the inn, but it did occur to me as a sort of possibility that he might have thought a move ahead of the game and anticipated you. And so it has proved. He went to Peake, and Peake gave him the boat.'

'I'd like to kick Peake's spine through his hat.'

'Many men have felt the same urge.'

'He wants kicking, this man Peake? People have noticed it?'

'Very frequently.'

Silence fell. Sir Buckstone was brooding. A bee buzzed past his nose and he gave it a cold look. He turned and started to stump to the gate.

'One really scarcely knows,' said Joe, following him, 'what to say about a man like Peake. You would have thought that anyone could have spotted that this fellow Bulpitt was up to something, asking for the boat. A child, one would have imagined, would have suspected that his motives were sinister. But not Peake.'

'Chap must be a perfect ass.'

'A very indifferent mentality, certainly. I don't know if you have met him. He has a sort of soppy expression.'

'He's gone and put us in the devil of a hole.'

'It is difficult to forgive him for that.'

'I wasn't thinking of forgiving him,' said Sir Buckstone. 'What I'm trying to work out is, what are we going to do?'

'Yes. The situation will require careful thought. I take it that these people have to be served personally? Bulpitt can't just slip them in an envelope and mail them to Tubby?'

'Personally, yes. Though Chinnery says you can throw 'em.'

'Throw 'em?'

'Chinnery's second wife's inhuman-cruelty papers were thrown at him. By this very fellow Bulpitt. He said "Ahoy" and threw them at Chinnery.'

'I don't see how he can repeat that performance this time, unless he is the very dickens of a hurler. I mean, if he is on the houseboat and Tubby is at the Hall – '

'But will your brother have the sense to remain at the Hall?'

'We must see to it that he does. I will take it upon myself to watch him like a hawk.'

'Thank you, Joe.'

'A pleasure, Buck.'

The hired vehicle which J. B. Attwater had promised came creaking round the corner and halted beside them. They climbed in and drove off.

'Yes,' said Joe, 'Walsingford Hall from now on must be looked upon as a beleaguered fortress, thanks to Peake.'

'Thanks to Peake,' said Sir Buckstone, breathing heavily.

'But I see no reason why, by the exercise of never-ceasing vigilance, we should not foil this Bulpitt indefinitely.'

'So long as we can hold him off till the Princess has bought the house – '

'Yes.'

'You see, she's my only hope. Women fatheaded enough to want to buy a house like Walsingford Hall don't grow on every bush.'

'Exactly. Well, I feel sure that we can stymie Bulpitt all right. Good heavens, two men of our intelligence against a fellow who chews gum and wears a hat like that! The thing's in the bag.'

'You really think so?'

'I'm sure of it.'

'You're a great comfort, Joe.'

'I try to be, Buck.'

'What astounds me,' said Sir Buckstone, after a few moments of silent brooding, 'is that it should be Miss Whittaker of all people who has brought about this frightful situation. Would you have thought that she was the sort of girl to go and do a thing like this?'

'I wouldn't, no.'

'Nor I. I was shocked. Shocked and astounded. Chinnery says I ought to give her the sack. But how can I give her the sack? I couldn't run the place without her for a day. Chaos. If she had stolen the silver or murdered me in cold blood, I'd have to keep her on just the same.'

'Awkward.'

'Very.'

'Embarrassing, you might say.'

'Most. Man who's being sued for breach of promise and girl who's suing him living in the same house. Creates a strained situation.'

'Stops the flow of conversation at meals.'

'Exactly. But what can I do?'

'It's difficult.'

'No, I've got to keep her on, but I shall be very reserved and distant in my manner when we meet. I'm not sure for the future if I shall say, "Good morning". Blast the girl!'

Joe nodded sympathetically.

'I can readily understand your emotion,' he said. 'But, of course, one must always look on both sides of a thing. She has a case. A woman scorned, you know.'

'Yes, that's true, I suppose.'

'It can't ever be really pleasant for a woman to be scorned, and when she's scorned by a muttonhead like young Tubby, I imagine the iron must enter pretty deeply into the soul.'

'No doubt.'

'So I don't altogether blame Miss Whittaker. The person whose behaviour amazes me is this man Peake. It leaves me positively breathless.'

'Me too.'

'One tries always to see the good in one's fellow-men, and generally one succeeds. But when it comes to Peake, the naked eye is baffled. You need a microscope. Just fancy letting Bulpitt have that boat!'

'Damn fool!'

Joe was looking grave.

'I wonder,' he said. 'It has only just occurred to me, but, weighing the evidence, don't you think it may be possible that he is more knave than fool?'

'Eh?'

'May he not have acted deliberately and of malice afore-thought? It seems highly probable to me, Buck, that Peake has been in league with Bulpitt from the start.'

'Good heavens, Joe!'

'It would explain a great deal.'

'Is he the sort of chap who would be in league with chaps?'

'Exactly the sort.'

'God bless my soul! And to think that I invited him to my house!'

'I wouldn't dream of having him anywhere near your house. Have you dogs at Walsingford Hall?'

'Eh? Oh, yes, a couple of dogs.'

'If Peake tries to get into the house, set them on him.'

'They're only spaniels.'

'Spaniels are better than nothing,' said Joe.

The hired vehicle drew up at the front door. Sir Buckstone was out of it like a rabbit. As always when in the depths, he yearned to get to his wife, so that she might apply to his bruised soul the healing ointment of her placidity. Joe, follow-ing more slowly, paid the driver and placed his suit-cases in the charge of Pollen. This done, he sauntered off to the terrace. Lunch, he presumed, would be served shortly, but there would be time before the meal for him to make himself acquainted with his new surroundings.

The terrace terminated in a low stone wall, along the top of which were dotted busts of the Caesars and other ancient worthies, placed there in the spacious days of Sir Wellington, when people liked that sort of thing. The one nearest Joe was that of the censor Cato, an unpleasant-looking man who suffered from having a long nose and no eyeballs, but had the saving virtue of possessing a very large bare upper lip, the sort of upper lip which calls imperiously to every young man of spirit to draw a moustache on it with a pencil.

Joe, fortunately, had a pencil on his person, and was soon absorbed in his work. So absorbed, indeed, that it was only a moment or two after it had been uttered that he heard the curious, sharp exclamation in his rear.

He turned. Jane Abbott was standing there.

If you will take down your copy of Sir Buckstone Abbott's 'My Sporting Memories' from its shelf and turn to page 51, you will find a passage describing in some detail the reactions of the author, at that time a novice to conditions on the Dark Continent, on discovering, while swimming in the River Limpopo, that mixed bathing regulations were in vogue there and that his dip was being shared by a couple of young crocodiles. It is a powerful piece of word-painting, leaving no doubt in the reader's mind that the narrator was genuinely stirred. And what seems to have impressed him most deeply was the eye of the crocodile on the left, which he describes as cold and penetrating and unfriendly.

Very much the same adjectives would have been applied to the eye which Jane Abbott was now directing at Joe Vanringham.

Joe, on his side, was momentarily quite a little taken aback. He had expected that, having gained access to Walsingford Hall, he would meet Jane – indeed, that was the whole idea – but the suddenness of her advent had startled him; and as he met her eye, which was like a blue icicle, he was aware of emotions similar in kind and intensity to those experienced by his host in mid-Limpopo. Sir Buckstone specifically mentions that on that occasion everything swam about him – not merely the crocodiles but the whole of that part of Africa which was visible to him at the moment; and for an instant everything swam about Joe. That stare of hers gave him the impression that something cold and sharp had gone through him and come out on the other side.

But he was not long in recovering himself. After his encounter with Miss Prudence Whittaker, he was in the position of a boxer with a hard fight under his belt or one of the survivors of the Charge of the Light Brigade. A man so recently come from the society of that Spirit of Frigidaire was not easily to be frozen by lesser freezers; and though Jane's eye was keen, it was not in the Whittaker class.

'Oh, there you are,' he said amiably.

Jane continued to stare. Her lips were parted, baring her teeth a little.

'What are you doing here?'

'I am in residence.'

'What?'

'This charming place of yours is now my home. I am one of your father's guests. If Walsingford Hall, like so many English country houses, is open to the public on Thursdays, the butler, as he shows the customers around, will be in a position, dating from today, to say "We are now approaching the banqueting hall. At the table you will observe, banqueting like billy-o, the great playwright, Joseph Vanringham." This added attraction, once the news gets about, should lead to many an extra shilling at the turnstiles.'

He paused, eyeing her closely.

'Correct me if I am wrong,' he said, 'but something in your manner suggests that you are not pleased to find me here.'

'I object to being followed.'

Joe was amazed.

'Followed? Do you think I came here following you? Whatever gave you that extraordinary idea? Nothing could be more delightful, of course, than meeting you again, but – Why, how could I possibly know that you lived here?'

'You might have suspected it when I told you I did.'

'You told me? But this is astounding. When?'

'At lunch yesterday.'

'Surely not? And yet – Wait ... Good heavens so you did.'

'Yes.'

'Yes, I recall the whole thing. It all comes back to me. I said – I remember now – I was sitting over here and I said, "Do you live in London?"'

'Yes.'

'To which your reply – you were sitting over there – was,

"No. I live at Walsingford Hall in Berkshire." Yes, yes, yes. You're quite right. Well, well, well. Astonishing how one forgets these things.'

'Very.'

'I can see how you were led into the error of supposing that I had followed you here. But there is a ready explanation of my presence.'

'I should be glad to hear it.'

'I came because my brother Tubby is staying at the Hall.'

'Oh?'

'Yes. I happened to run into him, and he was enthusiastic about the place. He raved about the food and the company. He told me not to miss a good thing, and had me all on fire. I felt that I must be in this. The squarest of meals, said Tubby, the most sparkling conversation during them, lovely scenery, splendid air, baths both h. and c. I tell you, he sold me Walsingford Hall all right.'

'Odd that you did not mention to me at lunch that you had met him.'

'I ought to have done so, of course, but you must remember that I was in a confused mental condition owing to having been up most of the night, revelling with triumphant hams. I did tell you that I had had a play produced the night before, with stupendous success?'

'You did.'

'Did I read you the notices?'

'No.'

'Would you care to hear them now?'

'I would not.'

'Just as you like. Let me know when you feel in the mood. Well, as I say, Tubby got me all worked up and I packed a bag and came along. I trust this simple, manly explanation has got across. You do believe that I hadn't the remotest notion in my head of coming here just because I wanted to see you again?'

'No, I don't.'

'I thought you wouldn't. Superficially, that Tubby thing seemed pretty watertight, but one cannot buck a woman's intuition. Very well, then, I will come clean. I did follow you down here. And why not? Why should you be so surprised at that?'

'I'm not surprised. Nothing that you could do would surprise me.'

'Oh, I wouldn't say that. You haven't seen me at my best. But to get back to it. Why wouldn't a man of sensibility want to take the earliest possible opportunity of apologizing to a girl for his uncouth behaviour in asking her to marry him as abruptly as I asked you? I blush to think of it. I had known you only for about twenty minutes, and it was unpardonable of me to have said what I did after twenty minutes. I should have waited at least an hour. Can you ever forgive me?'

'It is a matter of complete indifference to me –'

'Now you're being pompous again. Correct this tendency. It is your only fault.'

'Do you mind not talking to me like a governess?'

'I'm sorry.'

'Not at all. I just mentioned it. Good-bye.'

'Are you going?'

'Yes.'

'It's an odd thing; whenever we have one of these little get-together of ours, you always leave abruptly.'

'Not so very odd.'

'You're really deserting me, Ginger?'

'I am. And don't call me Ginger.'

'Ah, well,' said Joe, 'all that's beautiful drifts away like the waters. Still, I have my art!'

He turned again to Cato. The moustache was coming out well – a fine, flowing affair with pointed ends, not one of those little smudges. Cato now looked like a Mississippi gambler, and Jane was not proof against the spectacle. Her dignity, always easily undermined, suddenly collapsed. She uttered a little squeal of laughter.

'You are an idiot!'

'That's more the tone.'

'It's no good being furious with you.'

'I wouldn't try. How does that strike you?'

'A little more body to the left side,' said Jane, surveying Cato critically.

'Like that?'

'That's better. Oughtn't he to have whiskers too?'

'Whiskers most certainly. What a flair you have in these matters. I will attend to it immediately.'

'It's nice,' said Jane meditatively, 'to think what hell father's going to give you for this. He'll tear you into little pieces.'

'On the contrary, I anticipate that Buck will be tickled to death. He is a man of taste, and must appreciate the improvement.'

'Buck?'

'He asked me to call him that. "Buck to you, my dear Joe," he said. We are like ham and eggs. One of those instant friendships. In the circumstances, of course, very fortunate.'

'Why?'

'Because – Oh, just fortunate. And now,' said Joe, 'bring your pencil and let us see what we can do with a few more of these gargoyles. No.' he went on, as the booming of a gong sounded from the house, 'I fear we shall have to wait till after lunch. Meet me here at two-thirty.'

'I shall do nothing of the kind.'

'At two-thirty on the dot.'

'At two-thirty on the dot I shall be playing croquet with Mr Waugh-Bonner.'

'Who is he?'

'One of the inmates.'

'Do you get landed much with these inmates?'

'A good deal. Buck dodges them shamefully.'

'Then we will make it three-thirty on the tick.'

'No, we won't. At three-thirty I shall be dressing before starting out to pay social calls on the nobility and gentry of the neighbourhood.'

'Doesn't Lady Abbott attend to that sort of thing?'

'No, she doesn't. She just ignores the whole unpleasant matter.'

Joe regarded her sympathetically.

'It is becoming increasingly clear to me,' he said, 'that you are the Patsy in this joint. All the dirty work appears to be left to you. Never mind. It will be very different when you have a home of your own. With an indulgent husband, alert to gratify your every wish and take every burden off your shoulders, things will improve amazingly. You have a very bright future before you, Jane.'

They walked together to the house, Joe full of animation, Jane a little pensive. She was remembering the impression which she had formed of this young man at the luncheon table. He had struck her then as one of those who got what they wanted, and she was aware of a certain uneasiness.

She did not know it, but she was feeling very much as Mr Chinnery felt when pursued by Mr Bulpitt.

13

The information, received by her secretary and through the medium of Miss Prudence Whittaker relayed to Sir Buckstone Abbott, that the Princess Dwornitzchek, her mission in America concluded, would be arriving in England almost immediately, proved strictly in accordance with the facts. Her boat docked at Southampton on the morning following Joe Vanringham's descent upon Walsingford Hall, and on the evening of the day after that she celebrated her return by entertaining to dinner at her house in Berkeley Square a Colonel and Mrs Waddesley, whose acquaintance she had made on shipboard, and Adrian Peake.

The feelings of Adrian Peake when, reaching his flat after leaving the Goose and Gander, he had found on the table the wireless message from his patroness commanding his presence at the meal, had been mixed. There had been surprise, because he had not expected her back for at least another fortnight; relief, because he had not missed the invitation owing to being absent without leave; and a certain apprehension. As he stood now, fingering his white tie and watching her bidding farewell to his fellow-guests, it was this apprehension that predominated. A close observer would have detected in his demeanour anxiety and nervousness. Adrian Peake, he would have said, was not at his ease, and he would have been right.

As far as physical well-being was concerned, Adrian was, of course, in the pink. After prolonged abstinence he had at last renewed his acquaintance with the output of one of the best chefs in Mayfair, and, under the influence of caviar, clear soup, salmon, roast duck and a superb soufflé, had blossomed like a rose in summer sunshine. It was spiritually that he was below par. He was in the grip of that shrinking feeling which came upon him in the anteroom of his dentist. He was about to have his first tête-à tête with this formidable woman since he had seen her off on the boat to New York nearly a month ago, and he was acutely alive to the fact that he would be called upon to render a strict account of his actions during her absence. And what was agitating him was the fear lest some unguarded word, slipping from a tongue lubricated by unaccustomed Bollinger, might inform her that among those actions had been the plighting of his troth to Jane Abbott.

There had never been a time when such an announcement would have gone well, but to make it now would be to precipitate a situation of such peculiar embarrassment that his eyes swivelled in their sockets as he thought of it.

For Tubby's statement, though it had seemed to Jane the mere aimless babble that might have been expected from such a source, had been scrupulously correct in every detail. On the eve of her departure for America, as the result of just such another dinner as he had enjoyed tonight, Adrian Peake had also plighted his troth to the Princess Dwornitzchek.

That this seemingly fragile young man, so obviously unfitted for living dangerously, should have been capable of the hazardous feat of becoming engaged to two women simultaneously – and one of them a lady who even in repose resembled a leopardess – is not really so remarkable as it may appear at first sight. There is a simple explanation of his heroism.

Briefly, he had not, as has been said, expected Prospect No. 1 to return until a considerably later date, and by that time, he had hoped, he would have been able to establish himself solidly with Prospect No. 2. Once accepted as the official son-in-law-to-be of the wealthy Sir Buckstone Abbott, it would have been an easy task to have relieved himself, in a few regretful and apologetic words, of his obligations to the Princess Dwornitzchek. The telephone was invented for just such a purpose.

But now all this angry-father-with-horsewhip stuff had come up, and it was clear to him that those dreams he had had of a genial Sir Buckstone patting him on the shoulder and making large settlements must be written off as a total loss. His energies, he perceived, must now be devoted to consolidating the earlier deal. He was not devoid of sentiment and, given the choice, would much have preferred money with Jane attached to it to money that involved marriage with the Princess Dwornitzchek, but he was practical.

Tonight, before going to bed, it was his intention to write a well-expressed letter to Jane, pointing out the hopelessness of it all and suggesting that, in view of her father's attitude, it were best to end it all. This would clean up the situation satisfactorily, leaving no loose ends, and now the task before him was to be watchful and wary in his speech. Passing his tongue nervously over his lips, he prayed that that tongue would not betray him.

The door closed. The Princess came back to her seat. She was a large, sinuous woman, with a beautiful figure and a supple way of moving herself from spot to spot, and it was at moments like this, when she did that quick pad-pad across a room and sank into a chair, that she reminded the spectator most forcibly of a leopardess in its cage. Adrian, watching her, found his uneasiness increasing. He removed his finger from his tie and passed it along the inside of his collar.

'Thank God they've gone,' said the Princess. 'At last.'

This opportunity to postpone, if only for a while, the stock-taking from which he shrank was very welcome to Adrian. An expert in this woman's moods, he could see that the one prevailing at the moment was not amiable. Something, he perceived, had upset her. Her bright, rather prominent hazel eyes were glowing unpleasantly, her face was hard and her manner had now come to resemble that of a leopardess which has just been deprived of a T-bone steak. It seemed to him that a little light conversation on neutral subjects might ease matters.

'Who were they?'

'Some people I met on the boat. They took me to the theatre last night.'

'Oh, really? Which one?'

'The Apollo.'

'I forget what's on there.'

'A play called *The Angel in the House.*'

'I've heard about that.'

'What have you heard?'

'Oh, just that it's a big success. They say it will run a year.'

'Do they? I think it very unlikely.'

'Isn't it good?'

'No.'

'It's by some new man, isn't it?'

'It was written,' said the Princess, grinding her cigarette into the ash-tray with a vicious jab, 'by my stepson Joseph.'

Adrian began to understand her emotion. He was aware of her views on her stepson Joseph, and he appreciated how galling it must be for a woman who for years has been looking on a young man as a prodigal to discover suddenly that the prodigal has made good. It was too late to withdraw his flattering prediction about the play, but he could at least show that his heart was in the right place by disparaging its author.

'I don't like that fellow,' he said.

The Princess looked up. While conceding that this was the right spirit, she was surprised. She had not supposed that he and the fellow were acquainted.

'Oh?'

'No,' said Adrian. 'I hope he bumped his head.'

'What?'

'On the door of my – '

He broke off, appalled, biting the tongue which had just been about to add the word 'houseboat' and thus precipitate the exposure of all his cherished secrets. Champagne and roast duck, working on a mind enfeebled by too-long deprivation of those delicacies, had nearly led him into a fatal indiscretion.

'Flat,' he said.

'What on earth are you talking about?'

'The door of my flat. I hoped he would bump his head on the door of my flat. Somebody brought him to a cocktail party at my flat, and the top of the door is rather low and he is rather tall, and I was hoping that he would have bumped his head. But,' concluded Adrian, as brightly as he could manage, 'he – er – didn't.'

He produced a handkerchief and passed it across his forehead.

'Cocktail party?' said the Princess Dwornitzchek.

It did not need the metallic note in her voice to tell Adrian

Peake that in eluding one pitfall, he had tumbled into another. He remembered now, too late, that when seeing his betrothed off to America, he had assured her that it was his intention during her absence, to lead the life of a recluse – going nowhere, seeing nobody – in a word, pining in solitude until her return. He found it necessary to employ the handkerchief again.

'So you have been giving cocktail parties while I was away?'

'Only that one.'

'Lots of pretty girls, I suppose.'

'No, no. Just a few men.'

The sharp, discordant sound which proceeded from his companion's lips was technically a laugh, but it did not suggest merriment.

'Men! I suppose what has really been happening, if I only knew, is that, the moment my back was turned, you started making love to every woman in sight.'

'Heloise!'

'Not that it's the least use asking you, of course. You're such a liar.'

Adrian rose. For some time he had been experiencing a strong urge to be elsewhere, and these words seemed to offer a welcome cue for a dignified departure. His hostess's resemblance to a leopardess was now so vivid that the room seemed to have bars and an odd smell. Only the presence of a man in a peaked cap and a few bones lying about the floor were needed to complete the Regent's Park atmosphere.

'I think I had better go,' he said in a quiet, pained voice.

'Sit down.'

'I am not prepared to remain and – '

'Sit down.'

'You have hurt me, Heloise. We meet again for the first time after all these weeks, and you – '

'Sit down!'

He sat down.

'You're simply wasting your time,' said the Princess Dwornitzchek, 'pretending to be wounded and injured. Do you think I don't know what you're like? I don't trust you an inch.'

'Well, really!'

'Not an inch. There's nothing that would please you more than to make a fool of me.'

'I can only say that you seem to be in a very strange – '

'Well, you won't get much chance after we're married, because we are going to live in the country.'

'In the country!'

'I shall be able to keep an eye on you there.'

This seemed to Adrian, though one could scarcely have described him as sensitive, not a very nice spirit in which to begin a romantic life partnership, and he said so.

'My motto,' explained the Princess, 'is "safety first", and I am certainly not going to have you running around loose in London. Yes, I thought it might be rather a shock. Have some whisky.'

The advice struck Adrian as good. He crossed the room and became busy with the decanter. He helped himself liberally and drained half the glass at a draught.

Her words had been a death blow to all his dreams and aspirations. He loathed the country. Only in the gay whirl of big cities could he fulfil and express himself. Over the glass, the remainder of whose contents he was now absorbing, he stared at her blankly. His thoughts were sombre thoughts and bitter. He had known that a man who marries an imperious and autocratic woman from sound commercial motives must be prepared to take the rough with the smooth, but he had never anticipated that the former would be quite so rough as this.

'So you had better be getting measured for your little pair of leggings,' said the Princess with a facetiousness which he found jarring and in dubious taste.

'But, Heloise, have you thought this all out?'

Again his hostess laughed that sharp, discordant, disagreeable laugh.

'You bet I've thought it out.'

'I mean, have you considered what it will involve?'

'What will it involve?'

'Stagnation. The giving up of everything you enjoy. A brilliant woman like you, accustomed to being the centre of a circle of attractive, intelligent people in Mayfair, you would hate it. You would be miserable. You couldn't stand it. How can you possibly contemplate burying yourself in the country, hundreds of miles from London?'

'We shall not be hundreds of miles from London. The house I am going to buy is in Berkshire.'

'Berkshire?'

'A place called Walsingford Hall.'

It was fortunate for the well-being of the Princess Dwornitz-chek's drawing-room carpet that Adrian's glass had for some moments been empty, for at these words it leaped from his grasp like a live thing.

'Walsingford Hall!'

'You appear to know it.'

'I – I've heard of it.'

'From whom?'

'I – er – met its daughter. . . . I met Miss Abbott.'

'Where?'

'At a house down in Sussex.'

'Oh? So you went to stay at country houses as well as giving cocktail parties every night? Your life since I left England seems to have been one long round of gaiety.'

Something of the emotions of a bull in the arena had begun to come to Adrian Peake. He found himself wondering whether any amount of money could make this sort of thing worth while. But the recollection of the roast duck – and, above all, of that superb soufflé – stiffened his resolution.

'I didn't give cocktail parties every night,' he cried desperately. 'And I had to go to these people. I couldn't get out of it. It was a long-standing engagement. One has one's social obligations.'

'Oh, certainly. And Imogen Abbott was there?'

'Was that my fault?'

'I'm not blaming you. What did she tell you about Walsingford Hall?'

'She said it was revoltingly hideous.'

'It is not at all hideous. I like it. And I intend to buy it. I am going down there the day after tomorrow to stay for a few days and settle things. Tomorrow I shall be busy with lawyers and people. I suppose you saw quite a lot of Miss Abbott after that house party?'

'I never set eyes on her.'

'You didn't miss much. A colourless girl.'

'Very.'

'Though some people think her pretty, I believe.'

'In a way, perhaps.'

'Well, I'm not worrying about her. Pretty or not pretty, she has one defect which would repel you. She is as poor as a church mouse.'

'What?'

'Didn't you know? I should have thought that was the first thing you would have found out. The Abbotts haven't had a penny since some ancestors of theirs spent all the family money rebuilding the Hall in the reign of Queen Victoria. Sir Buckstone has to take in paying guests to make both ends meet. My buying the house will be a godsend to the man.'

Adrian passed his tongue over his lips. His eyes were round and glassy.

'I suppose so,' he said. 'Yes, I suppose it will. Er – well – '

'Are you going?'

'I think I'll be going.'

'Perhaps it is getting late. I'm glad we've had this little talk. Come and lunch here tomorrow. Good night.'

'Good night,' said Adrian.

He kissed her absently, and in the same distrait manner made his way down the stairs and allowed the butler to help him on with his coat. As he wandered through the streets to his flat, his mind was deeply occupied.

What an escape! He felt like a man who has been snatched back from a precipice. He had never expected to think kindly of Sir Buckstone Abbott after learning of his views on penniless suitors and horsewhips, but he did so now. But for the attitude which that excellent man had seen fit to take up toward him, by this time, he told himself, he might have been committed beyond recall to an alliance with a girl whose father could make both ends meet only by filling his home with paying guests. The thought chilled him to the marrow.

He could not help feeling a certain resentment toward Jane, the resentment of a man conscious of having been badly treated. It would be too much, perhaps, to say that he considered that he had been the victim of sharp practice, but he did think she might have made some laughing reference to the state of the family finances before allowing matters to proceed as far as they had gone. That remark of hers about lodgers could so easily have been amplified.

Once, in the days of his childhood, a visiting aunt had told Adrian Peake that if he went and looked in the cupboard in her room, he would find a lovely surprise. And when he had trudged upstairs – thinking it would be half a crown; hoping that it might be ten shillings; speculating even, for this was an aunt with a fur coat and a motor-car, on the possibility of it being a pound note – all he had found was a rubber ball – a beastly painted rubber ball which would have been dear at sixpence.

As he had felt then, so did he feel now. A little more candour, a little more openness at the outset, and what a lot of heart-burning men would be saved in their dealings with women.

He let himself into his flat and sat down to write that well-expressed letter to Jane. But scarcely had he dipped pen in ink when a frightful thought suddenly exploded in his mind, bring him to his feet with every nerve in his body quivering.

Tubby!

He had completely overlooked the fact that Tubby was in residence at Walsingford Hall.

The future unrolled itself before his eyes like a ghastly motion picture. Heloise had told him that she was going to the Hall the day after tomorrow. He saw her meeting Tubby, being informed by him that he, Adrian, had been living on the houseboat *Mignonette*, putting two and two together in that intelligent way of hers and, having brought the sum out at four, descending upon him with a demand for a full explanation.

His stomach seemed to turn on itself, as if strong hands were twisting it. Once let these things occur, and it was the end. He could say goodbye to a life of ease and plenty. That despite her knowledge of his character – on tonight's showing, a rather unpleasantly intimate knowledge – he exercised over the Princess Dwornitzchek a powerful attraction, he was aware. But there were limits beyond which his spell would cease to operate and that limit would be reached and passed if she ever found out about Jane.

There was, he saw, but one course before him – just one way of avoiding ruin and disaster. He must go down to Walsingford Parva on the morrow, get in touch with Tubby through the medium of the telephone – even in this crisis he did not contemplate calling in person at a house in which lurked Sir Buckstone Abbott and his hunting crop – and enjoin upon him secrecy and silence.

Adrian Peake went to bed. It was only when he woke next morning that he remembered that he had not yet written that letter to Jane.

He dealt with it after breakfast.

14

To say that the unexpected arrival of her brother Sam in the capacity of plasterer, desirous of plastering one of the guests beneath her roof, had upset Lady Abbott would be to use too forcible a verb. She was not a woman whom it was easy to upset, or even to disturb or ruffle. But, like some placid queen in whose realm civil war has broken out, she did react to the situation to the extent of feeling, in a dreamy sort of way, that, perhaps, something ought to be done about it. Not that she minded herself, but she could see that what had occurred was worrying her Buck and she hated him to be worried.

About an hour after lunch on the day following the Princess Dwornitzchek's small and intimate dinner party, accordingly, she heaved the sort of slight sigh which a philosophical martyr at the stake would have heaved, and, with the spaniels, James and John, at her heels, set out for the houseboat *Mignonette* to have a word in season with the intruder, looking like a stately galleon leaving port accompanied by a brace of skiffs.

The whole thing reflects great credit upon Lady Abbott, for she had never been an enthusiastic pedestrian. As a rule, if she wandered through the rose garden after breakfast and took a couple of turns up and down the terrace before dinner, she considered that she had done her bit as an athlete. Yet now she started off on the long half-mile hike down to the river without a thought of what the climb back up the hill was going to do to the muscles of her calves. Her great soul bore her on.

She found Mr Bulpitt sitting on the roof of the *Mignonette*. His rosy face and the sparkle of *joie de vivre* in his eyes suggested that he liked his new quarters. And so he did. It was the first time he had been on a houseboat, but he had settled down to the nautical life with the easy adaptability of a man whose circumstances had compelled him to spend a large part of his existence flitting through a series of American provincial hotels. His little knick-knacks were distributed cosily about the saloon, he had plenty of gum and it seemed to him that all the place needed now, to make it like home, was a Gideon Bible.

It was not immediately that he observed his sister's approach, for his gaze was riveted on Walsingford Hall. Unlike Joe Vanringham, who had looked at that curious edifice as if it had been a shrine, and Adrian Peake, who had gazed at it as if it had been the Mint, he scrutinized Walsingford Hall with the eye of the general of a siege force contemplating a fortress which he has come to capture.

The barking of James and John, who had never seen a man sitting on a roof before and suspected a Red plot, diverted his attention.

'Why, hello, Alice,' he said. He climbed cautiously down and embraced her affectionately. The spaniels, reassured by the spectacle, wandered off to sniff at molehills. 'Mighty nice of you to come and see me. I was kind of beginning to think there might be hard feelings.'

Lady Abbott disengaged herself; not angrily, for it was not in her nature to be angry with anyone, but with certain austerity. She was not in sympathy with her brother. She thought of poor old Buck, and how worried he was, and the picture that rose before her eyes of him frowning and chewing his pipe as he paced the terrace made her resemble a very easy-going tigress whose cub has been attacked.

'I've come to talk turkey, Sam.'

Mr Bulpitt's manner became guarded.

'Oh, yes?'

'Sam, you've got to lay off.'

Mr Bulpitt shook his head regretfully. He had feared this.

'I can't, Alice. It's a matter of professional pride. Like the North-West Mounted Police.'

A quarter of a century before, with the breezy vocabulary of the dressing-room at her disposal, Lady Abbott would undoubtedly have said something telling and effective about professional pride. But the wife of a Baronet, with the raised eyebrows of the county to consider, tends to lose the old pep as the years go by. So now she merely uttered a wordless exclamation.

'It is,' insisted Mr Bulpitt. 'Women don't understand these things.'

'I understand you've got a nerve, coming and trying to plaster people in your own sister's home.'

'To a plasterer whose heart is in his work,' said Mr Bulpitt sententiously, 'there is no such word as "sister".'

'So you won't lay off?'

'No, Alice. I'd do most anything for you, but the show must go on.'

Lady Abbott sighed. Remembrance of her childhood came to her, when Sam had always been as obstinate as a mule. She realized that no word of hers could soften this man, and, with her customary placid amiability, forbore to argue further.

'Well, suit yourself,' she said.

'Sure,' said Mr Bulpitt. 'Those'll be spannles, won't they?'

Lady Abbott admitted that James and John belonged to the breed mentioned, and silence fell for a space. As if by mutual agreement, they both lowered themselves to the carpet of buttercups and daisies. Mr Bulpitt gazed across the river, sentimentality in his eye. These idyllic surroundings appealed to him. There was something about them that reminded him of Bellport, Long Island, where he had once put the bite on a millionaire whose summer house was in that charming resort. He mentioned this to his sister.

'Jest the same sunny, peaceful afternoon it was, with the sky a lovely blue and the birds singing their little hearts out. He chased me half-way to Patchogue, I remember, with something in his hand that I have an idea was a pitchfork, though I didn't stop to make sure.'

Lady Abbott was interested.

'Then you're allowed to assault a process server?'

'You aren't allowed to. But,' said Mr Bulpitt thoughtfully, 'I've known it done.'

'Maybe you'd better be careful, Sam.'

'What do you mean?'

'I was thinking of this young Vanringham's brother. He's visiting us now.'

'What about him?'

'Oh, nothing. Except that he was telling Buck he used to be a box fighter.'

'Where was he ever a box fighter?'

'Out on the Pacific Coast a few years ago.'

'I've never heard of him. Probably one of these five-dollar prelim boys. Listen,' said Mr Bulpitt. 'One time I slapped a plaster on Young Kelly, the middle-weight challenger, in his own home. He was having supper with his brother Mike, the all-in wrestler, his cousin Cyril, who killed rats with his teeth, and his sister Genevieve, who was a strong woman in vaude-ville. Vanringham? Phooey! Just a novice.'

In spite of herself, Lady Abbott was impressed.

'You do live, Sam.'

'Only just, sometimes. What crossed my mind,' explained Mr Bulpitt, 'was the time I handed the papers to that snake charmer. Sixteen snakes of all sizes, and he sicked 'em all on to me.'

'When did you start this line?'

'Nine, maybe ten, years after I saw you last.'

'What do they pay you?'

'Not much. But it's not the money. It's the joy of the chase.'

'Sort of like big-game hunting, like Buck used to do?'

'That's it. You get a big kick out of plastering a man that thinks he's got you foiled.'

'I don't see how you're going to plaster Tubby Van-ringham.'

'I'll find a way.'

'It'll be no good your putting on false whiskers. You can't disguise that map of yours.'

Mr Bulpitt sneered openly at the idea of doing anything so banal as donning a disguise.

'And if you set foot in the grounds, Buck'll butter you over the terrace.'

For the first time, Mr Bulpitt seemed concerned.

'I hope you'll try to make his lordship understand that there's no animus. I like him.'

'He doesn't like you.'

'They don't often like me,' sighed Mr Bulpitt. 'It's the cross we of the profesh have to bear.'

Lady Abbott rose. She pointed a finger up at the Hall.

'How good's your eyesight, Sam?'

'Pretty good.'

'Can you see a big cedar tree up there? Follow the line of the house.'

'I see a tree. I know the one you mean. Noticed it when I was calling on you.'

'Well, young Vanringham's sitting under that tree with a good book, and he's got orders not to stir. So how you think you're going to get at him is more than I can understand.'

'That's where the science comes in.'

'You and your science!'

'All right, then, me and my science.'

There was hostility in Lady Abbott's eyes, but also a certain reluctant respect, such as the Napoleon type always extorts from women.

'Have you ever been beaten at this game, Sam?'

'Once only,' said Mr Bulpitt, with modest pride. 'It was my last job before this one. There was this guy Elmer B. Zagorin – the Night Club King, they used to call him, on account he ran a chain of night clubs in all the big cities – had fifty million dollars and refused to pay a bill for forty for hair restorer. Claimed it hadn't restored his hair. Boy! Did I chase that bird! Clear up and down the country for months and months and months. And he fooled me in the end.'

'He did?'

'Yes, sir. Died on me – weak heart – leaving a signed statement that I had made him very, very happy, because he hadn't had so much fun since he was a small child. Seems I had cured him of onwee. He'd grown kind of bored by wealth and riches,' explained Mr Bulpitt, 'like all these well-to-do millionaires, and hadn't been able to get a kick out of anything till I came along. Me on his heels all the time stimylated him.'

'Like these foxes that Buck says enjoy the chase more than anyone.'

'That's right. A great guy,' said Mr Bulpitt, reverently, as one laying a mental wreath on the Zagorin tomb. 'A shame we never met. I've a hunch I'd have liked him.'

There was a silence. Lady Abbott looked up at the Hall, as if calculating the weary distance she had to travel. She gave a little sigh.

'Well, good-bye, Sam. Pleased to have seen you.'

'Been nice seeing you, Alice.'

'Comfortable on that boat?'

'Sure. Snug as a bug in a rug.'

'Where do you eat?'

'Down at the inn.'

'I thought Buck had told them not to serve you?'

'They've got to serve me,' said Mr Bulpitt, with modest triumph. 'If they don't, those lose their licence. Lord Abbott can use his pull to make them ease me out of my bedroom, but when it comes to eats and drinks, I'm the public and they have no option. That's the law.'

'I see. Well, good-bye, Sam.'

'Good-bye, Alice.'

And having added a courteous word of advice about taking no wooden nickels, Mr Bulpitt watched his sister collect James and John and move majestically away across the water meadows.

Up at the Hall, Sir Buckstone Abbott was stumping up and down the front drive in the company of his friend Joe Vanringham.

The callous indifference of Nature toward human anguish has become such a commonplace that nowadays even the most reproachful poet scarcely bothers to comment on it. In literary circles it is pretty well taken for granted that the moment when Man is mourning is the very moment which Nature can be relied on to select for smiling her broadest. The rule held good now. Sir Buckstone's heart was heavy, but the skies did not weep in sympathy with him. The grounds of Walsingford Hall were flooded with golden sunlight.

Sir Buckstone walked with quick, short strides, with which Joe found it difficult to keep step, for his agitation was extreme. He had been in conversation with Mr Chinnery, and Mr Chinnery had made his flesh creep. On the subject of Sam

Bulpitt that much-married man could be really eloquent, and had been. Discussing Sam, he had drawn a picture of a kind of supernatural force against which it was futile to try to struggle, illustrating his arguments with anecdotes of the other's illustrious career. Some of these Sir Buckstone was now retailing to Joe.

'There was a fellow named Jorkins,' said Sir Buckstone, falling in his emotion into a sort of hop, skip, and jump, 'who used to try to fool him by going out of the back door, crossing an alley, getting into the basement of the house opposite, climbing on to the roof, walking along the roof tops to the end of the street and coming down through another house. You would have thought he would have been safe enough, taking precautions like that.'

'You would, indeed. But – ' said Joe, divining correctly that this was but Act I.

'But,' said Sir Buckstone, 'what happened? Bulpitt finds out what he's doing, and goes to a policeman and says, "Officer, a strange thing is occurring, which I think you ought to know about. I've seen a man coming out of a back door, crossing an alley, getting into the basement of the house opposite – " and, in short, so on. So the policeman lurks in wait for Jorkins – '

'Sees him going out of the back door, crossing an alley, getting into – '

'Precisely. And collars him at the end of the route, and says, "What's all this?" "It's quite all right," says the man. "All this may look odd, but the matter is readily explained. I am doing it for a bet. I am a respectable householder named Jorkins." "Oh, you are, are you?" says Bulpitt, popping out from the shadows. "Then these are for you!" And hands him the papers. What do you think of that?'

'Devilish,' agreed Joe.

'Fiendish,' said Sir Buckstone.

'Tubby must avoid the back door.'

'But he also comes to front doors.'

'Versatile,' said Joe.

'He comes carrying a bottle of champagne, and asks to see the man he's after. The butler, feeling that anyone will be glad of a present of champagne, suspects no trap. He admits the blighter, who proceeds to work his will.'

'Fortunately, we are in the country, where it might excite remark if men called at houses with bottles of champagne.'

'True. Yes, that is a point. But, my dear Joe, there is no end to the ingenuity of this man Bulpitt. Chinnery says that in order to serve a person in retreat at his seaside cottage, he has been known to put on a bathing suit and swim round to the fellow's private beach.'

'He can't get here by swimming.'

'No, that is so. But I fear the man. Do you know anything about the English law on these matters?'

'Not a thing, I'm afraid. Though I'll bet it's silly.'

'Chinnery says the American courts have ruled that a process server, though debarred from entering a house forcibly, may get in through an open door or window. If that is so in this country, it presents an appallingly grave problem. You can't keep all the windows shut in weather like this. And another thing. Have you spoken to your brother?'

'Yes.'

'What did you make of his attitude?'

'I know what you mean. All that out-thrust chin and let-her-sue stuff.'

'Precisely. When I was talking to him this morning he was extremely difficult. He appeared to court a breach-of-promise suit. Is he half-witted?'

'Well, you see, the whole thing is that Tubby regards himself as the injured party. His reason for breaking off the engagement was that he had reason to suppose that Miss Whittaker was double-crossing him and receiving presents on the side from a rival, and when I spoke to him, he kept saying that he had never heard of such nerve as his late betrothed was exhibiting and that there was nothing he would like better than to have the thing dragged into the pitiless light of day, so that the world might judge betwen this woman and him.'

'In that case, we might as well chuck in our hand.'

'Oh, no. I fancy it's all right now. I pointed out to him what would be the effect on our mutual stepmother of his being jerked before a tribunal for breach of promise, and he simmered down considerably. His passion for abstract justice waned. When I left him, he was seeing reason and had agreed to play ball. You need have no fear of Tubby breaking out.'

Sir Buckstone drew a deep breath.

'Joe,' he began, in a voice that quivered with gratitude. . . . 'Oh, hullo, my dear.'

Lady Abbott, limping a little, as marathon walkers will, had reached journey's end.

'Been for a walk, Toots?'

'I've been down seeing Sam.'

Sir Buckstone's face, which had brightened at the sight of her, darkened once more.

'Joe and I were just talking about him. What did he say when you saw him?'

'He said he was like the North-West Mounted Police.'

'He did, did he?'

'Yes, and that the show must go on.'

'He didn't happen to drop any sort of a hint as to what he was planning to do?'

'No. Well, you would hardly expect him to, would you? But I'll bet the little weasel's got something up his sleeve, all right. I told him young Vanringham was sitting under the cedar with a book and wasn't going to stir, but it didn't seem to discourage him. He just grinned, and said something about science. Oh, well, I guess everything'll be all right,' said Lady Abbott, equably. 'All we've got to do is watch out.'

And with these words of cheer, she passed on her way, anxious to get to her settee and put her feet up.

Sir Buckstone, a disciple of the Chinnery, or pessimistic, school of thought, was not greatly uplifted by her prognostication. The picture of the subtle super-plasterer crouching for a spring depressed him. And, as he now observed to Joe, breaking the moody silence which had followed upon Lady Abbott's departure, the worst thing about the whole infernal business was the suspense, the waiting, the feeling that at any moment the worst might befall.

Joe patted his arm sympathetically.

'You mustn't let it get you down, Buck. But I know just what you mean. Most trying for the nervous system. It must recall to you very vividly, I imagine, the old days when you were a big-game hunter. Many a time, no doubt, as you made your way through the African jungle – '

'There aren't any jungles in Africa.'

'There aren't?'

'No.'

'Negligence somewhere,' said Joe. 'Well, many a time, as you made your way through whatever substitute for jungles they have in Africa, you must have heard hoarse breathing off-stage and realized that you were being stalked by a local leopard, and I'm sure that the worst part of such an experience must have been the uncertainty of it all, the feeling that you could never know just when you were going to get the creature on your back collar stud. And so with this man Bulpitt. What, we ask ourselves, will his next move be?'

'Exactly.'

'And what do we reply? We reply that we're damned if we know. We can but, as Lady Abbott says, be on our guard. How simple,' sighed Joe, 'it would all have been if Peake had not let him have that houseboat.'

Sir Buckstone quivered.

'Joe,' he said, 'the more I think about it, the more convinced I am that you were right about Peake being Bulpitt's accomplice.'

'The evidence does seem to point in that direction.'

'There isn't a doubt about it. What brought the man down here? He came to prepare the way for Bulpitt. Why did he take the houseboat? Obviously, so as to ensure Bulpitt a base of operations. There can be no other explanation. Do normal innocent people take houseboats? Of course, they don't. What the devil would anyone want a houseboat for? The *Mignonette* has been a drug in the market since the day it was built.'

'Till Peake came along.'

'Precisely. Twenty years that boat has been sitting there empty, and suddenly, a few days before Bulpitt's appearance, Peake says he wants it. And laid his plans with fiendish cunning, mark you. He appears to have scraped acquaintance with my daughter Jane at some country house, and thus made it possible to worm his way in. Gor!' said Sir Buckstone. 'I'd like to horsewhip the fellow! ... What is it, Pollen?'

The butler had come out of the house and was moving softly past them, his objective apparently the cedar tree at the end of the terrace, beneath whch Tubby was sitting with his book. He halted.

'A telephone call, Sir Buckstone, for Mr Vanringham.'

'Eh? ... Somebody wants you on the telephone, Joe.'

'The younger Mr Vanringham, Sir Buckstone.'

'What!'

A far less sinister piece of information than this would have been enough to excite suspicion in the Baronet. In these dangerous days, if a fly had come buzzing round Tubby's head, he would have questioned its motives. He started visibly, and shot a meaning glance at Joe. Joe pursed his lips, grave and concerned.

'Who wants him?'

'If I caught the name correctly, Sir Buckstone, it was a Mr Peake.'

There was a sharp whistling sound. It was Sir Buckstone Abbott gasping. His eye, widening, once more encountered Joe's, and read in it a good man's horror at the low-down machinations of the wicked.

He pulled himself together. This was not a time for reeling under blows. It was a time for action.

'All right, Pollen,' he said, with an admirably assumed nonchalance. 'I'll answer it. Mr Vanringham's busy. Don't want to disturb him. ... Come, Joe.'

The telephone was in the hall. As Sir Buckstone picked up the receiver, the impression Joe got, watching his mauve face, was that he was about to bellow harsh words of violent abuse into it. But he had vastly underestimated the Machiavellian cunning of which members of the British Baronetcy are capable when the occasion calls. His companion's voice, when he spoke, was lowered to a respectful butlerine coo.

'Are you there, sir? I regret that I have been unable to find Mr Vanringham. Could I give him a message? ... Yes, sir ... very good, sir ... I will inform him.'

He hung up the receiver, puffing emotionally, while Joe stared, amazed at this exhibition of histrionic virtuosity.

'Buck! What an artist!'

Sir Buckstone had no time for compliments.

'He's at the inn!'

'The Goose and Gander?'

'The Goose and Gander. And he wants your brother to go down there at once and see him about something very important.'

Joe whistled.

'Black work!'

'A deliberate trap.'

'Can be nothing else but. What are you going to do?'

Sir Buckstone drew a laboured breath. Then his manner took on an ominous calm, like that of a cyclone gathering itself together before starting operations on the Texas hinterland.

'It will take me a quarter of an hour,' he said, 'to get to the Goose and Gander. Five minutes after that – Look about, my dear fellow, and see if you can see a hunting crop with an ivory handle. You can't mistake it. It should be on that chest over by the – Yes, that is it. Thank you, Joe.'

15

Mr Samuel Bulpitt was one of those thinkers whose minds are at their briskest when the body is in gentle motion. He liked to formulate his plans and schemes while strolling to and fro, as if on a quarter-deck, his hands clasped behind his back and some sentimental ballad on his lips. Many of his best coups had been thought out on that bush-bordered gravel path that runs beside the eastern border of Central Park at 59th Street, to the accompaniment of 'Alice Blue Gown' or 'What'll I Do?'

For some considerable time after Lady Abbott had left him, he had been walking up and down the towpath downstream from the houseboat *Mignonette*, crooning the latter of these two melodies. He was still doing so when Sir Buckstone set out on his punitive expedition to the Goose and Gander.

His mood, as he promenaded, was pensive. Bravely though he had scoffed in his sister's presence at the idea that the problem of establishing contact with a Tubby Vanringham who sat tight under distant cedar trees would present any difficulties to the expert mind, he had not really been so confident as he affected to be. The situation which confronted him, he could see, was different from those which he had handled so triumphantly in his native New York. The methods so effective there would not serve him here. It would be necessary to dish out something new.

Mr Bulpitt, as plasterer, resembled Adrian Peake in that he was a man who was at his best in urban surroundings. He liked to shout 'Fire!' on staircases in order to bring his prospects bolting out of the front doors of flats. He liked to bluff his way into offices under the pretence of being an important customer from the West. If a prominent actress happened to be his quarry, no one knew better than he how to wait at the stage door, a bouquet in one hand, the fatal papers behind his back in the other. ('Oh, how sweet! Are these really for me!' 'No, lady, but this is.') Put Mr Bulpitt in the heart of a big city and he could not go wrong.

But in the English countryside things were different. An Englishman's country home is his castle. It possesses stairs, but only those invited to tread them can use them as a base for shouting 'Fire!' It does not welcome customers from the West. Nor has it a stage door.

'What'll I do?' murmured Mr Bulpitt to his immortal soul. 'What'll I do, ti-um ti-um ti-ay?'

And he had fallen to wondering whether, scornfully though he had rejected the suggestion when it had been made, some form of rude disguise might not, after all, be his best plan, when the whole situation, as is so often the way on these occasions, suddenly lost its complexity. Out of the welter of his thoughts, springing fully armed like Minerva from the brow of Jove, there had emerged a scheme, a simple but ingenious device for the undoing of Tubby, which as a student of human psychology, he felt confident, would bring home the bacon.

He smiled contentedly. His crooning took on a gayer note, changing to 'Happy Days Are Here Again'. And it was at this moment that his attention was diverted by the sight of odd things happening upstream.

Until now, Mr Bulpitt had had this sylvan nook of old Berkshire to himself. Since his sister's departure, no human form had come to mar his peaceful solitude. But now there had appeared abruptly on the river-bank, coming from the direction of the village, a lissom, slender figure. It was approaching at a considerable speed and, as it drew nearer, he recognized it as that of the young man, Peake, his niece Jane's lowly suitor. And he was just about to advance in order to meet and introduce himself to one whose acquaintance he had long desired to make, when the other, reaching the houseboat, leaped up the gangplank and disappeared into the saloon.

Mr Bulpitt made for the *Mignonette* at his best pace, a puzzled man. He was at a loss to account for all this activity. He could not know that Adrian's actions apparently so eccentric, were based on the soundest common sense.

When Sir Buckstone arrived at the Goose and Gander, Adrian had been sitting in the front garden. He had not failed to observe the stocky individual with the flushed face and the purposeful eye who went stumping up the path into the inn, but he had given him only a momentary attention before allowing his thoughts to return to Tubby and the interview which, he trusted, would shortly take place. It was only when he heard a resonant voice from within asking for Mr Peake that he recalled that in the stocky individual's right hand there had been a most formidable hunting crop, and realized that for the first time he had set eyes upon the Sir Buckstone Abbott of whom he had heard so much.

There followed upon the realization a moment of paralysed inaction, and Sir Buckstone was already emerging from the inn and advancing on him like a pink-faced puma before he recovered himself sufficient to begin the race for life.

When he did act, however, he acted promptly. A jack rabbit of the Western prairies could have picked up some useful hints from him. Before the Baronet's first hoarse bellow had died away on the languid summer air, he was over the low hedge that fringed the garden and out in the road. The gate which separated the road from the water meadows he took almost in his stride. He then settled down to some plain, intensive running.

At first, when starting to run, he had no fixed plan, merely a sort of vague general desire to get away from it all. Then, just as the unaccustomed exercise was beginning to take its toll, the *Mignonette* came into view, offering a refuge. He supposed it to be still in the possession of Joe Vanringham, and he did not like Joe, but he was in no position to be choosy about refugees. Joe Vanringham might be lacking in many of the finer qualities, but he was sure he was not the man to cast out a fugitive desiring sanctuary. On the *Mignonette*, he felt, he would be safe.

His emotions, accordingly, when, a few moments after he had dived into the saloon and closed the door behind him, he heard a heavy step on the deck outside, accompanied by the puffing of heavy breath, were distressing. Who, he asked himself pallidly, was this man who puffed without? It could not be Joe, for Joe, whatever his spiritual defects, was in excellent physical condition, but – and here he quaked like a blancmange – it might quite well be his pursuer. With a sickening qualm he told himself that Sir Buckstone Abbott, after a brisk spin along a river-bank, would probably be puffing just like that. He looked about him for a safer hiding-place, but found none. The saloon, as has been said, was simply furnished, and had never been intended to afford cover for its occupants.

With leaden heart and with the flesh crawling upon his body as he thought of that hunting crop, he was preparing to meet his doom, when, from the towpath, a voice shouted: 'Hi! You damned Bulpitt! '

Life began to creep back into Adrian's numbed frame. The situation was still of almost the maximum stickiness, but the actual worst had not yet happened. Whoever the man outside the saloon door might be, he was not Sir Buckstone Abbott. The Baronet's voice, raised in anger, was easily recognizable by one who had once heard it. It was Sir Buckstone who was standing on the towpath, shouting: 'Hi! You damned Bulpitt! '

Many men might have been offended at being addressed in this curt fashion, but the mysterious individual on the deck showed no sign of annoyance. His voice, when he replied, was cheery, even cordial.

'Hello, your lordship! Nice day.'

His affability awoke no echo in Sir Buckstone Abbott.

'Never mind what sort of a day it is, and stop calling me "Your lordship", blast you. I'm a Baronet.'

'Isn't a Baronet a lord? '

'No, he isn't.'

The intricacies of the British system of titles seemed to interest the man who answered to the name of Bulpitt. When he next spoke, there was a genuine desire for knowledge in his voice:

'What's the difference?'

The question appeared to act as an irritant.

'Listen, you ghastly Bulpitt,' roared Sir Buckstone, 'I didn't come here to instruct you in the order of precedence. Where's Peake?'

'He's around.'

'Produce him.'

'Why?'

'I am going to thrash him within an inch of his life.'

That unpleasant feeling of bonelessness which he had experienced in the garden of the Goose and Gander surged once more over Adrian. The moment, it was plain, had come. The crux or nub of the situation had been reached, and his fate was now to be decided. With ashen face, he waited. Would Bulpitt yield? Or would Bulpitt stand firm?

Bulpitt stood firm.

'You're going to do nothing of the kind,' he replied severely. 'Don't you know better than that, a Baronet like you? Baronets,' said Mr Bulpitt, quite rightly, 'ought to be setting an example, not going around trying to beat the tar out of young fellows who can't help it if they're in love, can they?'

The rebuke was one which should have abashed the most hardened holder of a hereditary title, but it seemed merely to increase Sir Buckstone's displeasure. His voice rose.

'Stop drivelling, Bulpitt! And,' he continued with a sudden access of vehemence, 'put that plank back!'

The word 'plank' mystified Adrian for a moment. Then he remembered the strip of wood that linked the *Mignonette* with the shore, and understood. This admirable Bulpitt, whoever he might be, acting with a resourcefulness which did him credit, had apparently performed the nautical equivalent of raising the drawbridge.

That this was so was made plain by his next words, which were spoken in a tone of rather unctuous complacency:

'Now, if you want him, you'll have to jump.'

Sir Buckstone's reply was not fully audible, for emotion interfered with the precision of his diction, but Adrian understood him to say that this was precisely the feat which he proposed to attempt, and he waited anxiously to hear what his preserver would advance in rebuttal.

He need have had no concern. Mr Bulpitt was fully equal to the situation.

'If you do, I'll bop you.'

'You'll what?'

'I'll bop you over the head with this chair.'

'You won't!'

'I will.'

'You bop me over the head with chairs, and I'll summon you for assault.'

'You start jumping aboard my boat and I'll have you pinched for burglary.'

A silence followed this remark. It appeared to have left Sir Buckstone momentarily breathless.

'What the devil are you talking about?' he demanded at length.

'I know the law. A boat's the same as a house. You bust into a boat and you're a burglar.'

'I never heard such dashed nonsense in my life. It's my boat.'

'It's not any such thing, your boat. It's my boat. I'm the tenant. So you be careful. One jump, and I bop.'

The duel of two strong minds was over. Sir Buckstone Abbott was a lion of physical courage, and it was not from any apprehension of chairs descending on his head that he now decided to give up the struggle and leave the field to the enemy.

What swayed him was the fact that a legal point had arisen and that he was uncertain of his standing. He feared no foe in shining armour, but like all respectable Britons, he shrank from getting mixed up with the law. Rather than run any risk of actions and damages he preferred to sheath the hunting crop.

Possibly he consoled himself, like so many baffled Baronets in the fiction and drama of an earlier age, with the thought that a time would come. At any rate, he moved off, flicking moodily at the meadowsweet with the thong which he had hoped would have been put to a better use, and Mr Bulpitt, flushed with moral victory, lowered his chair and opened the door of the saloon.

'He's gone,' he said, rightly feeling that this was the point on which his guest would desire immediate assurance. 'Yes, sir. Had the sense to quit while the quitting was good.'

He regarded Adrian with a gaze that was not only kindly but full of admiration. Being naturally in ignorance of the motives which had led the young man back into the danger zone, he assumed that what had brought him was the overwhelming desire to be near Jane and he approved of his gallant hardihood. All the sentiment in Mr Bulpitt responded to the thought of the humble suitor braving fearful risks to contact his loved one. Adrian Peake reminded him of Romeo.

Perceiving that the young hero was still somewhat shaken, he went to the cupboard and produced a bottle, from which, before proceeding further, he poured a heartening draught. While Adrian choked over this, he resumed:

'How did you happen to run into his lordship?'

Adrian related briefly the scene in the inn garden. Mr Bulpitt shook his head. While applauding his companion's knightly courage, he seemed to be deploring his recklessness.

'You shouldn't have hung about there, right out in the open. Taking a big chance. Might have known that his lordship would have been tipped off that you were around and would come gunning for you. Got his spies everywhere, I guess. Well, you'll be all right now. He can't get at you here. You heard us chewing the rag? Well, I meant what I said. If he'd of tried to come aboard, I'd have bopped him. Yessir! It wouldn't have been the first time I'd bopped a guy with a chair. Or with a bottle,' said Mr Bulpitt, his eye dreamy as he mused on the golden past.

It occurred to Adrian that he had not yet thanked his preserver, and he endeavoured now to do so. But Mr Bulpitt waved aside his gratitude with an airy hand.

'Don't give it another thought,' he said. 'I told Imogen I was for you, and I am. It was her that put me wise to your little trouble. I saw you kissing her down here that day, and she told me you were the fellow she was going to marry. I'm her uncle.'

Adrian's eyes widened. The restorative which he had been consuming had been potent, and he was not sure that he had heard aright.

'Her Uncle Sam from America. Mother's brother. Which gets you wondering, maybe, why I'm on this boat, instead of being up at the big house. Well, I'll tell you. There's been a mite of unpleasantness, which we needn't go into now, and they don't seem to kind of want me as one of the family. . . . Have another drink?'

'No, thank you.'

'Sure?'

'No, really; thanks.'

'Well, there isn't one, anyway. That's the last of the bottle. Yes, Imogen told me you were her beau, and then I happened to overhear that young fellow telling you about her father being after you with his horsewhip, so I'd gotten all the facts and was ready for his lordship when he came along. I'm fond of that niece of mine, and anybody she's fond of is my buddy. You stay on this boat as long as you like.'

'It's awfully good of you.'

'Not at all, not-a-tall. I'm for you. I admire the way you came here, just to see her, knowing all the time that peril lurked.'

Adrian perceived that he must dissemble. His companion's hospitality, it was clear, was being offered to him purely in his capacity of Jane's betrothed. Once allow Mr Bulpitt to gather that there was an 'ex' attached to the word, and this sanctuary would be barred to him. And it was imperative that he remain in the neighbourhood until he had been able to get in touch with Tubby.

'Oh, well,' he said modestly.

'It was swell,' said Mr Bulpitt. 'And now I'll have to leave you for a while. Got to go along to the inn and see someone. Make yourself at home. I'll be back as soon as I can manage.'

16

The mellow afternoon was well advanced toward the cool peace of evening when Mr Bulpitt reached the Goose and Gander. He directed his steps to the public bar, and was glad to find it unoccupied except for the blonde young lady who stood behind the counter and played the role of St Bernard dog to the thirsty wayfarers of Walsingford Parva. It was she whom he had come to see.

She greeted his entry with a friendly smile. The daughter of J. B. Attwater's brother, who lived in London, she had been sent down by her parents to make herself pleasant and helpful to the proprietor of the Goose and Gander, who was the wealthy one of the family, and she had conceived a strong distaste for what she termed the dog's island in which she found herself. There seemed to her little to do in Walsingford Parva, and nobody with whom to do it. Her clientele, consisting, as it did, of worthy sons of the soil, who, after telling her it was a fine day, were inclined to relapse into thoughtful silences running anywhere from ten to twenty minutes, bored her. The one bright spot in her drab life was Mr Bulpitt.

Thirty years spent in kidding waitresses in quick-lunch restaurants from Maine to California had developed in Samuel Bulpitt an unsurpassed technique with the sex, and he had made himself a warm favourite with the Goose and Gander's temporary barmaid.

'The usual, Mr Bulpitt?' she said brightly.

'The usual,' assented Mr Bulpitt. 'Say, you've been doing your hair a different way.'

'Fancy you noticing that! How does it look?'

'Swell. Like Greta Garbo.'

'Do you really think so?'

'I'll say.'

'Back in London, most of the boys tell me I look more like Myrna Loy.'

'Well, there's a touch of her too. And Ginger Rogers ... Got a box of matches?'

'Here you are.'

'Show you a trick,' said Mr Bulpitt.

He did three, to her great satisfaction. An atmosphere of cosy cordiality thus achieved, he sat for some moments, sipping his beer in silence.

'We had some excitement here this afternoon,' said Miss Attwater. 'Missed it, of course, myself, but that's my luck. Myrtle told me about it. She's the girl with the adenoids.'

'Oh, yes?'

'Don't know what it was all about, but it seems Sir Buck-stone Abbott was chasing some young fellow with a horsewhip all over the garden.'

'You don't say!'

'And I said to Myrtle, "Well, I'm glad something exciting sometimes happens here," I said, "because of all the dead-and-alive holes – "' Don't' you find it a bit quiet for you, Mr Bulpitt?'

'When you get to my age, you'll like quiet.'

'Your age!'

'A hundred and four last birthday. I'm not saying I mightn't have found the place kind of motionless when I was going good.'

'I'll bet you've had some rare old times in your day.'

'You're not so far wrong there, girlie.'

'I expect you raised old Harry back in the reign of William the Conqueror.'

Mr Bulpitt, who, during these exchanges, had been debating in his mind how best to approach the subject which he had come to discuss, perceived that he had been given a cue. He allowed a thoughtful look to creep over his face, then emitted a low chuckle.

'What's the joke?'

'Oh, I was just thinking of something. Something that happened in the old days.'

'What?'

'Oh, nothing, really.'

'What was it?'

'Maybe it wouldn't amuse you,' said Mr Bulpitt diffidently. 'It was a sort of practical joke. Some people don't like them.'

'You mean like making an April fool of somebody?'

'That sort of thing.'

'What happened?'

'Well, it was this way,' said Mr Bulpitt.

The story which he told was long and rambling, and many might have considered that the characters in it, stated by him to have near died laughing, had been easily amused, but it went over well with his audience. J. B. Attwater's niece giggled heartily.

'You must have had lots of fun in those days,' she said.

'Oh, lots,' said Mr Bulpitt. 'I often look back and think what a barrel of fun we had. But there was a crowd of us then. That's why we could work stunts like that. It was one for all and all for one, like the Three Musketeers. You can't do nothing constructive by yourself. Often and often I wish I'd got some of the old gang around. Why, say, listen; there's a friend of mine up at the Hall I could play a swell joke on right now. Only what's the use? I can't do it alone. I'd need a girl to help me.'

'What sort of a girl?'

'Any sort, just so long as she wasn't dumb.'

'You mean foolish?'

'No, really dumb. I'd want her to talk to the guy over the telephone.'

'Couldn't I do it?'

Mr Bulpitt lowered his glass.

'I hadn't thought of you,' he said, untruly. 'Why, say, that's an idea. Sure you could do it. And it would be a bit of fun for you, seeing you're finding things kind of dull here.'

'What would I have to say?'

'I'd write it all down for you. It's like this. This friend of mine, his name's Vanringham.'

'I know. The gentleman that was staying here.'

'No, his brother. You want to get the right one. This one's T. P. Vanringham.'

'I see.'

'And he's a fellow that thinks all the girls are crazy about him. So here's the gag I want to pull on him. I want this girl – you, if you say you'll do it – to call him on the phone and make a date to meet him. Where would be a good place? I know. Say the second milestone on the Walsingford road. I've been there. There's bushes back of it. We'd need bushes.'

'Why?'

'To hide in and spring out of from. It's like this: You don't say who you are, y'understand; you're just a mystery woman that's seen him around and fallen for him in a big way, and you want to make a date. You tell him you'll meet him at the second milestone, and he gets all worked up and patting himself on the back, and along he comes, all in his best clothes, and then, instead of it being a lovely girl, it's me. I jump out from the bushes at him and say, "Hello, there!" And that'll be a big laugh.'

He chuckled richly, and Mr Attwater's niece chuckled, too, but only out of politeness. Privately, she was feeling a little disappointed. It seemed to her that a great deal of trouble was to be taken for a rather disproportionate result. But she could not say so, with Mr Bulpitt smiling his sunny smile and looking like a boy about to be taken to the circus. She was a warm-hearted girl, and his childlike innocence touched her.

'And listen,' said Mr Bulpitt, scribbling industriously. 'This is what you say.'

She read the script, and at once thought more highly of the scheme. It now began to seem to her rich in humorous possibilities. Mr Bulpitt's plot might be weak, but she liked his dialogue.

'You are a one,' she said admiringly.

'You'll do it?'

'Rather.'

'Then do it now,' said Mr Bulpitt.

Tubby Vanringham, seated beneath the large cedar which shaded the western end of the terrace of Walsingford Hall, had begun to find it hard to endure with fortitude the life of captivity which had been thrust upon him. A moody frown was on his brow and his gaze, fixed on the river gleaming coolly below him, was a wistful gaze, like that of Moses on the summit of Mount Pisgah. He was conscious of a growing ennui. The sight of those silver waters, in which he longed to be sporting like the porpoise he rather resembled, tantalized him. Missing his two swims a day had tried him sorely.

Nor was this the only deprivation that irked him as a result of the cramped and restricted conditions now governing his life. Jane Abbott, on this very terrace, had told him that he was the sort of man who was lost without a girl, and her intuition had not misled her. Even more than for the daily bathe, he found himself pining for feminine society.

In the matter of feminine society, Walsingford Hall was at the moment a little understaffed. There was Mrs Shepley, who wore spectacles; Mrs Folsom, who had large teeth; Miss Prudence Whittaker, whose extraordinary views on accepting presents from city slickers and deplorable tendency to initiate actions for heart balm ruled her out of consideration; and Jane. And though he would have been perfectly content to pass the last few days in Jane's company, the pleasure had been denied him. She seemed to have become monopolized by his brother Joe.

With the feeling that he might just as well have been on a desert island, Tubby tried again to interest himself in the book which lay open upon his knee. But once more he found it too deep for him. It was entitled 'Murder at Bilbury Manor', and was a whodunit of the more abstruse type, in which everything turns on whether a certain character, by catching the three-forty-three train at Hilbury and changing into the four-sixteen at Milbury, could have reached Silbury by five-twenty-seven, which would have given him just time to disguise himself and be sticking knives into people at Bilbury by six-thirty-eight.

The detective and his friend had been discussing this question for about forty pages with tremendous animation, but Tubby found himself unable to share their eager enthusiasm. The thing left him cold, and he was just wondering if the solution of the whole problem of coping with this interminable afternoon might not be to go to sleep till the dressing gong sounded, when Pollen came to inform him that he was wanted on the telephone, and this time, Sir Buckstone not being present, was able to deliver the message.

'Telephone?' said Tubby, instantly alert. Even this trivial break in the monotony was welcome to him. 'Who is it?'

'The lady did not give a name, sir.'

Tubby started. The terrace flickered before his eyes. Hope, which he had thought long since dead, stirred in its winding cloth.

'Lady?' he said, speaking in a husky, trembling voice. 'The lady?'

'Yes, sir.'

'Gosh!' said Tubby.

It was at a speed remarkable on so warm a day that he covered the distance to the house. Not even had he been a fiend in human shape trying to make the four-sixteen connexion at Milbury, could he had moved more nippily.

'Hello?' he breathed into the instrument. 'Hello.... Yes. This is Mr Vanringham.'

A musical voice, faintly Cockney in its timbre, spoke at the other end of the wire:

'Mr T. P. Vanringham?'

'Yup.'

The voice seemed to be combating a disposition to giggle.

'You don't know who I am.'

'Who are you?'

'Ah, that ud be telling.'

'Your voice sounds familiar.'

'I don't know why it should. We've never met.'

'Haven't we?'

'No. But I'd like to.'

'Me too.'

'I've seen you about.'

'Have you?'

'Yes. And,' said the voice coyly, 'I admired you so much.'

'Did you?'

'Oh, I did.'

Tubby was obliged to support himself against the wall. His voice, when he next spoke, shook as his legs were doing. Manna in the wilderness seemed to him but a feeble way of describing this.

'Say! Say, couldn't we meet sometime?'

'I'd love to, if you would. Would you?'

'You betcher.'

'We might go for a walk.'

'That's right.'

'But I don't want people to see me.'

'I get you.'

'They talk so.'

'Yes.'

'So, if you'd really like to – '

'I should say so.'

'Well, then, be at the second milestone on the Walsingford road at three o'clock tomorrow afternoon. I'll be waiting there. And when you come, make a noise like a linnet.'

'Why?'

'Because I'll be hiding, because I don't want people to see me, because they talk so.'

'I see. Sure. Yes, I understand. Like a what?'

'A linnet. The bird, you know. Then I'll know it's you, and I'll come out. Pip-pip,' said the mysterious unknown. The line was not in the script, but the scene had gone so well that she felt entitled to gag.

Tubby hung up the receiver. He was breathing tensely. It is always gratifying to a romantic young man to discover that the mere sight of himself has inspired uncontrollable admiration in a member of the other sex. He looked forward with bright anticipation to this meeting, so particularly attractive at a time when his heart was bruised and life had seemed to hold nothing but gloom and boredom.

It only remained to get straight on this linnet proposition. He took counsel of Pollen, whom he encountered as he was leaving the hall.

'Say, Pollen, do you know anything about birds?'

'Yes, sir. Birds have always been something of a hobby of mine. I find it interesting to observe their habits.'

'How are you on linnets?'

'Sir?'

'I mean, do you happen to know what sort of noise they make?'

'Oh, I beg your pardon. I did not follow you for a moment. Yes, sir. The rough song of the linnet is "Tolic-gow-gow, tolic-joey-fair, tolic-hickey-gee, tolic-equay-quake, tuc-tuc-whizzie, tuc-ruc-joey, equay-quake-a-weet, tuc-tuc-wheet."'

'It is?'

Tubby stood for a moment in thought.

'Oh, hell!' he said. 'I'll whistle.'

17

It has been well said of Baronets that, although you may defeat them temporarily, you cannot keep them down. That the reverse which he had sustained at the hands of Mr Bulpitt in their struggle over the body of Adrian Peake would leave Sir Buckstone Abbott permanently crushed, accordingly, was scarcely to be expected. Where a knight or an O.B.E. might have cracked under the humiliating experience of being driven from the field of battle, he merely became fuller of the belligerent feeling that something had got to be done about this Bulpitt blighter, and done immediately.

Brooding on his brother-in-law in bed that night, he saw that the root of the trouble lay in the fact that the latter was as artful as a barrel load of monkeys, and that where he, Sir Buckstone, had made his mistake was in trying to cope unaided with that snaky brain. What he needed, it was now clear to him, was the assistance and co-operation of other brains, equally serpentine, and by noon on the following day his plans were formed. He sought out his daughter Jane and instructed her to have her Widgeon Seven in readiness as soon as possible after lunch, to drive him over to Walsingford. It was his intention to catch the two-fifty-seven express there, and go to London to confer with his lawyers.

He had a solid faith in the acumen of the Messrs Boles, Boles, Wickett, Widgery and Boles, of Lincoln's Inn Fields, and was rather hoping that they might tell him that it would be quite in order for him to slip a couple of sticks of dynamite under the houseboat *Mignonette* and blow the bally thing to blazes.

Soon after two, in consequence, Jane was in the stable yard, putting the finishing touches of perfection to her loved one. And she had just twiddled at a nut with her spanner – for like all girls with a proper sense of duty towards their cars, she was a confirmed nut twiddler – and was starting to tighten it again, with a view to leaving it exactly as it had been before she touched it, when a shadow falling upon the flagstones at her side informed her that she was no longer alone and, looking up, she perceived Joe. He was gazing down at her with an expression that was half indulgent, like that of an affectionate father watching his idiot child disport itself, and half worshipping, as of one regarding a goddess.

'So here you are, young Ginger.'

'Yes,' said Jane.

She spoke a little brusquely, for she always disliked to be interrupted when communing with her Widgeon. Moreover, from the very inception of their acquaintance, Joe Vanringham had revealed himself as a man who proposed early and often, and she could see by his face, on which the worshipping expression had now begun to predominate to a rather marked extent, that he was about to propose again. This she wished, if possible, to prevent.

'Busy?'

'Very.'

He lighted a cigarette and surveyed her lovingly.

'What a messy little creature you are, to be sure,' he said. 'I suppose you know you've got a spot of oil on the tip of your nose?'

'I can wash it off.'

'But think of the wear and tear. Why put it there in the first place? What are you doing?'

'Working.'

'To some specific end, or just mucking around?'

'If you really want to know, Buck is going up to London, and I am getting the car ready to take him to Walsingford.'

Joe whistled.

'Walsingford, the Forbidden City? Are you really going to try to get there? No wonder you're tuning up the engine. Well, take plenty of pemmican, and be sure of your water supply. It was owing to the water giving out that Doctor Livingstone failed to get to Walsingford in '66. It's a pity, though.'

'Why?'

'I was hoping that you might have been free this afternoon to help me with a statue or two. The fascination of your society has caused me to fall behind in my work of late. The day before yesterday, snatching a few moments before breakfast I moustached up as far as the tenth plug-ugly from the end, but yesterday was a blank day. However, the job is progressing.'

'That's nice.'

'I thought you would be pleased. Yes, I'm getting along. Several of them – notably Marcus Aurelius and the god Jupiter – outsmarted me by being already whiskered to the eyebrows, but I have had good results with Julius Caesar and Apollo, and should welcome your critical opinion. And now,' said Joe, 'to a more tender and sentimental subject.'

'Oh, golly!'

'You spoke?'

'I said "Oh, golly!"' Jane rose and tucked the spanner away in its box. 'Are you really going to start that all over again?'

'I don't know what you mean by "start all over again". I've never stopped. Haven't you noticed how I keep on asking you to marry me? Every day. As regular as clockwork.'

'And haven't you noticed how, every time you do it, I tell you I'm engaged to someone else?'

'That has not escaped me, but I don't pay very much attention to it. In the manuscripts I used to read for dear old Busby, until our paths separated, the heroine was always engaged to someone else at the start. I wish I could have brought along a few of those manuscripts.'

'Good stuff?'

'Terrific. From a man steeped in their contents as I am, no method of ensnaring the female heart is hidden. I know just how it's done. I shall rescue you from a burning house, or from drowning, or from bulls, or from mad dogs, or from tramps, or from runaway horses. Or I might save your kitten.'

'I haven't a kitten.'

'A kitten shall be provided. I tell you, young Ginger – '

'Do ... not ... call me Ginger.'

'I tell you, young Jane, it is hopeless for you to try to escape me. You are as good as walking up the aisle already. You shake your head? Just you wait. A time will come – and shortly – when you will be doing so in order to dislodge the deposits of rice and confetti which have gathered in your lovely hair. If I were you, I'd cease to struggle.'

'Oh, I think I'll go on.'

'Just as you please, of course. But you're wasting your time. I feel that nothing is too good for you, and I intend that you shall have the best of husbands. And, believe me, you're going to get a pippin. One of the nicest chaps I know – loving, devoted, rich, fascinating – '

'Whom did you ever fascinate?'

'Whom didn't I? I bowl them over in their thousands. Did you notice Mrs Folsom at dinner last night?'

'What about her?'

'The way she looked at me when I was doing that balancing trick with the nut crackers and the wineglass. Poor, foolish moth, I said to myself.'

'I noticed the way Buck looked at you. He values that set of wineglasses.'

'It would take more than broken glassware to queer me with Buck.'

'He does seem fond of you, certainly. I wonder why?'

'That could have been phrased more tactfully. Yes, he esteems me as highly as I esteem him. Dear old Buck, there is nothing he would like better than to have me as a son-in-law, bless him.'

'What makes you think that?'

'He told me so, when I approached him yesterday to ask his formal permission to pay my addresses to you.'

'You didn't!'

'I certainly did. I'm old-fashioned. I disapprove of the casual modern practice of letting the girl's father in on the thing only in the vestry after the ceremony. Buck would simply love to have me as a son-in-law. But how can this be managed while you persist in that extraordinary habit of yours of refusing me every time I propose? I think I will now have another pop. You may have changed your mind since I last spoke.'

'I haven't.'

'You will eventually. Shall I draw a little picture for you? It is the opening night of my new play. The curtain has fallen to the accompaniment of thunderous applause. The whisper passes from mouth to mouth, "Another Vanringham success! How does the fellow do it?" There are insistent cries of "Author! Author!" and in response a well-knit figure steps on to the stage. This turns out to be me. I advance to the footlights and raise a hand for silence. A hush falls on the crowded house. I speak. "Ladies and gentlemen," I say, "I thank you, I thank you for this wonderful reception. I thank you one and all. But most of all I thank my wife, without whose never-failing sympathy, encouragement and advice, this play would never have been written."'

'Shifting the responsibility. A low trick.'

'"Ladies and gentlemen, I owe it all to the little woman!" Terrific applause, during which you take a shy bow from your box, and renewed salvoes as you coyly throw a rose at me. Doesn't that picture tempt you?'

'Not a bit. It would have to be something much more solid than a rose. And now do you think you could move your well-knit figure slightly to one side? I want to start the car.'

'What train is the boss catching?'

'The two-fifty-seven.'

'Then perhaps you had better be getting along. The spot of oil, by the way, has now extended to your left cheek.'

'Didn't your mother ever teach you not to make personal remarks?'

'Don't think I mind. I don't at all. I say to myself, "She is probably at this moment the grubbiest little object in Berkshire and will need thoroughly going over with soap and pumice stone, but she is the girl I love." All I meant was that you will require a wash and brush up before starting. I should not care for my future wife to be seen driving through an important centre like Walsingford looking like something excavated from Tutankhamen's tomb. Permit me.'

He placed his hands under her arms and hoisted her gently into the driver's seat.

'You know, young Jane,' he said, getting in beside her, 'one of the things I like about you is that you are so slim, so slight, so slender, so – in a word – portable. If you had been Mae West, I couldn't have done that. You can drive me as far as the terrace. I think I will put in a quarter of an hour among the statues.'

There is nothing like creative work in fine weather for releasing the artist spirit from the bonds of earth and putting it in tune with the infinite, and it was not long before a perfect contentment began to envelop Joe Vanringham. By a happy chance, the next in the line of statues awaiting his intention was that of the Emperor Nero, whose smooth bulbous face afforded his maximum of scope to the pencil; and, inspired, he gave of his best.

As he worked, he mused on the differences which a few brief days can make in a man's fortunes. Less than a week ago, he reflected, his position regarding Walsingford Hall had been that of a peri at the gate of Paradise, outside looking in. And now here he was, an honoured guest, able to hobnob daily with Jane Abbott, that wonder girl in whose half-pint person were combined all the lovely qualities of woman of which he had so often dreamed beneath full moons or when the music of the wind came sighing through the pines, or, for the matter of that, when the band was playing Träumerei.

As he started to attach a waxed end to Nero's moustache, he pondered on the strangeness of it all. How odd, he felt, that he should have fallen in love in this fashion, absolutely at first sight, like the heroes of those manuscripts to which he had alluded in his conversation with Jane. It was a thing he had heard of fellows doing, even outside novels published at their authors' expense by Mortimer Busby, but he had never supposed that he would do it himself. Too much sense, he had always maintained.

Yet here he was, level-headed old J. J. Vanringham, smacking into it with a whoop and a holler, just as if he had been his brother Tubby, who, from the age of fourteen onward, had been unable to see a girl on the distant horizon without wanting to send her violets and secure her telephone number.

Joe started. A shudder ran through him, as if he had been splashed with icy water. He stood motionless, gazing along the terrace. The Emperor Nero stared at him with sightless eyes, seeming to plead dumbly for the rest of his moustache, but he had no time to attend to emperors now. Thinking of Tubby and Tubby's tendency to love not wisely but too well had caused him to look at the spot beneath the cedar tree where the other should have been sitting, and, with a hideous shock to his nervous system, he saw that the spot was empty.

The chair was there. 'Murder at Bilbury Manor' was there. But not Tubby. He had vanished, and what Joe was asking himself was, 'Whither?'

It might be, of course, that the absentee had merely stepped into the house to replenish his cigarette-case or to look in the library for better and brighter mystery stories, and for a moment this thought eased Joe's agitation. Becoming slightly calmer, he scanned the terrace in the hope of finding someone who might have been an eyewitness of his brother's departure, and was glad to see that there was a clock-golfer clock-golfing on the putting green over by the main gate, through which, if he had been mad enough to leave the grounds, Tubby would presumably have passed.

He hurried toward this sportsman, arriving in his rear as he

shaped for a putt, and recognized in the seat of his bent plus-
fours the bold green-and-crimson pattern affected by his
fellow paying guest, Mr Everard Waugh-Bonner, a doddering
old museum piece whom, until now, he had always been at
some pains to avoid.

'Have you seen my brother?' he asked, in his concern rather
more loudly than was necessary at so close a range.

Mr Waugh-Bonner combined a startled leap with the com-
pletion of his shot, and, having missed the hole by some three
feet, turned, peering petulantly through a pair of those dark
spectacles which add anything from ten to twenty years to
their wearer's age.

'Hey?'

'My brother. Have you seen him?'

'You made me miss, shouting like that.'

'I'm sorry. But have you seen my brother?'

'I didn't even know,' said Mr Waugh-Bonner frankly, 'that
you had a brother.'

Time was pressing, but Joe saw that if a perfect understand-
ing was to be arrived at, he would have to start nearer the beginning.

'My name is Vanringham. My brother was sitting under the
cedar.'

'Hey? Oh, you mean that young fellow? You his brother?'

'Yes. Have you seen him?'

'Of course I've seen him.'

'Where?'

'Sitting under the cedar,' said Mr Waugh-Bonner, with the
manner of a man answering an easy one, and turned to
address his ball.

It seemed for a moment as if there might be murder at Walsingford Hall as well as at Bilbury Manor, but, with a powerful effort, Joe restrained himself from snatching the putter
from this obtuse septuagenarian and beating out his brains, if
you could call them that. He even waited until the other had
completed his stroke – another miss.

'He's not sitting there now.'

'Of course, he's not. How could he be when he's gone for a
walk?'

'Walk? Where?'

'Where what?'

'Which way was he heading and when did he leave?'

'Started out along the Walsingford road twenty minutes ago,' said Mr Waugh-Bonner, and snorted irritably as his companion left him like a bullet from a gun. He disliked all young men, but he hated jumpy ones.

18

Mr Bulpitt and Adrian Peake had lunched on board the houseboat *Mignonette* off bottled beer and sandwiches from the Goose and Gander. It had been a silent meal, for Mr Bulpitt, absorbed in his plans, had spoken little, and Adrian, laden with care, had not spoken at all. Brooding on the fact that every minute was bringing nearer the Princess Dwornitzchek's arrival at Walsingford Hall and that he had not yet succeeded in getting in touch with Tubby had begun to sap his morale.

From a reverie of unexampled unpleasantness he awoke to find that his host was asking him a question. Mr Bulpitt was a man who, when not eating or sleeping, was generally asking questions. He now swallowed the last fragment of sandwich, wiped his mouth on a pink handkerchief and opened the barrage.

'Say, tell me. How did you come to know Imogen?'

Adrian explained that they had been fellow guests at a week-end party. Mr Bulpitt asked what week-end party.

'It was at a house belonging to some people named Willoughby.'

'Nice folks?'

'Very.'

'Friends of yours?'

'Yes.'

'Friends of hers?'

'Yes.'

Mr Bulpitt nodded. He was getting into his stride.

'What happened? Did you fall in love at first sight?'

'Yes.'

'Came like a thunderbolt?'

'Yes.'

'All in a flash?'

'Yes.'

'Well, that's the best way, isn't it?'

'Yes.'

'And you kept it a secret?'

'Yes.'

'Her idea, maybe?'

'Yes.'

'She wanted you to have time to fight the world and wrest a fortune from it?'

'Yes.'

'And then his lordship found out about it?'

'Yes.'

'And came after you with a horsewhip?'

'Yes.'

Mr Bulpitt sighed. He seemed to be deploring the impetuosity of the English landed classes.

'He shouldn't have done that. Love's love, isn't it?'

'Yes.'

'Sure it is,' said Mr Bulpitt. 'You can't get away from it. I don't hold with this keeping your hearts asunder. Of course, his lordship has a different slant on the thing, and I see his view-point. You're kind of strapped for money, aren't you, Mr Peake?'

Adrian admitted that his resources were not large.

'That's what's biting Lord Abbott,' said Mr Bulpitt sagely. 'He don't get the sentimental angle. The way he looks at it is that his daughter – his ewe lamb, as you might say – '

He rolled a bright eye inquiringly at Adrian. Adrian endorsed the phrase with a nod.

'The way he looks at it is that his ewe lamb has gone and given her heart to a lowly suitor, and he's out to put the bee on it. Those haughty English aristocrats are like that. Tough babies. Comes of treading the peasantry underfoot with an iron heel, I guess. You can't blame him, I suppose; it's the way he's been raised. He just can't get into his nut that love conquers all. Say, I used to sing a song about that. What was it now? Oh, yes.' In pursuance of his invariable policy when about to become vocal, Mr Bulpitt closed his eyes. 'Yes, that's how it went: "You may boast of the pride of your ancient name, you may dwell in a marble hall, but there's something that's greater than riches and fame, yeah, Love that conquers all."'

On the final note, with the air of a man who has performed an unpleasant but necessary task, he opened his eyes and fastened them on Adrian in an affectionate goggle.

'Listen,' he said. 'You don't have to worry about Lord Abbott. Let him eat cake. You just follow the dictates of your heart and go right ahead and marry the girl. And you needn't fuss about where the money's coming from. I'm fond of that niece of mine. I want her to be happy. So the day she marries, I'm going to settle half a million dollars on her. Yes, sir!'

For some moments silence reigned in the saloon of the *Mignonette*, and Mr Bulpitt would not have had it otherwise. He knew that he had been sensational, and it would have been a disappointment to him to be repaid with a casual 'Oh, yes?' He regarded Adrian with approval. He had expected him to take it big, and he was taking it big.

As a matter of fact, the latter's faculties had virtually ceased to function. He did not know it, but his emotions were almost precisely those experienced by the unfortunates whom, in his hot youth, Mr Bulpitt had bopped over the head with bottles. The eyes had become glazed, the limbs rigid and the breathing stertorous. It was lucky that he had finished lunch, for the announcement, if absorbed simultaneously with Goose and Gander ham sandwich, would undoubtedly have choked him.

A full minute had passed before he was able to control his vocal cords, and even then the control was only partial. His voice, when he spoke, came out in a sort of sepulchral gasp, as if he had been a spirit at a seance talking through a megaphone.

'Half a million dollars!'

'That's what I said.' Mr Bulpitt paused for a moment, twiddling his fingers. 'A hundred thousand pounds,' he added, with the rather exhausted look of the man who has been dividing by five in his head. 'That's nice sugar. A young couple could start setting up house on that.'

Adrian Peake was now blowing invisible bubbles.

'But – but are you rich?'

He could not help asking the question, though aware that it

was a foolish one. A man who is not rich does not go about giving people half a million dollars. If the urge to do so comes upon him, he resists it, feeling that it is best to keep the money in the old oak chest. However, Mr Bulpitt did not appear to be annoyed.

'Sure,' he replied affably. 'I got plenty.'

'But a hundred thousand pounds!'

'I had a notion it would shake you up some,' said Mr Bulpitt, well pleased. 'Don't you worry, sonny. I won't miss it. I'm a millionaire.' He rose and dusted crumbs from his waistcoat. 'Well, time I was off. I got a date.'

'But –'

'Don't thank me. A pleasure. What's money for, if you don't use it bringing two young hearts in springtime together?'

And with this admirable sentiment, accompanied by a benevolent smile, Mr Bulpitt went to the closet where he kept the Whittaker-Vanringham papers, took them out, eyed them lovingly for a moment and made for the door. Looking at his watch, he was glad to see that the hour was not so advanced as he had supposed. There would be plenty of time to stop in at the Goose and Gander for a post-prandial refresher before proceeding to keep his tryst with Tubby. He had an idea that that establishment's draught beer was superior to its bottled, and wished to put this theory to the test.

He left behind him a young man from whose life the sunshine, a moment ago shining with such prodigal warmth, had suddenly been banished. Adrian Peake had just remembered that well-expressed letter which he had written to Jane, severing their relations. It was this that had caused ecstasy to change so abruptly to despair.

The thought of that letter affected him like some corrosive acid. He writhed in agony of spirit. Not since the historic occasion when Lo, the poor Indian, threw the pearl away, richer than all his tribe, and suddenly found out what an ass he had made of himself, had anyone experienced such remorse as now seared Adrian Peake. He felt like a man who, having succeeded in unloading his holdings in a shaky mining venture, reads in the paper next morning that a new reef has been located and that the shares are leaping skyward.

But these young fellows who need the stuff are no weaklings.

Though crushed to earth, they rise again. For several minutes, Adrian Peake sat slumped in his chair, overwhelmed by that old bopped-on-the-head feeling. Then, like sunlight peeping through the clouds, there came into his eye a purposeful gleam. He had seen the way.

Two minutes later he was on the towpath, hastening towards the Goose and Gander.

It would be a grudging and churlish spirit that could withhold its admiration of Adrian Peake at this crisis in his affairs. Experience had shown him that the Goose and Gander was a place where at any moment Sir Buckstone Abbott might pop up with his hunting crop. No one knew better than he that his steps were taking him into perilous territory. But he did not waver. His flesh might shrink, but his soul was resolute. There were no writing materials on board the houseboat *Mignonette*, and the Goose and Gander was the only spot he knew of where these could be obtained. And in order to procure notepaper and envelope and write another well-expressed letter and send it up to the Hall by hand, he was prepared to risk all.

He had just reached the gate which led to the road when from the other side of the hedge there came the sound of an approaching car, and a moment later a two-seater had sped past him. It turned the corner and vanished quickly in the direction of Walsingford, but not so quickly that he was not able to see that Jane was at its wheel and that at her side sat her father, the hunting-crop specialist.

A delicious relief surged over Adrian Peake. What this meant was that there was now no possibility of a distasteful interruption on the part of the emotional Baronet, and it also meant that, with Jane out motoring to some unknown destination, he need not hurry over the composition of that letter. He could take his time and polish his phrases, secure in the knowledge that it would reach the Hall before her return.

It was almost at a saunter that he entered the parlour of the inn, and almost nonchalantly that he dipped pen in the curious black substance that passed for ink at the Goose and Gander. Presently, the nib was racing over the paper – or as nearly racing as a nib can that for some months past has been used by smokers for cleaning out pipes. He became absorbed in composition and the stuff came out as smooth as oil.

158

He implored Jane to dismiss from her mind entirely that other communication, which, he presumed, she had by now received from him. It had been written he said, in one of those fits of black depression which come at times to the best of men. He mooted the suggestion that he must have been mad when he wrote it. But today, he assured her, the cloud had cleared away and he was able to see clearly once more.

Admitting, he wrote, that it would be ideal if their union could be solemnized with the consent and approval of her father, surely his disapproval ought not, in these modern days, to be permitted to stand in their way. Sir Buckstone, he gathered, objected to him because he was poor. But money was not everything. Love, said Adrian, conquers all.

It was a good letter. He thought so as he re-read it, and he was still thinking so when he handed it, with half a crown, to J. B. Attwater's young son, Cyril, whom he found playing trains in the garden, with instructions to take it up to the Hall and leave it there.

Having watched the child start off, he turned away toward the public bar. His literary labours had engendered quite a respectable thirst.

J. B. Attwater's niece was at her post behind the counter, dreaming of London as she listlessly served out a half pint of mild and bitter to an elderly gentleman in corduroy trousers whose rich aroma suggested that his was a lifework that lay largely among pigs. At the sight of Adrian, she brightened perceptibly. He was a stranger to her, for during the brief period when he had been taking his meals at the inn, their paths had not happened to cross, but his appearance was so metropolitan that she warmed to him at once, and when the man in corduroy trousers had finished his refreshment and withdrawn, trailing pig smells behind him like clouds of glory, she embarked immediately upon affable conversation.

'You're from London, aren't you?' she asked when they had agreed that the day was warm and were pretty straight on the prospects of the fine weather holding up.

Adrian said that his home was in London.

'So's mine,' sighed Miss Attwater. 'And I wish I was there now. Making a long stay in these parts?'

'Not long.'

'You're up at the Hall, I suppose?'

'No. I'm on a houseboat.'

Miss Attwater was interested.

'Mr Bulpitt's houseboat?'

'Yes. Do you know Mr Bulpitt?'

'He comes in here regular. There's a nice gentleman.'

'Yes.'

'Always merry and bright and full of fun. He was in for a quick one not half an hour ago. And while I remember,' said Miss Attwater, reaching down behind the counter and coming up with a paper in her hand, 'he left this behind him. Put it down by his glass while we were talking, and forgot to take it away with him. I only noticed it after he'd gone. You might give it to him when you see him.'

Adrian took the document. It was blue in colour and legal in aspect. It held no message for him, for, owing to the liberality of the Princess Dwornitzchek and others, he had never seen a summons, and he put it away in his pocket with only a casual glance. Miss Attwater passed a cloth meditatively over the counter.

'I wonder what he was doing with that,' she said. 'If you want to know what I think, Mr Bulpitt's what I call a man of mystery.'

'Oh, yes?'

'Well, what's he doing here at all, to start with? I don't know if you've noticed, but he's an American gentleman.'

Adrian said that he had observed this.

'Well, what's an American gentleman doing, living on a houseboat in a dead-and-alive hole like this? I asked him straight out, and he just laughed and sort of turned it off. And I asked Uncle John if he knew, and he was very short with me.'

'Yes?'

'Bit my nose off. Told me to mind my own business and let the customers mind theirs. Set me thinking, that did. It's my belief that Mr Bulpitt's up to something. Could he be one of these international spies you read about?'

Adrian suggested that there was not very much in Walsingford Parva for an international spy to spy on.

'No, there's that, of course,' said Miss Attwater.

Another client intruded at this point, compelling her to sink the conversationalist in the business-woman. When he had gone, she resumed, still on the subject of Mr Bulpitt, but touching upon another facet of his many-sided character.

'He's a card – Mr Bulpitt. Has he played any of his jokes on you yet?'

'Jokes?'

'Practical jokes. He's a great one for practical joking. He was telling me about some of the ones he used to play on people over in America. I wouldn't live with him on a houseboat, I can tell you. I'd be afraid he'd push me into the water or something, or put a rat in my bed or something. He's gone off to play a joke on a fellow now.'

'Yes?'

'Yes. He's going to jump out of a bush at him.'

'Jump out of a bush?'

'Yes. When the fellow makes a noise like a linnet.'

'But why?'

'Ah!' said Miss Attwater. 'Now you're wanting to know something I can't tell you. He says it'll be a big laugh, but I think it all goes deeper than that. I think there's more behind it than we can guess. That's what I mean about him – he's a man of mystery.'

A positive inrush of customers now took place, and it was plain to Adrian that nothing more in the nature of intimate conversation was to be hoped for, he finished his tankard and left.

As he walked back to the houseboat, he found himself a prey to a certain uneasiness. It is never pleasant for a highly-strung young man to discover that he is accepting the hospitality of what appears to be a border-line case. On his own showing, Mr Bulpitt was a man who thought nothing of bopping people with bottles. He now stood revealed as a jumper-out of bushes. One could not help asking oneself where this sort of thing would stop. Nobody, of course, minds a genial eccentric, but the question that was exercising Adrian Peake was: How long would this jumping bopper remain genial?

Profoundly thankful that today would see the end of his visit, he reached the *Mignonette* and climbed the gangplank. As his foot touched the deck, the door of the saloon opened and a nude figure came out, holding a towel.

It was Tubby Vanringham.

Tubby was the first to recover from the shock of this unexpected encounter. He was surprised to see Adrian, having
supposed that he was many miles away, but he had too much
on his mind to worry about the activities of a fellow like
Adrian Peake. If he was here, he was here – that was how
Tubby felt. He dashed a bead of perspiration from his forehead and said, 'Oh, hello.' Adrian echoed the remark, and
there was silence for a moment.

'Going to have a swim,' said Tubby.

A less-observant man than Adrian would have seen at a
glance that he needed one. In spite of the warmth of the afternoon, he had evidently been moving swiftly from point to
point, and his condition was highly soluble. In Mr Bulpitt's
powerful, if slightly nauseating, phrase, he was sweating like
a nigger at election.

'I'm warm,' he said.

'You look warm.'

'I feel warm.'

'Been walking fast?'

'Running fast,' corrected Tubby. 'All the way from the
second milestone on the Walsingford Road.'

'What? Why?'

'So as to get here and tear up – ' An idea seemed to
strike Tubby. 'Say, listen,' he said. 'You used to have this
boat. Is there any place on it except the saloon where a fellow
could keep papers? I've gone over the saloon with a fine-tooth
comb, and they're not there.'

'Papers?' Adrian remembered that that girl at the inn had
given him a paper of some kind. He felt in his pocket. 'Could
this be what you are looking for?' he asked obligingly, stepping forward with outstretched hand.

The effect of the words and their accompanying action upon
Tubby was remarkable. He had been standing with the towel
draped about his waist in the normal manner of an American
gentleman chatting with a friend. He now sprang backwards
with a convulsive leap, as if he had observed snakes in his
path, and threw himself hastily into an attitude of self-defence.
His fists were clenched and his gaze menacing.

'You come a step closer,' he said, 'and I'll beat your block off!'

Adrian's bewilderment was extreme. It seemed to be his fate today to mix with eccentrics, and in the case of this one, he had no hesitation whatever in discarding the adjective 'genial'. In describing Tubby Vanringham, it was the last word a precisian like the late Gustave Flaubert would have selected.

He gaped blankly.

'What do you mean?'

'You know what I mean.'

'But I don't.'

'Oh, no? I suppose Bulpitt didn't give you that to slip to me?'

'He left it at the inn. The barmaid gave it to me.'

Tubby's austerity relaxed a little, but he remained wary.

'Well, all right. Maybe you're on the level. But I'm not taking any chances. Tear it up and drop it in the river.'

'But it belongs to Bulpitt.'

'I'll say it belongs to Bulpitt! Go on. Tear it up.'

'But really – I mean – '

'Do you want a poke in the beezer?' asked Tubby, approaching the matter from another angle.

Except the sudden appearance of Sir Buckstone Abbott with his hunting crop, there was nothing Adrian could think of that he desired less. His misgivings concerning the destruction of property belonging to his host remained acute, but if the alternative was a poke in the beezer, then the property must be destroyed. He was not sure what a beezer was, but the operative word in his companion's remark had been the verb 'poke'. He followed his instructions meticulously, and a moment later the fragments of the blue document were floating sluggishly downstream like an armada of paper boats.

The sedative effect of this upon Tubby was very gratifying to a peace-loving man. All trace of animosity now left the nudist. He drew a deep breath of relief and asked Adrian if he had got a cigarette. Having secured this, he asked him if he had got a light. Having been given a light, he said, 'Thanks'. The thing had virtually become a love feast.

'Sorry I got tough,' he said. 'You see, I wasn't sure that darned thing couldn't be served by proxy.'

'But what was it?'

'A summons.'

'A summons?'

'For breach of promise.'

'But what was Bulpitt doing with it?'

'Trying to serve it on me. And will you believe,' said Tubby, flushing darkly as he thought of the loathsome stratagem, 'the old devil actually got a girl to phone me and date me up for the second milestone on the Walsingford road. And when I got there and started making a noise like a linnet, out he came bounding from the bushes. It jarred a couple of years' growth out of me.'

He noted with pleasure that his companion's eyes were bulging and that his jaw had fallen slightly – with horror, no doubt, as any honest man's would have done, at this revelation of the depths of duplicity to which humanity can sink. For the first time in their acquaintance, he found himself thinking well of Adrian Peake. A twerp, yes, but a twerp with proper feelings.

'And pretty soon,' he went on, a sombre satisfaction now creeping into his voice, 'I jarred a couple of years' growth out of him. Because what do you think happened? Just as I was saying to myself that this was the end, he suddenly pulled up short and started feeling in his pockets. And when I said, "Well, come on. Get it over with," he gave a sort of silly laugh and told me he'd have to call the thing off for today, because he must have left the papers on the boat. And I felt that this was where I got a bit of my own back for all that alarm and despondency he had been causing me.'

An odd gurgling sound proceeded from Adrian Peake. It was not loud enough or compelling enough to divert Tubby from his narrative.

'I socked him on the snoot. Yes, ma'am, I hauled off and let him have it squarely on the schnozzle. And then I took him by the collar and shook him like a rat. His false teeth came out with a pop and vanished into the undergrowth, and I wouldn't have been surprised if his eyes had come out too. Because I shook him good. And then I left him lying there, and came running to the boat to find the papers and tear them up. And now they are torn up, and it'll take him days, maybe, to get another set. By which time – '

Adrian at last found speech.

'But is this man Bulpitt a process server?'

'Sure.'

'But isn't he rich?'

'Of course he's not.'

'He told me he was a millionaire!'

'He was kidding you.'

The sickening probability – nay, the certainty – that this was so made Adrian Peake feel absolutely filleted. Into his reeling mind there flashed what that girl at the inn had said about Mr Bulpitt's inordinate fondness for practical joking, and he perceived the hideous tangle which his too-trusting nature had led him to make of his personal affairs.

Lured on by the man's apparent genuineness, he had poured out his heart to Jane in a well-expressed letter and sent it up to the Hall by courtesy of Cyril Attwater. And unless some beneficent earthquake had engulfed Cyril or kindly bears had come out of the bushes and devoured him, that letter must even now be lying on some table, waiting her return.

Adrian Peake took one shuddering mental glance at the position of affairs and looked away again. Brief as it was, that glimpse of his predicament had made him feel absolutely sick. He had never been really happy at the thought that he was engaged to two women at once, but until now he had always had the consolation that no written evidence existed of his obligations to Jane, and that a verbal agreement can always be denied by a man who keeps his head.

'Well, I guess I'll have my swim,' said Tubby.

'I think I'll come in too,' said Adrian.

He was feeling as if he had contracted some form of prickly heat, and cold water seemed to offer at least a temporary relief.

19

Meanwhile, unknown to Adrian Peake, though it is improbable that he would have cared if he had known, for his was rather a self-centred nature, other people in the immediate neighbourhood were having their troubles. On the short stretch of road that lay between Walsingford and Walsingford Parva, quite near to one another and getting nearer with every stride which Joe Vanringham took and every revolution of the wheels of Jane Abbott's two-seater, there were, on this sunny afternoon, no fewer than three hearts bowed down with weight of woe. One was Joe's, the second was Jane's, the third Mr Bulpitt's. This constituted a local record, for that sleepy thoroughfare was, as a rule, almost empty of pedestrians and traffic.

Joe was suffering from remorse. It gnawed him to the bone. Swinging along the highway at his best speed, he was experiencing all the pangs of one who has sold the pass or been asleep at the switch. His familiarity with his brother's notorious fatheadedness, he told himself, ought to have warned him that it would be insanity to relax his vigilance for even the brief space of time required for proposing to Jane in stable yards. When you were guarding a fellow like Tubby, it was not enough to dump him in a chair and give him a mystery novel and expect him to stay put. You had to stand over him with a shotgun. He felt that he had lightly betrayed a sacred trust which had been reposed in him; and musing, in the intervals of wishing that the weather had been a little cooler and more suited to track work, he mourned in spirit.

Jane was not so much mourning in spirit as boiling with fury. Her eyes, dark and stormy, were alive with quite a good deal of the old crocodile glitter.

The afternoon post had arrived just as she was starting out on her drive to Walsingford, bringing with it the first of Adrian Peake's well-expressed letters.

She had not been able to read this communication until some ten minutes ago, on the departure of her father's train, and its contents were, in consequence, fresh in her mind. She could, indeed, have recited them verbatim, and she pressed her foot on the accelerator, anxious to reach the Hall and discuss the situation with Joe. From time to time her tight lips parted and moved, and it seemed as if flame might come from between them. This was when she was murmuring to herself some of the things she intended to say to him when they met.

The distress of Mr Bulpitt, crawling about the road by the

second milestone, differed from that of Joe and Jane, being in its essence physical rather than mental.

The punch administered by Tubby to his snoot, though it had been a vigorous one and had caused that organ to bleed rather freely, had not disturbed Mr Bulpitt to any great extent. He was a man who had taken many such a punch in his day, on just that spot. Indeed, in the really active years of his professional career he had come to look upon the sort of thing which had just been happening to him as pure routine. What did occasion him concern was the fact that his teeth had strayed from their moorings. Lacking them, he felt like Samson after his hair had been shorn. A man may rise on stepping stones of punched snoots to higher things, but he is lost without his bridgework.

The shaking which Tubby had given him had blurred his mind a little, dulling his usually keen grasp of affairs, but he had a sort of recollection of having seen the missing molars, when they set out on their travels, lay a nor'-nor'-easterly course, and it was in this direction that he was proceeding when Jane came along in her car. There was a squealing of brakes and a flurry of dust as she drew up beside him. She opened the door and jumped out, agitated in the extreme. Mr Bulpitt, on all fours and smeared with blood, presented a distinctly horrifying spectacle, and hers had been a sheltered life. Except for the time when the cook had cut her thumb opening a tin of sardines, she had never been brought face to face with tragedy.

In the sunken features on which her eyes rested, it is not surprising that she did not recognize the round, rosy countenance of her Uncle Sam. She had seen him only once, and then under very different conditions. It was in the light of an anonymous hit-and-run victim that she regarded him, and it was thus that she introduced him to Joe, when the latter came panting up a short while later.

She was glad to see Joe. Adrian Peake in his letter had specifically named him as the source from which he had learned that Sir Buckstone Abbott was thinking in terms of hunting crops, and she knew what motives had led him to give the information, but in spite of that she found his presence welcome. However black his soul might be, his body was comfortingly muscular; and somebody muscular to help her get the sufferer into the car and off to the doctor was what she had been wanting ever since her arrival on the scene.

Her own efforts to that end had been foiled by the coy refusal of Mr Bulpitt to assume a perpendicular position. With a quiet firmness, in spite of all her persuasion, he had remained on all fours, questing about like a dog that has scented game. It had not yet occurred to Mr Bulpitt that anyone might suppose that he was hurt. All he wanted was to be left alone to conduct his research work. He had endeavoured to explain this to Jane, and it was the horrible, wordless, yammering sound which he had produced that, even more than his appearance, had struck a chill to her heart.

But though she was relieved to see Joe, she did not intend that even in this supreme moment there should be any mistake about her displeasure. The fact that he had appeared so opportunely did not in the slightest degree modify her opinion that his behaviour had been abominable and that if ever a young man had justified a girl in drawing herself up to her full height, such as it was, and speaking like a Princess to an offending varlet, he was that young man. It was with a cold hauteur that she addressed him.

'Mr Vanringham, this man has been knocked down by a car.'

Joe took in the situation in a flash. He was a little out of breath, but even with bellows to mend, he was gallant, self-sacrificing and the perfect gentleman. He had read a sufficient number of the novels published at their authors' expense by Mr Busby to know what your man of honour does on an occasion like this. He takes the rap, like Cecil Trevelyan in *Hearts Astir* and Lord Fotheringham in *'Twas Once in May*. A swift, intelligent glance at Mr Bulpitt, who was now rooting in the undergrowth by the milestone, and he had drawn Jane aside and was speaking in a low, tense voice.

'I was driving. Remember. That's our story, and we must stick to it. I was driving – '

'You silly ass,' said Jane, who found his heroism trying. 'You don't think I did it, do you?'

'Didn't you?'

'Of course I didn't. He was like that when I came up.'

Joe scrutinized Mr Bulpitt. The grass by the milestone having yielded no treasure, he was now crawling along the edge of the road with the air of a Nebuchadnezzar in search of better pasture.

'Like that?'

'Yes.'

'On his hands and knees?'

'Yes.'

'Circling and sniffing?'

'Yes, yes, yes, yes, yes. A car must have knocked him down and gone on.'

'I suppose so.'

'Do you think he's dying?'

'He doesn't seem any too bobbish.'

'He said something, but he didn't speak properly.'

'Much stirred, no doubt. On these occasions a man's coarser side will come to the surface.'

'I mean I couldn't understand him. He just sort of gargled. He must have got concussion.'

'Where's the nearest doctor?'

'There's Dr Burke in the village, but he might be out now. He goes his rounds in the afternoon.'

'How about Walsingford?'

'There must be lots of doctors there, but I don't know where they live.'

'We had better drive there and ask. . . . Hello's, he's getting up.'

Mr Bulpitt had risen and was coming toward them. It had suddenly occurred to him that the quest was not being conducted in the most scientific manner. Three heads are better than one. With his niece Jane and the young fellow whom he had now recognized as T. P. Vanringham's brother to fall in and work under his directions, he had all the material for an organized search party. He mentioned this.

'Say, I can't seem to find my teeth,' he said. 'I wish you two would come and lend a hand. They're around here somewheres.'

He was aware, as he spoke, that his diction lacked something of its customary bell-like clearness, but it surprised him, nevertheless, to see Joe give a shocked start and look at Jane, who looked back and said, 'There!' And his astonishment was increased when, a moment later, a sinewy arm passed itself about his waist and he found himself lifted gently and placed in the car. And before he could find breath for comment, Jane was at the wheel, Joe had swung himself into the dickey, and the car was backing and turning, and then speeding smoothly along the road to Walsingford.

A passionate sense of bereavement came upon Mr Bulpitt as he was snatched away. He was convinced that a little more intensive searching would have produced solid results, and he endeavoured to voice a protest.

A kindly hand came from behind him and patted his shoulder.

'It's quite all right,' said Joe. 'Sit back and wait for the medical treatment. Just relax.... Say, I know this bird,' he added, scanning the twisted face. 'He's living on the house-boat. His name's Bulpitt.'

'What! Why, so it is!'

'You know him?'

'He's my uncle.'

This was news to Joe. Nothing in the attitude of Sir Buck-stone Abbott toward their passenger had suggested that the latter was his brother-in-law. Lacking to rather a marked extent that easy cordiality which one likes to see in Baronets toward their wives' kinfolk, it had resembled more that of a man confronted with a snake which is no relation.

'Was your mother's name Bulpitt?'

'Yes.'

'I think she did well to change it to a sweet name like Abbott. He's really your uncle, is he?'

'I said he was.'

'Well, step on the gas, or he'll be your late uncle.'

The car sped on. It seemed to Joe a suitable moment for pointing out a psychological aspect of the matter which might have escaped her notice.

'You know,' he said, steadying Mr Bulpitt with a hand on his back and leaning forward, 'deplorable though this incident is, we must remember that it has its brighter side. It has brought you and me very close together. There is nothing like the sharing of a great emotional experience for doing that. It forms a bond. It knits. After this, you will find yourself thinking differently of me.'

It is not easy for a girl to give a man a long level look, if she is driving a car and his head is just behind her left shoulder, but Jane did her best. The fact that it nearly dislocated her neck did not improve her frame of mind.

'You would be lucky if I did.'

'What do you mean?'

'I will tell you after we have seen the doctor.'

'Tell me now. It may be my imagination, but there seems to me something strange about your manner. It has an odd curtness. Almost abrupt. Is something the matter?'

'Yes.'

'But what? What has happened? Why, the last time we met, you were allowing – I might say encouraging – me to put my arm round your waist. In the stable yard, you remember.'

'When I was in the stable yard, I had not read the letter which I found waiting for me on the hall table.'

'A letter?'

'It came by the second post.'

A certain uneasiness began to steal upon Joe. In itself, of course, there was nothing unusual in the fact of her having received mail by the second post. He had, indeed, while conversing with her in the stable yard, seen the postman flash by on his bicycle. But he seemed to sense something sinister in her tone. Moreover, though that look of hers had been brief and wobbly rather than long and level, it had been long enough to enable him to discern the glitter in her eye.

'Oh, yes?' he said.

'It was from Adrian Peake.'

Joe removed his hand from Mr Bulpitt's back and began slowly to scratch his chin. A far less astute man than he would have been warned by this statement that trouble was in the air. He was well aware that the twerp Peake, having taken pen in hand, might quite conceivably have touched on topics with great potentialities of embarrassment in them.

However, as usual, he did his best.

'From Adrian Peake, eh? Now, let me see, who is Adrian Peake? Of course; yes, I remember. I have a sort of slight acquaintance with him. . . . I wouldn't drive so fast, if I were you.'

Jane drove faster.

'Mr Vanringham, did you know that Adrian was the man to whom I was engaged?'

'Now, how in the world could I have known that?'

'I imagine Tubby told you. Did he?'

'Well, as a matter of fact, yes. Yes, now that I recall it, he did.'

'I thought so. And did you tell Adrian that he had better go away, because my father was furious with him and was looking for him with a horsewhip?'

Joe sighed. All this was making everything very difficult.

'Why yes,' he said. 'I had been meaning to tell you about that. Yes, that's right.'

'Thank you. That is all I wanted to know.'

With tight lips and tilted chin, she increased her pressure on the accelerator. A wordless cry proceeded from Mr Bulpitt, whom a rough spot in the road had caused to bound in his seat like ice in a cocktail shaker.

'I think what he is trying to say,' suggested Joe, 'is that we should all be more comfortable if you would slow down a little. Try to hold the thought that you are driving an ambulance rather than a Juggernaut.' He leaned farther forward as the advice was taken. 'And now to go back to what we were talking about,' he said. 'I'm glad you have brought this matter up, because I have been wanting to explain. You concede that all is fair in love and war?'

'I don't.'

'That makes my explanation rather difficult, then. I acted on the assumption that it was. It seemed to me that only by eliminating Peake at a fairly early point in the proceedings could I secure the leisure and freedom from interruption which I required. You know how it is when you are trying to show yourself to a girl at your best and there's another fellow hanging around. I had an idea that my little ruse would send him shooting off like a rabbit, and it did. Indeed, few rabbits would have acted so promptly.'

'You have ruined my whole life.'

'I don't see how.'

'Adrian has broken off the engagement.'

'He has?'

'Yes.'

'Well, that's fine.'

'Don't talk like that! '

'I will talk like that. You don't love him.'

'I do.'

'You don't.'

Jane's lip, already much bitten that afternoon, received another nip.

'Well, we will not discuss the point.'

'Pompous,' said Joe warningly.

'Will you stop calling me pompous! '

'I'm sorry.'

Once more, regardless of Mr Bulpitt's creature comforts, she trod on the accelerator, and Joe, about to speak further, saw that it would be useless now to continue to put forward reasoned arguments. He leaned back and gave himself up to thought.

He was a good deal affected by the irony of it all. Here was the girl he loved, tilting her chin at him and mutely allowing him to gather that his standing with her was approximately that of some slug or worm, and all because he had told Adrian Peake that her father was after him with a hunting crop. And you couldn't get away from the fact that her father was. If ever since the world began a Baronet had been desirous of laying into a twerp with the blunt instrument in question, Sir Buckstone Abbott was that Baronet and Adrian Peake that twerp. The only possible criticism the sternest judge could make of his actions was that he had slightly antedated his information.

He awoke from his reverie to find that the car had stopped. Some moments back, scattered houses had come into view, to be succeeded by other houses, less scattered, and for the last few minutes they had been running through a grove of uninterrupted red brick. This in its turn had given way to shops, public houses and all the other familiar phenomena of the principal street of a flourishing country town. It was outside one of these public houses, not far from an empty green charabanc against whose bonnet a uniformed driver leaned smoking a cigarette, that Jane had brought the two-seater to a halt. Joe hopped down from the rumble seat and stood waiting for orders.

Jane's face, he was sorry to see, was still cold and set. She jerked her head imperiously at the driver of the charabanc.

'Ask him where the nearest doctor is.'

'He won't know. Something tells me he is a stranger in these parts himself.'

'Then go and ask in the public house.'

'Very well. Can I bring you a little something from the bar?'

'Would you mind hurrying, please?'

'Watch!' said Joe. 'Gone with the wind.'

And Jane, relieved of his noxious presence, was free to devote her mind to the mystery of this sudden reappearance of her Uncle Sam – a problem which, as Sherlock Holmes would have said, seemed to present several features of interest.

Of the peculiar circumstances which had rendered Mr Bulpitt so unpopular with her father, Jane was entirely ignorant. Sir Buckstone had shrunk from letting her know that her family tree was tainted by the presence among its branches of plasterers, and – a still more compelling reason for silence – he did not wish her to be in a position, on the Princess Dwornitzchek's arrival, to let fall some incautious remark, such as the best of girls are apt to do, which would put that lady in possession of the facts.

Secrecy had seemed to him best, and he had accordingly answered her inquiry as to what had become of her uncle since she had talked with him in the dining-room, with the statement that business had called him back to London. She had been left with the impression that as soon as his business was completed, Mr Bulpitt would be coming to live at the Hall.

And now it appeared that he had been in the neighbourhood all the time, his headquarters the houseboat *Mignonette*.

There could be only one solution to this. Recalling her father's emotion at the prospect of having to place his relative by marriage on the free list, Jane saw what had happened. Torn between the sacred obligations of hospitality and an ignoble desire to save a bit on the weekly books, he had allowed love of gold to win the battle. Instead of a cosy bedroom at the Hall, he had given his brother-in-law a houseboat which, even when new, had scarcely been fit for human habitation.

Sitting there at the wheel of her Widgeon Seven, Jane blushed with shame for her parsimonious parent. This infamy, she felt, must end. If Conscience was unable to convince him how wrong it was to behave like a comic-supplement Scotsman, the matter must be taken out of his hands. From the doctor's door she proposed to drive Mr Bulpitt straight to Walsingford Hall and there deposit him, to be nursed back to health and strength. Even Buck, she felt, obsessed though he was by that Aberdonian urge of his to keep expenses down, would have to admit that this broken man could not be left alone on a houseboat.

She had reached this conclusion, and was feeling brighter and happier, as girls do when they have made up their minds to start something, when a voice spoke, a high-pitched, squeaky voice, like that of a ventriloquist's dummy, and she became aware that she was being addressed by the driver of the charabanc. He had left his post and was standing a few feet away, gazing at Mr Bulpitt with undisguised interest.

'I beg your pardon?' she said – a little coldly, for she had wanted to be alone with her thoughts. Moreover, Joe's outstanding villainy had given her a temporary prejudice against men. With every wish to be broad-minded, a girl cannot welcome conversation with members of a sex which includes people like Joe Vanringham.

The driver of the charabanc was a small, sharp-nosed individual who looked like a pimply weasel. As he stood staring at Mr Bulpitt, every pimple on his face was alive with curiosity. The injured man was now leaning back with closed eyes in a kind of dull stupor of resignation. He had come to the conclusion that nothing could bridge the gulfs of misunderstanding which yawned between himself and his rescuers, and that his only course was to be patient till he had seen the doctor, whose trained senses would immediately detect where the trouble lay. Following Joe's advice, he was relaxing. And he presented such a striking resemblance to a newspaper photograph of the victim of a hatchet murder that the Weasel, who had opened his remarks with the words 'Lor Lumme,' proceeded immediately to probe into first causes.

He pointed an interested cigarette.

'Woss the matter wiv 'im?'

If he had hoped for a burst of animated girlish confidences, he was disappointed. Jane's manner remained cold and reserved, and she replied aloofly:

'He has been hurt.'

'I'll say he's been hurt! Lord love a duck! Wot happened? Javvernaccident?'

'No,' said Jane, and her foot began to tap on the floor of the Widgeon. It seemed to her that Joe had had time by now to ascertain the addresses of ten doctors.

Her response evidently struck the Weasel as childish. His manner took on a touch of severity, like that of a prosecuting counsel who intends to stand no nonsense from an evasive witness. He frowned and placed his cigarette behind his ear, the better to conduct the cross-examination.

'Wodyer mean?' he demanded.

Jane gazed into the middle distance.

'Wodyer mean, you didn't tavvernaccident?' persisted the Weasel. 'You muster radernaccident. Look at the pore bloke. 'Is features are a masker blood.' He paused for a moment, awaiting a reply. 'Bleedin' profusely,' he added. Then, with stiffness: 'I said 'is features was a masker blood.'

'I heard you,' said Jane.

Her brusqueness affected the Weasel unpleasantly. Even at the beginning of this interview, he had been in none too amiable a mood, owing to the fact that his passengers, absorbed in their own selfish thirsts, had poured into the public house, intent on slaking them, without thinking to invite him to join them in a gargle. He was now thoroughly stirred up and ripe for the class war. Jane's was a delicate beauty which, as a rule, made men with whom she came in contact feel chivalrous and protective. It merely awoke the Weasel's worst feelings. There had been a patrician hauteur in her voice which made him wish that Stalin could have been there to give her a piece of his mind.

'Ho!' he said.

Jane said nothing.

'Ask you a civil question, and you bite at a man.'

Jane did not reply.

'Think you're everybody,' proceeded the Weasel, in Stalin's absence doing his best to handle the affair with spirit, but a little conscious that the latter would have said something snappier than that.

Jane gazed before her.

'It's women like you that cause the Death Toll of the Roads,' said the Weasel bitterly.

'Woddidesay?' inquired a new voice.

''E said that it's women like 'er that cause the Death Toll of the Roads,' replied another. And, looking round, Jane perceived that what had begun as a duologue had become a symposium.

As a centre of life and thought, the High Street of Walsingford, like the High Streets of other English country towns, varied according to the day of the week. On Saturdays and market days it was virtually a modern Babylon, at other times less bustling and congested. This was one of its medium afternoons. There were no farmers in gaiters prodding pigs in the ribs, but a fair assortment of residents had turned out, and half a dozen of these, male and female, were now gathered about the two-seater. And once more, much as she disliked him, Jane wished Joe would return.

As the eyes of those present fell upon Mr Bulpitt, a startled gasp of horror arose.

'Coo!' said a citizen in a bowler hat.

'Look at 'im!' said a woman in a cricket cap.

'Yus,' cried the Weasel, driving home his point, 'look at 'im. Bleedin' profusely. And does she care?'

The man in the bowler hat seemed staggered.

'Don't she care?'

'No! Don't give a damn, she don't.'

'Coo!' said the man in the bowler hat, and the woman in the cricket cap drew in her breath with a sharp hiss.

Jane stirred indignantly in her seat. There are few things more exasperating to an innocent girl who prides herself on the almost religious carefulness of her driving than to be thrust into the position of a haughty and callous artistocrat of the old pre-Revolution French régime, the sort of person who used to bowl over the children of the proletariat in his barouche and get fists shaken at him, and she found her temper mounting.

And she was about to deliver a hot denial of the charge,

when it suddenly occurred to Mr Bulpitt, who had been listening with some interest to the exchanges, to try to put everything right with a brief address to the crowd. He rose, accordingly, and began to speak.

The result was sensational. His appearance alone had been enough to purify the citizenry of Walsingford with pity and terror. That awful, wordless babble appalled them.

'Coo!' said the man in the bowler hat, summing up the general sentiment.

The Weasel was looking like a prosecuting counsel who has produced his star witness and completed his case. He took the cigarette from behind his ear and pointed it dramatically.

''Ark! Trying to talk, but can't. Jaw dislocated, if not broken.'

'What he wants,' said the clear-seeing man in the bowler hat, 'is to tell us 'ow it 'appened.'

'I know 'ow it 'appened,' said the woman in the cricket cap. 'I saw the 'ole thing.'

At any unpleasantness involving an automobile there is always to be found in the crowd which assembles a woman of the type to which this one belonged, not necessarily in a cricket cap but invariably endowed with the quick and imaginative mind that goes with that rather eccentric headgear. When bigger and better revolutions are made, women of this kind will make them.

She had got the ear of her audience. The crowd, sated with gazing upon the victim, gave her a ready attention.

'You saw it?'

'R. Saw the 'ole thing from beginning to end. Came round the corner at fifty miles an hour, she did.'

'Driving to the public danger?' asked the man in the bowler hat.

'You may well say so!'

'Coo!' said the man in the bowler hat. 'Comes of bits of girls like her 'aving cars. Didn't ought to be allowed.'

'A menace,' agreed the Weasel vengefully. 'Causes the growing mortality. And what does she care? Not a damn.'

'S'pose she thinks the road belongs to 'er.'

'R. Fifty miles an hour round the corner. And didn't even toot her rorn.'

'Didn't even toot her rorn?'

'Couldn't be bothered. So what chance had the pore gentleman got? She was on him before he could so much as utter a cry.'

'If I was 'er father,' said the Weasel, abandoning his impersonation of a prosecuting counsel and becoming the judge pronouncing sentence, 'I'd give her a spanking. And I've a good mind to do it, even if I'm not.'

The words definitely enhanced the delicacy of the situation. It was the first suggestion that had been made in the direction of a practical move, and it was greeted with a murmur of approval. Censorious looks were cast at Jane, and it was while she sat trying to crush down a growing apprehension which her proud spirit resented that Joe came out of the public house.

'Sorry I've been so long,' he said. 'The boys and I got discussing the situation in Spain.'

He stopped. It was borne in upon him that the situation in Walsingford also called for attention. In addition to the foundation members, the crowd had now become augmented by a number of rather tough eggs from the biscuit factory down the road. Walsingford is the home of the Booth and Baxter Biscuit, and those engaged in its manufacture appeared to have been selected more for their muscular development than for their social polish. They were large, hearty fellows in shirt sleeves whose instinct, when confronted with the unusual, was to make rude noises and throw stones. They had not yet begun to throw stones, but the noises they were making were so undisguisedly rude that Joe, at a loss to understand their emotion, leaned across Mr Bulpitt and addressed Jane in an interested aside.

'What's all this? A civic welcome? But how did they know who I was?'

Jane was in no mood for persiflage, particularly from such a source. His advent had stilled to some extent the fluttering of her heart, but she disliked having to converse with him. It irked her that the peculiar circumstances made it impossible for her to look through him in silence.

'It's my uncle,' she said curtly.

Joe looked at Mr Bulpitt, surprised.

'They want to give him the freedom of the city?'

'They think we knocked him down.'

'Oh?' said Joe, enlightened. 'But we didn't.'

'No.'

'Well, then, here's a thought. Tell 'em so.'

'That woman in the cap keeps saying she saw us.'

'I'll soon put that right. . . . Ladies and gentlemen,' said Joe, stepping on to the running board, and broke off to thrust Mr Bulpitt back into his seat, the latter having once more got the idea that a few simple words from himself were all that was required to remove these misunderstandings.

He could have made no more unfortunate move. As the injured man disappeared like a golf ball dropping into a hole, all that was best and most chivalrous in the crowd rose to the surface. There was a howl of fury which caused the local policeman, who had just been about to turn into the street, to stop and tie his bootlace.

'Shame!'

'Wotcher doin' to the gentleman?'

'Leave the pore old feller alone!'

'Aren't you satisfied with 'arf killing him?'

Joe was a man whom a rough and eventful life had taught that, no matter how great your personal charm, there are times when the honeyed word is not enough, but must be supplemented by the swift dash for the horizon.

'I think you had better get out of here,' he said. 'As our revered Buck would say, the natives seemed unfriendly, so we decided not to stay the night. This is the time of year when the inhabitants of Walsingford go in for weird rites and make human sacrifices to the sun god Ra. This renders them jumpy. You remember, I warned you against coming here.'

Jane agreed with him. She looked at the crowd. After the recent outbursts, a momentary lull had fallen upon its activities, the calm before the storm. It had split into groups which seemed to be discussing the situation and attempting to decide upon plans for the future. The biscuit makers, wearying of making funny noises with their mouths, were looking about them for stones.

'Yes,' she said. 'All right. Get in quick.'

Joe shook his head. She had not understood him.

'"You". Not "we". I will remain and fight a rearguard action.'

Jane's nerves had been a good deal frayed by the unpleasant ordeal of the last ten minutes. They now gave way abruptly.

'Oh, don't be a fool!' she snapped.

'Your retreat must be covered. Recognized military manoeuvre.'

'Come on. Get in. What's the good of posing as the young hero and pretending that you can do anything against a mob like that? You can't tackle fifty men.'

'I shan't try. I'll give you a bit of advice which will be useful to you next time you get into a street fight. Pick on the biggest man in sight, walk straight up to him with your chin out, give him the eye and ask him if he calls himself a gentleman. While he's thinking out the answer, paste him on the jaw. I can guarantee this. It works like magic. The multitude, abandoning its intention of lynching you, form a ring and look on contentedly. After a couple of rounds, half of them are on your side. I've picked my man. That bird in shirt sleeves at the back there, who seems to be searching for a brick. And the joke is that I can see, even from here, that he is not a gentleman. When I spring my question he will be all taken aback and flustered. He won't know which way to look.'

Jane followed his pointing finger, and sat appalled. The individual to whom he was directing her attention was of such impressive proportions that, had he not decided to earn a living among the biscuits, he might quite easily have become a village blacksmith. She quailed at the sight of the muscles of his brawny arms.

'He'd kill you!'

'Kill *me*? The hero?'

'You can't fight a man that size.'

'The bigger they are, the harder they fall.'

Jane's teeth came together with a click.

'I'm not going to leave you.'

'You are.'

'I won't.'

'You must. This poor bit of human wreckage – pardon me, Mr Bulpitt – can't be left indefinitely without medical assistance. Besides, what good could you do?'

Jane contrived a faint and tremulous smile.

'I could lend moral support.'

His eyes met hers, and she saw that they were glowing.

'Ginger,' he said, 'there is none like you, none. You're a girl of mettle and spirit, a worthy daughter of Buck the Lion Heart. But I just don't want you around. Off you go, and don't come back. Have no concern for me. I shall be all right. One of these days remind me to tell you what I did to Philadelphia Jack O'Brien.'

Jane let in the clutch and the Widgeon Seven began to move slowly forward. A howl of disapproval arose, to be succeeded by a silence. It was broken by a clear voice inquiring of somebody outside Jane's range of vision if he called himself a gentleman.

20

The town of Walsingford, though provided almost to excess with public houses, possesses only one hotel of the higher class, the sort that can be considered a suitable pull-up for the nobility and gentry. This is the Blue Boar, and it stands immediately across the street from the humbler establishment outside which Joe Vanringham had put his embarrassing question to the man in shirt sleeves. The fastidious find it a little smelly, for the rule against opening windows holds good here as in all English country-town hotels, but it is really the only place where a motorist of quality can look in for a brush-up and a cup of tea. Nowhere else will you find marble mantelpieces, armchairs, tables bearing bead ferns in brass pots and waiters in celluloid collars.

It was at the Blue Boar, accordingly, that the Princess Dwornitzchek, reaching Walsingford on her way to the Hall, directed her chauffeur to stop the Rolls-Royce in order that she might refresh herself before proceeding to her destination. Tea and toast were served to her in the lounge, near a window looking out on the street.

Of the fact that stirring things had been happening in this street only a few minutes before her arrival no indication existed now. The crowd had melted away, some of it into the public house, the rest about its personal affairs. The woman in the cricket cap had gone to see a sick niece, the man in the bowler hat to buy two pounds of streaky bacon at the grocer's. The charabanc, with the Weasel at its helm, was now some miles away along the London road. A perfect tranquillity prevailed once more.

Tranquil was also the word which would have described the Princess Dwornitzchek, as she sat sipping her tea in the lounge. The room was stuffy, but its closeness did not offend her. The tea was not good, but she had made no complaint. She was as nearly in a mood of amiability as it was possible for her to be. And this was strange, for she was thinking of her stepson Joseph.

Joe had been much in her thoughts these last two days, ever since she had seen his play at the Apollo Theatre. She was anxious to meet him. And she was glancing absently out of the window, wondering where he was and how contact could be established with him, when he suddenly emerged from the door of the public house opposite, at the head of a group of men who either did not own coats or had preferred not to put them on.

Some sort of festive gathering appeared to be breaking up. Even from where she sat, it was impossible not to sense the atmosphere of joviality and camaraderie. Snatches of song could be heard, and an occasional cheer, and the popular centre of the gay throng was plainly Joe. Whatever the party might be, he was unmistakably the life and soul of it. His hand was being shaken a good deal, and his back slapped. There was one extraordinarily large man with a black eye who gave the impression of being devoted to him.

But the pleasantest of functions must end, and presently, with a few parting words and a wave of the hand, Joe detached himself from the group and made for the Blue Boar; to stop, as he drew near to it, and stand for a moment staring. His eye, raised to the window, had been arrested by the spectacle of the Princess on the other side sipping her tea.

Then he moved on again and disappeared up the steps that led to the door, and a moment later was crossing the lounge to her table.

It was not immediately that either spoke. When a stepson who has left home in anger and a stepmother who has done all but actually speed his going with a parting kick meet again after an extended separation, there is bound to be a constraint.

Joe was the first to speak. 'My dear Princess!'

He was compelled to admit, as he looked at her, that his principal emotion was one of grudging admiration. She was the only person in the world whom he really disliked, but there was no getting away from it that she was wonderful. In some miraculous manner, she had contrived, or seemed to have contrived, to stay the hand of time. She was still, to the outward eye, exactly the same age she had been five years ago, when she had expressed the hope that he would starve in the gutter; eight years ago, when she had first begun to afflict his father; and in all probability ten years before that. She had made it her object in life to achieve perpetual youth, and she had succeeded.

It was not in the Princess Dwornitzchek to remain for long unequal to a situation. She smiled up at him pleasantly, thinking what an impossible young thug he looked. For his recent activities had left Joe a little dishevelled. You cannot brawl with biscuit makers and remain natty.

'Well, Joseph. It seems a long time since we met.'

'Quite a time. But you're as lovely as ever.'

'Thanks. I wish I could say the same of you.'

'I was never your type of male beauty, was I?'

'You were at least clean.'

'You find me a trifle shop-soiled? I'm not surprised. I've just been having a fight. I came in here for a wash.'

'Would you like a cup of tea?'

'I think not, thanks. You might poison it.'

'I came out without my poison today.'

'You didn't know you were going to meet me. It just shows how one should be prepared for everything. Well, if you will excuse me for a minute, I'll go and make myself fit for your society.'

He turned and left the room. She called to the waiter and paid her bill. She was still smiling as she did so, and she tipped the man lavishly. This unexpected meeting had set the seal on her mood of contentment. Presently Joe returned.

'You look much better now,' she said. 'So you have been having a fight?'

'With a delightful fellow named Percy. I didn't get his other name. We went three rounds, in the course of which I blacked his eye and he nearly broke one of my ribs, and then we decided to kiss and make it up. When I saw you, I had just been standing beer to him and a few personal friends. You look very happy, Your Highness.'

'Do I?'

'And I don't wonder. Running into an old friend like this. I suppose you were surprised to see me here.'

'Very.'

'I, on the other hand, was expecting to meet you shortly. I am staying at Walsingford Hall, and heard that you are expected.'

'How do you come to be staying at the Hall?'

'I thought it would be nice being with Tubby. He needs a brother's care.'

'How did you know he was there?'

'Oh, these things get about. He tells me you are thinking of buying the Hall.'

'Yes.'

'My visit will be a short one, then.'

'Extremely short. Are you going back there now? If so, I can give you a lift.'

'Thanks.'

'Unless you have any more street fighting to do?'

'No, I'm through for the day. I hear you have been revisiting New York.'

'Yes. I returned the day before yesterday. I had to go over and see my lawyer about my income tax. The Treasury people were making the most absurd claims.'

'Soaking the rich?'

'Trying to soak the rich.'

'I hope they skinned you to the bone.'

'No. As a matter of fact, I came out of it very well. Have you a cigarette?'

'Here you are.'

'Thank you. Yes, I won out all along the line.'

'You would!'

Once again, Joe was conscious of that reluctant admiration which he had felt at their meeting, and, with it, of the baffled resentment which so often came to those who had dealings with this woman. The effortless ease with which she overrode all obstacles and went complacently through life on the crest of the wave offended his sense of dramatic construction. She was so obviously the villainess of the piece that it seemed inevitable that eventually the doom must overtake her. But it never did. Whoever had started that idea that Right in the end must always triumph over Wrong had never known the Princess Dwornitzchek.

He watched her as she sat there smoking and smiling quietly at some thought that seemed to be amusing her, and tried to analyse the murderous feelings which she had always aroused in him. She was, as he had said, undefeatable, and he came to the conclusion that it was this impregnability of hers that caused them. She had no heart and a vast amount of money, and this enabled her to face the world encased in triple brass. He had in her presence a sense of futility, as if he were a very small wave beating up against a large complacent cliff. No doubt the officials of the United States Treasury Department had felt the same.

'It's maddening,' he said.

'I beg your pardon?'

'I was only thinking that there seems to be no way in which the righteous can get at you.'

'You look as if you would like to strangle me.'

'No, no,' protested Joe. 'Just beat you over the head with one of these brass pots and watch you wriggle.'

She laughed.

'You appear still to be the same engaging young man.'

'I imagine we've neither of us changed very much.'

'Your circumstances seem to have changed. The last I heard of you, you were a sailor on a tramp steamer.'

'And after that a waiter. And after that a movie extra and a rather indifferent pugilist. I was also, for a time, a bouncer in a New York saloon. That was one of my failures. I started gaily out one night to bounce an obstreperous client, and, unfortunately, he bounced me. This seemed to cause the boss to lose confidence in my technique, and shortly afterwards I sailed for England to carve out a new career. Since then I have been doing pretty well.'

'I am glad to hear that.'

'I bet you are. Yes, I got a job on a paper, and held that for a while, and then I became a sort of stooge or bottle-washer to a publisher of dubious reputation named Busby.'

'You have had quite a full life. Shall we go?'

They started to cross the room.

'And since when,' she asked, 'have you been a playwright?'

'You've heard about my play?'

'I have seen it.'

Joe's sense of futility diminished. He glowed a little. It was as if he had been a sportsman shooting at a rhinoceros with an air-gun and one of the pellets had caused the animal to wince. It was true that if his companion had winced, he had not observed it, but he knew her to be a woman who hid her feelings.

'Already? This is very gratifying. What did you think of it?'

'I suppose some people would call it clever.'

'The better element are unanimous on that point. Shall I read you the notices?'

'No, thank you.'

'It's an extraordinary thing. Nobody seems to want to hear those notices. Pretty soon I shall be beginning to think there's a conspiracy. How did it go when you saw it?'

'Very well.'

'House full?'

'Packed.'

'And they seemed to be enjoying it?'

'Immensely.'

They came out of the hotel.

'My favourite scene,' said Joe, 'is the one in the second act between the ghastly stepmother and her stepson. Did they like that?'

'Very much.'

'Did you?'

'It amused me.'

'That's good. I aimed to entertain.'

'I have been hoping to meet you, Joseph,' said the Princess, 'because I wanted to discuss that play of yours. We can have a nice, cosy talk about it in the car.'

She slipped gracefully into the Rolls-Royce. Joe followed her. As she settled herself in her seat, he saw that she was smiling that quiet smile again, and, but for the absurdity of supposing that there was any possible way in which she could now do him a mischief, it might have made him uneasy.

He knew that smile from the old days.

21

It was just as Joe and the Princess Dwornitzchek were preparing to leave the hotel that a panting two-seater entered the High Street and began to proceed along it at a slow crawl, the girl at the wheel peering keenly to right and left like Edith searching for the body of King Harold after the Battle of Hastings. Defying orders, Jane had returned to the front. She had conveyed Mr Bulpitt at racing speed to the Hall, handed him over to Pollen with instructions that he be put to bed and the doctor telephoned for immediately, and had then turned and spurred her Widgeon Seven back to Walsingford.

The comatose peace of the High Street, empty now except for a Rolls-Royce standing outside the Blue Boar, a child trundling a tin can along the pavement with a stick, and a dog making a light snack off something it had found in the gutter, filled her with mixed feelings. She was relieved at the absence of the Weasel and his supporting cast, but it alarmed her to see no sign of Joe. He could not have started to walk back to the Hall or she would have met him on the road, and the only other explanation of his disappearance that presented itself to her was that he had stopped one from the village blacksmith and been carried off to hospital.

It was with growing anxiety that she cruised down one side of the street, and she was returning up the other, when from out of the hotel there came a tall majestic woman in whom she recognized the Princess Dwornitzchek, and in her wake, Joe looking as good as new. A glance was enough to tell her that whoever might have been stopping things, it was not he. They entered the Rolls-Royce, which immediately drove off. She and the child and the dog had the street to themselves again.

The sight affected her oddly. Until this moment, admiration for Joe's prowess as a warrior had caused her to forget his other, darker side. Her heart, which had been aching with concern and apprehension, now hardened again, and he resumed his role of the serpent who had done his best to ruin her life's happiness, the sinister plotter who had told Adrian Peake that her father was swishing the hunting crop. Once more she had become aware that she was exceedingly angry with Joe.

The short drive home did nothing to soften her mood, and it was with her mind full of deleterious thoughts that she ran the two-seater into the stable yard. Only when, going to the house, she encountered Pollen on the front steps did she pigeon-hole them for future reference. The sight of the butler brought it back to her that there were inquiries to be made after the patient. In the press of other matters, she had almost forgotten about her Uncle Sam.

'How is Mr Bulpitt, Pollen?'

'Getting along nicely, miss. He is in the Blue Room.'

'Has the doctor seen him?'

'Yes, miss.' A soft smile played over the butler's face. 'It appears that the gentleman has sustained no injury. He merely lost his teeth.'

Jane stared at this iron man, bewildered. His air was that of one announcing a purely minor disaster. And while you naturally expect the emotion of a butler who is speaking of someone else losing his teeth, to differ in degree from that of a butler who has lost his own, this perplexed her.

'His teeth were knocked out?'

'They fell out, miss. False teeth. The gentleman gave minute instructions as to where they were to be found, and I have dispatched the knife-and-boot boy on his bicycle to recover them.'

Here Pollen, who yielded to none on his appreciation of the humorous, especially if it was in the old broad tradition of the music hall, lost his professional poise completely. The soft smile became a grin. And from behind the hand that shot up to hide it there proceeded an odd gurgling sound like the rough song of the linnet.

A moment later, he was himself again and had reassembled the features.

'I beg your pardon, miss,' he said. And it was with the exaggerated austerity which comes to butlers who momentarily yield to their lower selves that he extended a hand with a letter in it.

'A note for you, miss.'

Jane took it, and for an instant felt only a shrinking distaste. Clean when it had left Adrian Peake's hand, the envelope was now rather liberally smeared with foreign matter. Everywhere on its surface was to be detected the sepia maelstrom of young Cyril Attwater's clammy thumb. Then her heart gave a jump. She had recognized the handwriting.

'When did this come?'

'Shortly after you had left to take Sir Buckstone to the train, miss. It was delivered by hand by a small lad from the village.'

Jane's heart gave another jump. The significance of the words had not escaped her. If notes from Adrian were being delivered by hand by small lads from the village, it must mean that he was in the neighbourhood.

'Oh? Thank you, Pollen.'

The butler inclined his head gracefully, silently indicating his pleasure at having been able to be of service, and Jane opened the envelope.

We who have been privileged to peep over Adrian Peake's shoulder as he penned the letter which she was reading are already aware of its compelling qualities. Coming to Jane all fresh and new, the effect of those impassioned sentences was overwhelming.

There had been moments since the perusal of the first of his communications when, in the intervals of raging inwardly against Joe, she had caught herself thinking none too kindly of Adrian. To a girl of her spirited nature, courageous herself and an admirer of courage in others, the thought of him being frightened by her poor darling Buck had not been an agreeable one. The realization that mere whisper of impending hunting crops had been sufficient to drive him from her side had seemed to her to suggest the existence of flaws in a character which she had wanted to think perfect.

But now, with this second, soul-stirring epistle, he had redeemed himself. It was with glowing eyes that she read it, and with tripping feet that she hurried to the telephone. She rang up the Goose and Gander, and was answered by its proprietor. And some rough indication of the state of her feelings may be gathered from the fact that J. B. Attwater's voice, though husky from years of drinking port in his pantry in the service of Sir Buckstone Abbott, sounded to her like beautiful music.

'Oh, Mr Attwater, this is Miss Abbott.'

'Good afternoon, miss.'

'Good afternoon. I want to speak to Mr Peake,' said Jane, suitably, considering her emotion, abandoning prose and breaking into poetry.

'Mr Peake, miss?'

'Isn't he staying at the inn?'

The question was one which a man of exact speech had to turn over in his mind. The last Mr Attwater had seen of Adrian Peake, the latter had been jumping his garden hedge and making off across country at a high rate of speed. It was a debatable point whether this could be correctly described as staying at the inn.

He decided to temporize.

'The gentleman is not residing at the Goose and Gander, miss. But he was in here this afternoon.'

'When do you expect him back?'

Again J. B. Attwater had to pause and ponder.

'He left no word as to his plans, miss.'

'Oh? Well, when you see him, will you ask him to telephone me. Thank you, Mr Attwater.'

'Not at all, miss.'

Jane left the telephone, well content. She would have preferred to have been able to speak to Adrian in person, but no doubt he would be ringing up at any moment, to suggest a place of meeting. She went out in the garden, and the first thing she saw there was Joe Vanringham leaning against the wall of the terrace, his hands in his pockets and his shoulders hunched. He appeared to be in some sort of a daydream.

Adrian's letter had brought about another change in Jane's mood. When last she had seen Joe, as has been shown, it had been dark and dangerous. Lips had been bitten and nasty remarks stored up for future delivery. But now, in a world of sunshine with the clouds cleared away and the bluebird singing once more, she could feel no animosity even towards a J. J. Vanringham.

She could, however, make him feel foolish and as ashamed of himself as was within the power of one so deaf to the voice of Conscience, and it was her intention to do so. Extremely silly he would feel, she considered, when he learned how futile had been his low plottings. She hurried to where he stood, and he looked up, his eye for an instant dull and absent. Then it lightened, and he grinned his familiar grin.

'Hello, Ginger,' he said.

It seemed to Jane that before coming to the principal item on the agenda paper, it would be only civil to make some reference to the late conflict. She was a fair-minded girl, and he had unquestionably borne himself well at the battle of Walsingford.

'So there you are.'

'Here I am.'

'Did you win?'

'A draw. Stakes returned to the punters.'

'You didn't get hurt, did you?'

'Only a bruised knuckle. Towards the conclusion of the exchanges I feinted with my left and brought up a snappy right to the heart, only to discover that my opponent was wearing over it, under his shirt, a locket containing a photograph of the woman he loved.'

'What?'

'I assure you. He showed it to me later in the pub. You wouldn't have suspected a man like that of the softer emotions, would you? But so it was. Her name is Clara. A rather pie-faced girl, if you ask me, though I didn't wound him by telling him so. The locket was made of sheet iron or something, and was about the size of a young soup plate. A nasty crack it gave me.'

Jane's heart was touched. It was in her service, she reminded herself, that the wound had been sustained.

'Shall I bathe it for you?'

'No, thanks. A mere scratch. But next time I fight, I shall pick a misogynist.'

'And he didn't hurt you except for that?'

'No, no. A most enjoyable afternoon. By the way, I suppose you are wondering how I got back so soon.'

'No. I saw you.'

'Saw me?'

'Driving off with the Princess. I came back, you see.'

Joe's eyes gleamed.

'I knew you were a heroine. Ginger, will you marry me?'

'No. I thought I had told you that before.'

'I have an idea you did. I will now relate the story of Bruce and the spider.'

'No, you won't. Where did you meet the Princess?'

'She was tucking into tea at the hotel across the way, and I ran into her when I went there for a wash.'

'Was it very awkward?'

'Not at all. Conversation flowed like water.'

'Well, I'm glad you weren't hurt.'

'Thanks.'

'Though you deserved to be. Telling poor Adrian all those lies.'

'Oh, that? Yes, I know what you mean.'

'I should hope so. Well, what I have come to say,' said Jane, unmasking her batteries, 'is that you aren't as clever as you think you are.'

'Nobody could be.'

'Trying to drive Adrian away.'

'Trying?'

Jane's mouth tightened. She was conscious of a return of her earlier mood. She resented the cock of the eyebrow which had accompanied his remark. Her amiability waned, and she spoke with much the same cold hauteur which had made so bad an impression on the Weasel.

'It may interest you to know that I have had another letter from Adrian.'

'From the Fiji Islands? He should be somewhere near there by now.'

'From the Goose and Gander.'

'In the village? Or an establishment of the same name in Tierra del Fuego?'

'You had better read it.'

'No, please. I don't read other people's letters. Tubby, yes. Joe, no.'

'Read it.'

'Well, if you insist.'

He took the letter and glanced through it. He looked up. His face was expressionless.

'So what?'

'You see what he says. He wants me to marry him.'

'You're going to marry me.'

'You? You're just a clown.'

'Perhaps. But if you imagine that I am not sincere when I tell you I love you, you're making a mistake.'

'Adrian's sincere.'

'Adrian,' said Joe, 'is a worm and a rotter, and I shouldn't think he knows what sincerity means.'

There was a silence.

'After that,' said Jane, 'perhaps you will give me back that letter. I don't want to hear any more. And' – her voice shook – 'I don't want to speak to you again.'

Joe smiled a twisted smile.

'I thought you were going to say that,' he said. 'Well, you won't have the chance. I'm leaving.'

'Leaving?'

'In half an hour.'

Something seemed to stab at Jane's heart. Nothing could have been more illogical, and she realized it, but, nevertheless, she knew that this sudden cold feeling that seemed to go deep down into her was dismay.

'Leaving?'

With a shock it came to her that in these last days their intimacy had been growing like a gourd. A moment before, she had been filled with a cold fury. She had told herself that she hated this man. But now it seemed to her as if she were losing a part of herself.

'Leaving?'

'I must, I'm afraid. I have a living to earn.'

'But –'

He nodded.

'I know what you're thinking. The play. Money pouring in all the time, as I told Buck. Well, I'm sorry to say the old masterpiece is no more. It comes off tonight.'

'But – but I thought it was such a success.'

'It was. But it gave offence to my lady stepmother, and as

we were driving here in the car, she informed me that she had bought it, and was closing it down.'

Jane was staring.

'Bought it?'

'Lock, stock and barrel. The entire production. American rights, movie rights, everything. Heaven knows what it must have cost her, but she can afford it. She told me that she objected to having a vulgar lampoon running all over the world for her friends to snigger at. One sees her point.'

'The beast!'

'Oh, I don't know. She had a good deal of provocation. I was always willing to admit that it was raw work, putting her into the opus as I did, and I must say I can't help rather admiring her for this devastating come-back.'

Jane was in no mood to share this detached, sportsmanlike attitude.

'She's a hellhound.'

'But a Napoleonic one. Like Napoleon, she sees the enemy's weak point and goes straight at it, crumpling him up and causing him to fly from the field in rout. You see me now about to fly from the field.'

'But where are you going?'

'To California.'

'California?'

'Sun-kissed Hollywood. The night of the opening I was introduced to some kind of a liaison officer working the London end for one of the big studios, and he signed me up there and then. It was that kind of a hit, peace to its ashes. The original idea was that I was to sail in about a month, but now that this has happened, I shall have to get them to speed things up. I don't want to arrive at the Beverly Hills Hotel and find that my stepmother has bought the studio and suppressed that.'

An aching sense of desolation was gripping Jane. The sun had gone down behind the trees, and a little twilight wind was blowing through the world. She felt chilled and empty.

'Hollywood's a long way away.'

'A very long way.'

'Oh, Joe!'

Their eyes met. She gave a cry as his hand came out and gripped her arm.

'Jane, come with me! Jane, let's get married and go together. You know we belong to each other. I knew it the moment I saw you. We were made for each other. It's only once in a lifetime that you meet anyone you can feel that about. You never get a second chance. It was a miracle, our meeting. If we throw it away, there won't be another. Will you come, Jane?'

'I can't, Joe.'

'You must.'

'I can't, I can't. How can I let Adrian down?'

'You don't mean – '

'Well, can I?'

'But, Jane, are you standing there calmly proposing – Do you seriously mean that you're going back to that worm?'

'He's not a worm.'

'He is, and you know it.'

'I know this. He needs me.'

'Oh, my God! Needs you!'

'He does. You read that letter. Can't you see how impossible it is for me to throw him over after that? I know Adrian. He's weak. Helpless. He relies on me. If I let him down, he would just go to bits. I've felt it all the time. He's like that. You're different. You're tough. You can stand on your own feet.'

'No.'

'Yes. You could get on without me.'

'What do you mean, get on? I could go on breathing and eating and sleeping. I suppose I could get on, as you call it, without sunshine or music or – Jane, for heaven's sake pull yourself together. You're behaving like a half-witted, self-sacrificing heroine out of a Busby novel.'

'If I am it's because it's the way I am. I can't break promises. I can't welsh.'

'Oh, for God's sake!'

'It's no use blustering, Joe. That's the trouble with you. You come roaring into people's lives and wanting to snatch them up on your saddlebow and you think that's all there is to it. I can't go through the rest of my life hating and despising myself. If I let Adrian down, I should feel as if I had deserted a puppy with a broken paw.'

'This is absolute insanity.'

'It's how I feel, now I've read his letter.'

'I believe you're still in love with him.'

'No. I don't think so. And yet I may be. There are little things about him, little things he does, the way he looks sometimes – Oh, you must know what it's like when someone has once got under your skin. It must have happened to you. There must be some woman before you met me whom you can never really get out of your thoughts.'

'There was one in San Francisco.'

'Well, there you are. However long you live, you will always remember her.'

'You bet I will. Especially in frosty weather. She dug two inches of a hat-pin into my leg. Talk about getting under the skin!'

'You make a joke of everything.'

'And you laugh at it. And if there's a better recipe than that for living happily ever after, name it. Don't you see that that's just why we belong to each other, because we can laugh together? Jane, my lovely Jane, in heaven's name what sort of foundation to build your life on is a sloppy pity?'

'It's more than that.'

The twilight wind had dropped. Stars were peeping out above the trees. In the valley below, the river gleamed like dull silver. Joe turned and stood looking down at it, his hands resting on the terrace wall.

He gave himself a little shake.

'So you're really going back to him?'

'I must.'

He laughed.

'So it's all over. I had a feeling all along that it couldn't be real. Just summer moonshine. Poor old Joe! And we thought we were going to get him off this season!'

'Joe, won't you try to make this not quite so difficult for me?'

He moved back to the wall. Cato, resplendent in his gambler's moustache, gazed at him with sightless eyes. He pointed.

'I never did finish those statues. I shall have to leave them to you.'

'Joe, don't!'

He shook himself again, like a dog coming out of the water.

'I'm sorry. I'm ashamed of myself. I don't know where you ever got the idea that I was tough. I'm just a kid, kicking and screaming because he can't get the moon. I've no right to try to make you unhappy. This is not the old Vanringham stoicism. All right, I can take it. It's just one of those jams where somebody's got to suffer, and I'm the one. Good-bye, Jane.'

'Are you going already?'

'I have packing to do. J. B. Attwater's cab is calling for me in a few minutes.'

'Can't I drive you?'

He laughed.

'No. Thank you very much, but no. There are limits to my fortitude. If I found myself alone in your car with you, I couldn't answer for the consequences. Jane, may I say something?'

'What, Joe?'

'If ever you feel differently, let me know.'

She nodded.

'But I don't think I shall, Joe.'

'You may. If you do, telephone me any hour of the day or night. If I've left, cable me. I'll come running. Good-bye.'

'Good-bye, Joe.'

He turned abruptly and started toward the house. Jane moved to the wall and stood looking down at the river. Its silver had changed to grey.

There came the sound of wheels on the gravel behind her. She looked over her shoulder. The cab from Walsingford station had drawn up at the front door and Sir Buckstone Abbott was getting out.

22

Lady Abbott lay on the settee in her boudoir with her shoes off – her habit when at rest. She was doing a crossword puzzle. Through the open window at her side, the cool evening air poured in, refreshing to a brain which was becoming a little heated as it sought to discover the identity of an Italian composer in nine letters beginning with *p*. She had just regretfully rejected Irving Berlin because, despite his other merits, too numerous to mention here, he had twelve letters, began with an *i*, and was not an Italian composer, when there was a sound outside like a mighty rushing wind and Sir Buckstone came bursting in. His face was red, his eyes bulging and his grizzled hair was disordered, for he had been passing his fingers through it in the stress of his emotions.

'Toots!' he cried.

Lady Abbott looked up fondly.

'Oh, hello, Buck, dear. When did you get back? Buck, do you know an Italian composer in nine letters beginning with *p*?'

Sir Buckstone dismissed the whole musical world with a fevered wave of the hand.

'Toots, something has happened so frightful that the brain reels, contemplating it!'

It was now plain to Lady Abbott that her beloved husband was having one of his worries. She suggested a remedy which had been tried and proved many a time during the twenty-five happy years of their married life.

'Have a whisky and soda, honey.'

Sir Buckstone shook his head violently, to indicate that the time had gone for mere palliatives.

'I've just been talking to Jane.'

'Oh, yes?'

'Out there on the drive. She came up to me as I was getting out of the cab. Do you know what she has done?'

'Puccini!' cried Lady Abbott. She started to write, then checked herself with a placid 'Tut! ... Only seven,' she said wistfully. Sir Buckstone danced a step or two.

'I wish you would listen, instead of fooling about with that thing!'

'I'm listening, sweetie. You said Jane had done something.'

'I did. And do you know what?'

'What?'

'She has brought that brother of yours into the house. That bally plasterer. Told me so herself. After all the pains I've taken, after the sedulous care with which we have protected young Vanringham from his insidious wiles, Jane has brought him into the house.'

Lady Abbott was unquestionably interested. She did not go so far as to raise her eyebrows, but a keen observer would have seen that they quivered slightly.

'When did she do that?'

'This afternoon. She has some rambling story about finding him knocked down by a car on the Walsingford road. She brought him here and Pollen tells me he's in the Blue Room at this very moment, drinking my beer and smoking one of my cigars. Refreshing himself! Getting himself into shape for pouncing on young Vanringham! And the Princess in the Red Room!'

Lady Abbott was tapping her teeth with the pencil. Something seemed to be perplexing her.

'Had he any clothes on?'

'Clothes? What do you mean, clothes?'

'What people wear.'

'Of course, he had clothes on. What are you talking about? Do you suppose that even your brother would go roaming about the Walsingford road in the nude?'

'Well, it's very odd,' said Lady Abbott. 'Because I stole Sam's clothes.'

Sir Buckstone's eyes, already bulging, became almost prawn-like.

'You stole his clothes?'

'Yes. This afternoon. It seemed a good idea.'

'What the devil are you talking about, Toots?'

'You see, after you had left to catch your train, I started thinking about how worried you were, and I went down to the houseboat again to have another talk with Sam and try to get him to act sensibly, and he must have been in swimming, because there was nobody on board the boat and there were clothes lying around the saloon. And I suddenly thought that if I took them away, he would have to stay on the boat and couldn't come prowling after young Vanringham. So I scooped them all up and dropped them in the river.'

Sir Buckstone's eyes lit up. He gazed at her with the loving, admiring look of a man whose helpmeet tells him that in his absence she, too, has not been idle.

'Toots! What a splendid idea!'

'Yes, wasn't it?'

'How did you happen to think of that?'

'Oh, it came to me.'

The light faded from Sir Buckstone's eyes. He was facing the hard facts again.

'But, dash it, how does he come to be in the Blue Room, then?'

'You said Jane brought him.'

'I know, I know. But what I mean – I suppose what you dropped in the river was just his spare suit.'

'I don't believe Sam would have a spare suit. He was never a dressy man.'

'He must have had. He was certainly wearing clothes when Jane found him. If he hadn't been, she would have mentioned it.'

'Yes, that's true.'

'At any rate, there he is, in the Blue Room, sucking down beer and biding his time. What are we to do?'

Lady Abbott thought this over.

'Oh, I guess everything will be all right,' she said.

Sir Buckstone was not a man who often thumped tables – although, like all Baronets, he had table-thumping blood in him – but he felt obliged to do so now. As a rule, he drew comfort from his wife's easy optimism, but now her favourite formula merely heightened his blood pressure to a point where only sharp physical action could bring relief. Crossing the room to a small table bearing a framed photograph of himself in the uniform of a colonel in the Berkshire Territorials, he brought his fist forcibly down upon it. It was a fragile thing of walnut, and it collapsed in ruin. Glass from the photograph frame sprayed over the carpet.

Reason returned to its throne. He stood gaping at his handiwork.

'Good Lord, Toots! I'm sorry.'

'Never mind, darling.'

'I lost my self-control.'

'Don't give it another thought, sweetie. Ring for Pollen.'

Sir Buckstone pressed the bell, then went to the window and stood looking out, rattling his keys in his pocket. Lady Abbott, whose brow had wrinkled thoughfully for a moment, wrote down 'Garibaldi' and rubbed it out. The door opened and Pollen appeared.

'Oh, Pollen, some glass has become broken.'

The butler had already observed this, and was pursing his lips in respectful sympathy.

'I will bring a maid, your ladyship.'

Sir Buckstone turned, still rattling.

'Where's Mr Bulpitt, Pollen?'

'In his bedroom, Sir Buckstone.'

A very faint feeling of relief came to brighten the Baronet's sombre mood. He had expected to hear that the intruder, refreshed with beer, had left his base and was out scouring the grounds in search of Tubby.

'What's he doing?'

'When I last visited the Blue Room, Sir Buckstone, in response to the gentleman's ring, he was about to take a bath. He inquired of me whether, in my opinion, he would have time before dinner for another pitcher of beer.'

Sir Buckstone produced a sort of obligato on the keys. It was intended to convey nonchalance.

'He's coming down to dinner, then?'

'That was the impression I gathered, Sir Buckstone.'

'Thank you, Pollen.'

The butler withdrew, and Sir Buckstone turned to Lady Abbott with a wide gesture of despair.

'You see! Coming down to dinner. That means he'll plaster young Vanringham over the soup. And the Princess looking on and saying, "What the devil?" from the other side of the table. A pleasant prospect!'

Lady Abbott, who had just thought of Mussolini, poised pencil over paper for an instant, then shook her head.

'Why not stop him coming down to dinner?' she asked, absently.

A quiver ran through Sir Buckstone, and he shot a wistful glance at the wrecked table, as if regretting that it was no longer in shape to be thumped. Deprived of its co-operation, he found an outlet for his feelings in thumping his leg.

The action did him good. When he spoke, it was almost mildly.

'How?' he said.

Lady Abbott's thoughts had wandered off to Italian composers again. Then she appeared to realize that she had been asked a question.

'How? Why, steal his clothes while he's in his bath. Then he won't be able to come down to dinner.'

Sir Buckstone seemed about to speak, but he checked himself and stood staring. There are moments when words are inadequate.

Over his weatherbeaten features there began to spread a look of reverence. Twenty-five years ago, when he had whisked this woman off in a hansom cab to the registrar's to link his lot with hers, he had known that he was getting the sweetest and loveliest girl on earth, but even then, intoxicated with love though he was, he had not thought particularly highly of her intelligence. If somebody had asked him at that moment if his bride was one of America's brightest brains, he would have replied frankly that in his opinion she was not, adding that he didn't give a damn, either. What he had supposed himself to be marrying was what a future age was to call a 'dumb blonde', and he liked it.

And now he was stunned to perceive that in this mate of his the wisdom of American womanhood had come to its finest flower.

'Good God, Toots!' he said, awed.

Lady Abbott rose.

'I'll go and do it now. Then your poor little mind will be at rest.'

'But, Toots, half a minute.'

'What, honey?'

'He'll get some more.'

'Not if you tell Pollen to see that he doesn't.'

'But how can I explain to Pollen?'

'You don't have to. That's the beauty of English butlers. You just tell 'em. Sit down, sweetie, and put your feet up. I'll be back in a minute.'

Sir Buckstone did not sit down and put his feet up. He was far too emotionally stirred for that. He stood rattling his keys, and was still rattling them when Pollen returned, shepherding before him a small under-housemaid who bore brush and dustpan. Under the butler's silent supervision, she cleaned up the wreckage and was directed from the room with a jerk of the head. The butler, about to follow, was halted by a cough, and gathered that his employer desired speech with him.

'Oh – er – Pollen,' said Sir Buckstone.

He paused. The thing, he saw, wanted putting in just the right way.

'Oh, Pollen – er – what with one thing and another – '

He paused. Then he caught the butler's eye. It was a respectful eye, but one which intimated unmistakably that its owner would be glad if this little scene could be speeded up a trifle. In the time immediately preceding dinner, a butler's position is that of the captain of a ship in a stormy weather. He wants to be on the bridge. Sir Buckstone, aware of this, came to the point without further preamble.

'Oh, Pollen, her ladyship has just stepped up to Mr Bulpitt's room and taken his clothes.'

'Yes, Sir Buckstone?'

'A joke,' explained the Baronet.

'Indeed, Sir Buckstone?'

'Yes. Just a little joke, you understand. Too long to explain now, but the point is, if Mr Bulpitt rings for you and asks for some more, don't give 'em to him.'

'No, Sir Buckstone.'

'Spoil the joke, you see.'

'Yes, Sir Buckstone.'

'On no account is he to have clothes till further notice. You understand?'

The door closed. Sir Buckstone emitted a long, deep breath. A great weight seemed to have rolled off him. He picked up the paper and scanned the crossword puzzle which his Toots had been trying to solve. 'An Italian composer in nine letters beginning with *p*' was, he gathered, what had been stumping the dear girl, he took the pencil and in a firm hand wrote down the word 'Pagliacci.'

Each helping each, was the way Sir Buckstone looked at it.

23

The emotions of a man who comes out of a bathroom, all pink and glowing, and with a song on his lips, to find that in his absence from the bedroom adjoining it, some hidden hand has removed his clothes may be compared roughly to those of one who, sauntering along a garden path in the dusk, steps on the teeth of a rake and has the handle shoot up and hit him in the face. There is the same sense of shock, the same fleeting illusion that Judgement Day had arrived without warning.

Mr Bulpitt, re-entering the Blue Room some ten minutes after Lady Abbott had left it, experienced all these emotions – all the more poignant because his recent happy reunion with his teeth had left him with the complacent feeling that he was now safe from the molestation of Fate. And he was just singing 'Pennies from Heaven' and saying to himself, 'And now to put on the good old pants!' when he saw that he had been mistaken and that Fate still had weapons in its armoury. The Blue Room was equipped with every convenience; there were in it a chaise-longue, an arm-chair, two other chairs, a chest of drawers, some attractive eighteenth-century prints, a small bookcase and a writing-desk with plenty of notepaper and envelopes, but it contained no pants. Nor, for the matter of that, coat, waistcoat, underwear, cravat, socks and shoes. Even the hat, designed for the use of Western American college students, had vanished. And Mr Bulpitt, though a man of infinite resource and sagacity, found himself unequal to the situation. Climbing into bed and modestly wrapping the sheet about his shoulders, he gave himself up to thought.

After some moments of meditation, he did what every visitor to a country house does when untoward things have been happening in his bedroom. He rang the bell, and presently Pollen appeared.

The interview that followed was not very satisfactory.

'Say, look,' said Mr Bulpitt. 'I don't seem to have any clothes.'

'No, sir.'

'Can you get me some more somewhere?'

'No, sir.'

'Sure you can,' urged Mr Bulpitt encouragingly. 'Hunt around.'

'No, sir,' said the butler. 'Sir Buckstone has issued instructions that you are not to be provided with clothes, sir. Thank you, sir.'

He left Mr Bulpitt perplexed in the extreme, and the latter

was still between the sheets, trying to adjust his mind to these rather odd goings-on, when Sir Buckstone came bustling in, looking radiant. No more affable Baronet had ever bubbled over with geniality in a Blue Room.

'Why, hullo, Mr Bulpitt!' he cried. 'Where did you spring from? I thought you told me that you had gone to live on your houseboat. Get tired of camping out, did you, eh? Not so much of the gypsy in you as you fancied, eh, ha, what? Well, glad you changed your mind and decided to try my poor hospitality. Wasn't aware that I had invited you, but make yourself at home. This is Liberty Hall.'

Mr Bulpitt had a one-track mind.

'Say, look,' he said. 'I don't seem to have any clothes.'

'Gad, yes,' replied Sir Buckstone cheerily. 'That's right, isn't it? You haven't, have you?'

'That butler guy told me you told him I wasn't to have any.'

'That's right, too. My dear old chap, what do you want clothes for? You've gone to bed. Stay there and get a nice rest.'

'Have you got my clothes?'

'Toots has. It was her idea. Now, there's a girl with a brain, my dear Bulpitt. You must be proud that she is your sister. What she felt, you see, was that if you hadn't any clothes, you couldn't be up and about, serving young Vanringham with those papers. Thought it all out herself.'

'But I haven't any papers.'

'Oh, no?'

'I left them at the inn.'

'Oh, yes?'

His host's intonation was so sceptical that Mr Bulpitt bridled.

'Would you doubt my word?' he asked.

'I would,' replied Sir Buckstone.

There seemed to Mr Bulpitt little to be gained from further exploration of this avenue. He turned to another aspect of the situation – one which had been much in his thoughts:

'How long have I got to lie up in this darned room?'

'Till I've sold the house.'

Mr Bulpitt's jaw dropped. He had seen quite a good deal of Walsingford Hall in these last few days and a clear picture of it in all its forbidding hideousness was etched on his mental retina.

'But, gee, that may mean for years! You aren't going to keep me here for years?'

'No worse for you than for the Man in the Iron Mask, my dear chap. However, as a matter of fact,' said Sir Buckstone, relenting, 'I don't expect it will be as long as that. I hope to conclude the negotiations after dinner.'

'Who's buying it?'

'The Princess Dwornitzchek. Von und zu Dwornitzchek, to be absolutely accurate. She's young Vanringham's stepmother. She arrived this evening. That's why Toots felt – and I agreed with her – that you would be better – ha – in cold storage, as it were, than roaming about the house with those papers. No woman likes to see her stepson plastered for breach of promise. It annoys her, takes her mind off buying houses.'

'But I told you I hadn't got any papers.'

'Yes, I remember. You did, didn't you?'

Mr Bulpitt sighed resignedly.

'And when do I eat?' he asked.

'A tray will be sent up to you.'

'Oh, yeah? Raw beef, I suppose, and half-warmed brussels sprouts?'

Sir Buckstone seemed piqued.

'Nothing of the kind. There's a chicken casserole tonight,' he said proudly. 'And dashed good it will be, no doubt. I heard my daughter instructing the cook. She arranges our menus. It was Jane who brought you here, I understand?'

'Yes,' said Mr Bulpitt. 'A sweet girl.'

'One of the best,' agreed Sir Buckstone cordially.

Mr Bulpitt was in sore straits, but he was a man who could forget self when he saw an opportunity of saying a seasonable word on behalf of distressed damsels. He removed a bare arm from under the sheet and pointed his fingers accusingly at his host.

'You're treating that little girl very badly, Lord Abbott.'

Sir Buckstone stared.

'Who, me? I've never treated Jane badly in my life. Apple of my eye, dash it. What do you mean?'

'Sundering two young hearts in springtime.'

'It isn't springtime. Middle of August.'

'It amounts to the same thing,' said Mr Bulpitt firmly. 'Chasing the man she loves with a horsewhip.'

There had been only one man in Sir Buckstone's past whom he had chased with a horsewhip. He gaped incredulously.

'You aren't telling me Jane's gone and fallen in love with this blighter Peake?'

'She loves him devotedly. You know that.'

'I don't know anything of the sort. What you say has come as a stupefying shock to me. And I don't believe it, either. Sensible girl like Jane? Nonsense. She couldn't love Peake. Nobody could love Peake.'

'She does. And let me tell you one thing, Lord Abbott. You may boast of the pride of your ancient name, you may dwell in a marble hall, but there's something that's greater than riches and fame – '

'What are you talking about? Marble? Red brick; and glazed, at that.'

'Yeah, Love that conquers all,' concluded Mr Bulpitt. 'And I'm for her. Get that into your nut. I'm on her side, and when she marries, I intend to – '

He had got thus far when, from the regions below, there proceeded a loud booming noise, and Sir Buckstone started and ceased to listen. No Englishman, whatever the importance of the subject under discussion, will give it his attention when he hears the dinner gong.

'Ha!' cried Sir Buckstone, in much the same manner as the Biblical character who spoke that word among the trumpets, and made for the door more like Jesse Owens than a Baronet.

'Hey, wait!'

'I can't wait.'

'But I'm telling you sump'n.'

'Tell it me later,' said Sir Buckstone. 'Can't wait now. Dinner!'

He disappeared, and Mr Bulpitt was alone with his thoughts once more.

It is impossible for a man of Samuel Bulpitt's astuteness to be alone with his thoughts for long without something happening in the way of plans and schemes. Already, with his razor-like intelligence, he had perceived that, his own clothes having gone, he must somehow contrive to secure others, but it was only now that he saw whence these might be obtained. He might not be universally popular in this house, but he did have one friend at Walsingford Hall, though they had never actually met – Miss Prudence Whittaker, to wit, his exertions on whose behalf had led him into his present trouble. His first move, he decided, must be to get in touch with Miss Whittaker.

He had reached this conclusion, and was debating in his mind the best way of establishing the desired contact, when the door opened and there entered, in the order named, a savoury smell, a large tray and a very small under-housemaid. The smell was floating in front of the tray, and the under-housemaid was attached to the back of it. The procession halted at his bedside.

'Your dinner, sir,' said the midget, unnecessarily, for his inductive sense had already led him to this conclusion.

'Thank you, baby, thank you,' said Mr Bulpitt, releasing all his charm and starting to employ the technique which had made him so beloved throughout America's quick-lunch emporia, which we have seen winning the heart of Mr Attwater's niece at the Goose and Gander. 'What might your name be, girlie?'

'Millicent, sir. And Mr Pollen says he thought you would like beer.'

'Tell Mr Pollen, Millicent, that he hit it in one. Beer is what I wouldn't like anything except. I want lots of beer and Miss Whittaker.'

'Sir?'

'How do I contact Miss Whittaker?'

'She's gorn out, sir,' replied the under-housemaid, charmed by his cordiality.

'What, at dinner-time?'

'She has high tea over at the vicarage Wednesdays. There's a lit'ry society there,' said the under-housemaid, as if she were naming some strange beast. 'Miss Whittaker goes to it Wednesdays and has high tea.'

'Stealing home when?'

'She won't be back before nine. Did you wish to see her, sir?'

'I can't see her. There's a reason. But if you would be a kind little girl and slip her a note – '

'Oh, yes, sir.'

'Atta baby! I'll have it ready for you when you come for the tray.'

It was not immediately that Mr Bulpitt addressed himself to literary composition, for he never allowed anything to come between himself and the fortifying of his inner man. The casserole finished, however, and the beer disposed of, he lost no time in hopping out of bed and going to the writing desk. When the under-housemaid returned, the note was ready for her.

It had not been an easy note to write. Its author, striving for a measured dignity of phrase, had begun by making the mistake of trying to word it in the third person, only to discover an 'I' and a couple of 'me's' insinuating themselves into the third sentence. Switching to the more direct form, he had had happier results, and what was now in the under-housemaid's custody was something which would, in his opinion, drag home the gravy.

It wavered in style between the formal and the chummy, beginning 'Dear Madam' and ending 'So you see what a spot I'm in, ducky,' but it did present the facts. An intelligent girl, reading it, would be left in no doubt that Mr Bulpitt had been deprived of his clothes through the machinations of Sir Buckstone Abbott and his minions and hoped that she would come and discuss the matter with him through the door of his bedroom.

A glance at the clock on the mantelpiece had just told him that the hour was a quarter to nine, when there was a knock on the door and a voice spoke his name in an undertone.

'Mr Bullpott?'

He was out of bed with his lips to the panel in an instant, and a moment later the Pyramus and Thisbe interview had begun.

'Hello?'

'Is that you, Mr Bullpott?'

' —pitt,' corrected Pyramus. 'Miss Whittaker?'

'Yay-ess. I got your note.'

'Can you get the clothes?' asked the practical-minded Mr Bulpitt.

'I will secure them immediatelah. What size?'

This baffled Mr Bulpitt for a moment. In the circumstances, he could scarcely invite the girl to come in and measure him. Then inspiration descended on him.

'Say, look – I mean listen. I'm just around Lord Abbott's build.'

'Sir Buckstone Abbott's?'

'Call him what you like. The point is, we're about the same shape. Go and scoff one of his nibs' reach-me-downs.'

'Sir Buckstone Abbott's?'

'That's right. Still talking about him. Fetch 'em quick and leave them outside on the mat and knock. Get me?'

'Quate.'

'Right,' said Mr Bulpitt, and went back to bed.

Although her voice had been audible through the woodwork, it had, of course, been impossible for Mr Bulpitt to watch the play of expression on the face of his visitor during this conversation. Had he been able to do so, he would have observed that his request that she purloin clothes belonging to Sir Buckstone Abbott had not been well received by Miss Whittaker. Her eyebrows had risen and she had pursed her lips. A well-trained secretary does not rifle her employer's wardrobe, and the suggestion had frankly shocked the girl.

It was for this reason that, leaving the door of the Blue Room, she did not proceed to the Baronet's quarters, but hastened instead to the modest apartment which had been assigned to Tubby Vanringham.

She would have preferred to go elsewhere, for even though she supposed that he was at the dinner table and, so, unlikely to interrupt her search, she disliked the idea of having any association with him, even the somewhat remote one of stealing his clothes. But she had no choice. Mr Bulpitt had specifically stated that in build he resembled Sir Buckstone Abbott, and Tubby was the only other man on the premises who shared this distinction. Colonel Tanner was long and stringy. So was Mr Waugh-Bonner. So was Mr Profitt. And so, oddly enough, was Mr Billing. Only by calling on Tubby's resources could a reasonable fit be secured.

She crept into the room and switched on the light and made her way to the hanging cupboard. Her heart was beating quickly as she plucked a pair of trousers like fruit from the bough, but not so quickly as it was to beat a moment later, when a sudden exclamation from behind her caused her to turn, and she saw their owner standing in the doorway.

Tubby was lightly clad in a towel and a small Union Jack, and he would not have approached even as closely as that to the standards of the well-dressed man, had he not possessed a stronger will than Adrian Peake, and so been able to dominate him when it came to the division of the few wearable objects which Lady Abbott had left behind her after visiting the houseboat *Mignonette*. Adrian had had to make out with a piece of sacking.

For a long instant, Prudence Whittaker stood staring, as terror wrestled with outraged modesty within her. Then, uttering a low, honking cry like that of some refined creature of the wild caught in a trap, she staggered back against the wall.

24

Into the emotions of Tubby Vanringham and Adrian Peake when, returning from their swim, they discovered what had taken place on board the houseboat *Mignonette* during their absence, it is not necessary for the chronicler to go with any wealth of detailed analysis, for he has already indicated how men react to such discoveries. It is enough to say that both had taken it big. Their sense of loss was, indeed, even deeper than that of Mr Bulpitt, for he had at least had a comfortable bed to which to retire while shaping his plans for the future. Only after a search through the saloon had yielded an unopened bottle of whisky had Tubby been able to face with anything approaching a cool, reasoning mind the situation in which he found himself.

It was rather an inferior brand of whisky, for J. B. Attwater, who had supplied it to Mr Bulpitt, specialized in draught ale and did not bother much about the rest of his cellar, but it had bite and authority. It stimulated the thought processes. And it was not long, in consequence, before Tubby remembered that in his bedroom at Walsingford Hall he had left behind him a large and varied wardrobe, and realized that if he was prepared to wait patiently for the psychological moment and did not shrink from a walk across country in bare feet, it would be possible for him to avail himself of this.

There would, he knew, come a time, between the hours of eight and nine, when the residents of the Hall would be at dinner, leaving nobody loitering about the stairs and corridors to observe the entry of two young men, one in a towel and a Union Jack, the other swathed in sacking. From that moment, it may be said that the sun had begun to shine through the clouds for Tubby Vanringham.

For Adrian Peake, who had not had his fair share of the bottle and shrank from the idea of venturing near Walsingford Hall in any kind of costume, it had shone more faintly. Indeed, it was only the horror of the prospect of being left indefinitely on the boat with only a piece of sacking to keep him warm that had finally nerved him to undertake the perilous journey. But in the end he had accompanied Tubby, and was now in retirement in the cupboard in Sir Buckstone's study, awaiting the moment when his leader should return laden with garments. Seated in pitch darkness on a bound volume of the 'Illustrated Country Gentleman's Gazette', he was hoping for the best.

After that first brief exclamation from Tubby and that first sharp scream from his room-mate, there had fallen a silence. Tubby had become anxious about the stability of the Union Jack and was clutching it nervously, and it was Miss Whittaker who eventually opened the conversation. In the struggle between panic and offended modesty, the latter had now gained the upper hand. Lowering the trousers which she had been holding before her like a shield, she drew herself up coldly.

'How dare you come here dressed like that?' she demanded.

In a situation that called above all things for the tactful and conciliatory word, she could scarcely have selected a question less calculated to ease the strain. The injustice of it cut Tubby like a knife. His eyes rolled. His face became a deeper pink. He raised his hands heavenwards in a passionate gesture, to lower them immediately and grab at the Union Jack.

'Well, I'm darned! How dare I come here? I like that. My own room! How dare you come here, is what I want to know. What are you doing in my room?'

'Never mind,' said Prudence Whittaker.

It was another unfortunate remark, and it affected Tubby as powerfully as her previous one. He did not raise his hands, for he had had his lesson, but they twitched, and his eyes revolved as freely as before.

'So that's the attitude you take, is it? After all that has occurred, I come here and find you sauntering coolly about my bedroom as if it belonged to you, and when I ask you civilly what you're doing there, all you reply is – What's that you've got hold of?' he asked, breaking off and eyeing the trousers sharply. He seemed unable to believe his eyes. 'Pants? What are you doing with my pants?'

Even in this supreme moment, Prudence Whittaker could not let this pass.

'Trousers,' she corrected.

'Pants!'

'Don't make such a noise.'

'I will make such a noise. We're going to have a showdown. There's something sinister about this. What are you doing with my pants?'

Prudence Whittaker was beginning to feel the strain. Her tiptilted nose quivered like a rabbit's.

'I – I wanted them,' she said.

'I see.' Tubby's manner became heavily satirical. He sneered unpleasantly. 'Fancy-dress ball, I suppose? You required pants for your costume, eh, and felt that we were such buddies that I wouldn't object if you came and swiped mine? Just strolled in and helped yourself. He won't mind! Of course he won't. I see.'

'I wanted them for someone.'

'Oh, yes? Who did you want them for?'

'Whom,' corrected Miss Whittaker.

'Who,' thundered Tubby.

'Hush!'

'I won't hush. Who did you want them for?'

'Mr Bulpitt.'

'What?'

'He has lost his.'

Once more, she had said the wrong thing. It was impossible for Tubby to register emotion more intensely than he had been doing, but he maintained his previous high level. On the word 'What?' he had quivered as if he had been harpooned, and as he spoke he continued to quiver:

'Bulpitt! You wanted them for Bulpitt? Well, that's the top. That's the pay-off. Don't try to beat that, because you'll never be able to Bulpitt! That's a honey. You introduce this slavering human bloodhound into my life, you incite him to harry and pursue me till I feel like Eliza crossing the ice, and then you calmly sneak my pants to give to him! A little present, with compliments of T. P. Vanringham, eh? A slight testimonial from one of his warmest admirers. Just a trifling something from an old pal to keep among his souvenirs. Of all the – '

He had to pause to master his feelings, and it was as he did so that there flashed upon him an idea so bizarre, so stunning that he choked and could not proceed. He stood there rigid, blinking dazedly and putting two and two together. Then life returned to his paralysed frame and speech to his trembling lips.

'I see it all! It was Bulpitt! '

'I don't know what you mean.'

'You and he are that way. You love the little son of a bachelor.'

'You're quate absurd.'

'You can't get out of it like that. "Quate absurd", forsooth! He's the man. He's the guy. He's the fellow who sent you that jewellery. Is he? Come on, now. This is where we probe that jewellery sequence to the bottom. Is he the bird? Is he? Is he? '

'I refuse to discuss the mattah.'

'You do, do you? '

He turned quickly, and Miss Whittaker uttered a piercing cry.

'Unlock that door! '

'I won't.'

'Mr Vanringham, let me go immediatelah! '

'I'll do nothing of the kind. We're going to sift this – sift it to its foundations. You don't leave here till you have told all. And let me mention that if you persist in this – this – ' Tubby paused. He knew that there was a phrase which exactly expressed what he wished to say, and later he remembered that it was 'recalcitrant attitude', but at the moment he could not think of it. He went back and reconstructed his sentence. 'And let me mention that if you persist in refusing to come clean, I'll poke you in the snoot.'

It was a policy which had suggested itself to him once or twice since this interview had begun, and he had found himself more and more drawn to it. It had worked wonders, he reminded himself, in the case of Mr Bulpitt, and who could say that it would not prove equally effective now? Snoot-poking, moreover, is a thing which grows on a man. Once let him acquire the appetite, and he becomes like the tiger that has tasted blood. Just as such a tiger goes about calling for more blood and refusing to be put off with just-as-good substitutes, so does he yearn for more snoots to poke. He gets the feeling that he wants to do it to everyone he meets, sparing neither age nor sex.

Prudence Whittaker's fortitude was ebbing. Kensington trains its daughters well, sending them out into the world equipped for almost every emergency. But there are limits. It requires a poise which even Kensington cannot inculcate to enable a girl to bear herself composedly when confronted with cave men in locked rooms. Prudence Whittaker had an elementary knowledge of ju-jitsu – she knew the grip required for quelling footpads – but she felt herself helpless against a menace like this.

'Theodore!' she cried, quailing visibly. She had never been personally poked in the snoot, but she had seen it done in the pictures and had always thought that it looked most unpleasant.

Tubby remained the man of chilled steel.

'Less of the "Theodore",' he replied sternly, 'and more facts about this Bulpitt piece of cheese. How long have you known him? Where did you meet him?'

'I have not met him.'

'Tchah!'

'I haven't.'

'Then why did he send you jewellery?'

'He did not send me jewellery.'

'He did too.'

'He did not.'

'So,' said Tubby, 'you persist in your recalcitrant attitude!'

A throbbing silence fell. Tubby's chest was swelling beneath its towel, and he had begun to flex the muscles of his arms. And so plainly did these phenomena, taken in conjunction with the gleam in his eyes and the way he was puffing out his cheeks, indicate that he was working up steam and would shortly be in a position to begin, that Prudence Whittaker cracked under the strain. With a wailing cry, she flung herself on the bed and burst into tears.

The effect on Tubby was immediate. The toughest male becomes as wax in the presence of a crying woman. He stopped puffing out his cheeks and looked at her uncertainly. It was plain that a situation had arisen which cramped his freedom of action.

'That's all very well,' he said weakly.

The sobbing continued. His discomfort increased. And he was fast approaching the point where the melting process would have been complete, when his eye, roving uneasily about the room, fell on the trousers lying on the floor. He went to them, picked them up, put them on, and instantly felt a marked improvement in his morale.

'That's all very well,' he said, more resolutely.

He crossed to the chest of drawers and took out shirt and tie. A few moments later, fully clad, he was his own stern self again.

'That's all very well,' he said, the dominant male once more. 'Just like a girl, thinking she can square anything by crying.'

Words, an observation of some nature, caught his ear through the sobs. He turned sharply.

'What was that?'

It appeared that Miss Whittaker had reproached him for being so unkind, and he took the point up with a forceful briskness which he could never have achieved in a towel and a Union Jack.

'A fellow's got a licence to be unkind when the girl he loves starts cheating on him,' he said austerely. 'I can tell you it pretty near broke me up when I found you were two-timing me that way. Letting another guy send you jewellery. And Bulpitt of all people.'

'He didn't send me jewellery. Nobody sent me jewellery.'

'I was there when the package arrived.'

'There wasn't jewellery in that parcel. It – it was something else.'

'Then why wouldn't you let me see it?'

'Because I didn't want you to.'

'Ha!' said Tubby, with one of those hacking laughs of his.

A far less spirited girl than Prudence Whittaker would have resented having 'Ha!' said to her in such a tone. Add a hacking laugh, and it is not to be wondered at that she ceased to weep and sat up with cold defiance in her eye.

'If you really wish to know,' she said, 'it was a nose thing.'

Ever since three o'clock that afternoon, when, pausing at the second milestone on the Walsingford Road and making a noise as nearly resembling the rough song of the linnet as was within the scope of one who had never been a good bird imitator, he had observed Mr Bulpitt bound from the bushes at the roadside, Tubby Vanringham had been under a severe and continuous mental strain. It was possibly this that now rendered him slow at the uptake. He did not know what a nose thing was, and said so.

Prudence Whittaker's face was pale and drawn. She was revealing a secret which she had hoped to withhold from the world – one, indeed, which she had supposed only wild horses would have had the power to draw from her – and the agony was intense. But she spoke out bravely.

'A thing for changing the shape of the nose.'

'What?'

'I saw an advertisement in a magazine,' she went on in a low, toneless voice. 'Ugly noses of all kinds remedied, it said. Scientific yet simple. Can be worn during sleep. You had to fill up the coupon and send it off with ten shillings, so I filled it up and sent it off. And the thing arrived while we were talking. How could I tell you what it was?' Her voice broke and her eyes started to fill with tears again. 'I thought you would have trusted me.'

The reproach was a keen one, and at another time Tubby would have winced beneath it. But now he was too bewildered to be aware of reproaches.

'But what the heck did you want to change the shape of your nose for?'

She averted her face and picked at the coverlet.

'It turns up at the end,' she whispered, almost inaudibly.

He stared, amazed.

'But I like it turning up at the end.'

She looked at him quickly, incredulously, a new light dawning in her eyes.

'Do you?'

'Of course I do. Gee, whiz! That's what makes it so wonderful.'

'Oh, Theodore!'

'Why, it's great. It's swell. You don't want to touch a nose like that. Leave it be. It's perfect. It's terrific. It's colossal. Do you mean that that was really all there was in that packet?'

He was groping his way to where she sat, stumbling like a blind man. Once again, he was puffing out his cheeks, but in how different a spirit.

'Oh, hell, what a fool I've been!'

'No, you haven't.'

'Yes, I have.'

'It wasn't your fault.'

'Yes it was.'

'No, it wasn't. I should have told you.'

'No, you shouldn't.'

'Yes, I should.'

'No, you shouldn't. I ought to have trusted you. I ought to have known that you would never – Oh, Prue, I've been so miserable.'

Her head was on his shoulder, and he buried his face in her hair. They clung together, and as they clung something flicked at Tubby's mind. He had a sense that there was something he was forgetting, some task which he was leaving undone.

Not kissing her, because he was kissing her.

Not hugging her, because he was hugging her.

Then he remembered. Adrian Peake was still sitting in the cupboard in Sir Buckstone's study, waiting for him to bring his clothes.

He hesitated. Then an arm stole about his neck, and he hesitated no longer. This golden moment must not be marred by thoughts of Adrian Peake. Adrian was all right. Probably perfectly boop-a-doop. Later on would be plenty of time for thinking about Adrian.

'Prue, listen. I'll never say "Yup" again.'

He had said the one thing needed to complete her happiness, removed the one obstacle that stood between them. Greatly as she loved him, she had always winced at the thought of what he was going to reply at the altar, when the clergyman said, 'Wilt thou, Theodore, take this Prudence?' A 'Yup' at such a moment would have jarred her sensitive soul to its foundations. She raised her lips to his. Continue along these lines, she was feeling, and there might quite conceivably come a time when she would even be able to persuade him to eat his boiled eggs from the shell instead of broken up in a glass.

'Nor "mustah". And from now on, when I dig into a plate of cold beef, it'll be with tomarto ketchup on the side.'

A sudden quiver ran through Tubby. The words had started a train of thought. It was as if his stomach had been a Sleeping Beauty and that crack about cold beef the kiss that had wakened it to life. For there was no mistake about it having been wakened to life. It was up and shouting. Until this moment, having been practically pure spirit, he had been able to ignore the frequent complaints which it had been endeavouring to communicate with G.H.Q., but now connexion was established. He continued to fold her in his arms, but it was with a growing feeling that he wished she had been a steak smothered in onions.

She was nestling against him, her eyes closed, a blissful smile on her lips.

'I could sit like this for ever,' she murmured.

'Me, too,' said Tubby, 'if I wasn't so darned hungry. I haven't had a thing since lunch.'

'What?'

'Not a thing. I got back to that houseboat at haff past – harf parst three, and ever since then – '

Prudence Whittaker could be a dreamer, but she knew when to be practical.

'You must be starving!'

A 'Yup' trembled on Tubby's lips. He crushed it down.

'Yay-ess,' he said. 'How's chances for a bite to eat?'

'We'll go and find Pollen. He will get you something.'

And so it came about that Pollen, relaxing in his pantry over a glass of port after serving coffee to the diners above-stairs, found his sacred moment interrupted. He was uprooted and sent to forage. And presently he returned with a groaning tray, and Tubby fell on its contents with gleaming eyes.

And it was while the others were standing watching over him, Prudence Whittaker like a mother, and Pollen as much like a father as could be expected of a butler who has had his after-dinner port drinking cut short, that there suddenly came swelling through the house, reverberating, down back stairs and along stone-flagged passages till it reached the pantry, a noise – a brassy, booming noise so like the Last Trump that Prudence Whittaker and Pollen, after looking at each other for an instant with a wild surmise, hurried from the room to investigate.

Tubby remained where he was. In competition with the knuckle end of a ham, plenty of bread and a pitcher of beer, mysterious noises meant nothing to him.

25

The momentary impression which the butler and Prudence Whittaker had received that what they had heard was the Last Trump was a mistaken one. The noise had come from the foot of the main staircase which connected the hall with the bedrooms, and what had caused it had been the circumstance of Colonel Percival Tanner beating the gong which stood there. And it may be said at once that the verdict of History will be that he was perfectly justified in doing so. The motivating force behind his action had been the discovery of Adrian Peake in the cupboard in his bedroom.

It is one of the inevitable drawbacks to a narrative like this one that the chronicler, in order to follow the fortunes of certain individuals, is compelled to concentrate his attention on them and so to neglect others equally deserving of notice. As a result of this, Colonel Tanner has until now been somewhat thrust into the background. So much so, indeed, that it is possible that the reader may have forgotten his existence, and it may be necessary at this point to refresh his memory by mentioning that he was the gentleman who, on the morning when the story began, was talking to Mr Waugh-Bonner about life in Poona.

He was a man who talked a great deal about life in Poona, and he liked, when possible, to supplement the spoken word with a display of photographic snapshots illustrating conditions in those parts. He held, and rightly, that there is nothing like seeing the thing for driving home a description of a banyan tree and that an anecdote about old Boko Paunceford-Smith of the East Surreys gains in point if the auditor is enabled to see old Boko in his habit as he lived; the same thing applying, of course, to an anecdote about young Buffy Vokes of the Bengal Lancers. And it was because he thought that these photographs would interest the Princess Dwornitz-chek, to whom he had been talking about life in Poona during dinner, that, at the conclusion of the meal, he had gone to his room to fetch his album.

And the first thing he had seen on opening the door of the cupboard in which he kept it was Adrian Peake. Enough to make a retired Indian Army officer beat a dozen gongs.

The fact that Adrian, who had started the evening in one cupboard, was finishing it in another is readily explained. It was not so much that he was fond of cupboards as because, finding himself in this room and hearing footsteps approaching the door, the cupboard had seemed to him the logical place in which to hide.

In supposing that his vigil in Sir Buckstone's study would leave Adrian Peake in a condition capable of being described as boop-a-doop, Tubby had erred. He had not been there long before he began to have an illusion that he had been sitting on the bound volume of the 'Illustrated Country Gentleman's Gazette' since he was a small child. He became a victim to what Mr Bulpitt would have described as onwee, and more and more it began to impress itself upon him that as a force for supplying him with clothes Tubby was not to be relied on, and that if anything constructive was to be done in that direction, he must do it himself.

He had emerged, accordingly, and made for the stairs. Unacquainted though he was with the topography of Walsingford Hall, he was aware that in every country house the bedrooms are on the upper floors and, hastening upstairs, he had chosen at random the first door that presented itself, hoping that it would contain suits and not frocks.

It had not only contained suits, but suits that might have been made to his measure, and the speed with which he inserted himself into one of them would have drawn favourable comment from a quick-change artist. For the first time since his encounter with Tubby on the deck of the houseboat *Mignonette*, there came to him something which might be termed a lightening of the spirit. It would be an exaggeration to describe it as happiness, for the future, he recognized, was still dark and uncertain. But it was unquestionably relief. *V*-shaped depressions might be lowering on the horizon, but at least his nakedness was covered.

It was at this point that he heard the footsteps outside.

Adrian Peake was far from being the type that remains cool and calm in every crisis, but a man who has once taken to hiding in cupboards acquires a certain knack. Where another might have stood congealed, he acted. Another moment and he was inside, trying not to breathe. And he was standing there, festooned in summer suits, when the cupboard door opened. A hand came groping in, apparently reaching for the shelf above his head, but before it could arrive there, it touched his face. Upon which, a voice uttered a sound like a paper bag bursting, and the hand drew back as if it had rested on something red-hot. Adrian received the impression that his visitor was startled.

And such was indeed the case. Colonel Tanner was a man who in his years of service under the English raj had grown accustomed to finding strange objects in his sleeping quarters, accepting without disquietude the tendency of such Indian fauna as Afridis, snakes, scorpions and even tigers to stroll into his tent as if it had been a country club to which they had paid the entrance fee. 'A cobra, eh?' or 'An Afridi, what?' he had said to himself, and had proceeded to deal with each case on its merits.

But retirement had robbed him of this easy nonchalance. After all these peaceful years in the old homeland, this thing came on him as a complete surprise, and in his emotion he jumped back some six feet, finishing by tripping over a footstool and falling into the fireplace.

It was the crash of his body in the fender and the accompanying clatter of fire-irons that brought Adrian the reflection that by swift action on his part an embarrassing interview might be avoided. Whoever had touched his face was plainly fully occupied at the moment in sorting himself out from pokers and tongs, and so in no frame of mind to arrest a sudden dash for safety. He had burst from the cupboard and was through the door and in the passage before the colonel had finished taking coal out of his hair. He turned to the right and came, at the end of the passage, to a door. He opened it, and found himself on stairs. Back stairs, apparently, which were just the sort he wanted. He passed through, closing the door behind him.

Colonel Tanner, having at last extricated himself from the fireplace, brushed the coal dust from his trousers and went down to the hall and started beating the gong. It seemed to his direct soldierly mind the simplest and most effective method at his disposal for rousing the house and informing its occupants that there were burglars on the premises.

The beating of the gong in a country house is so exclusively the prerogative of the butler, and so rigidly confined to the half hour before dinner and the moment when that dinner is ready to be served, that when its note rings out after dinner has been concluded, the natural inference on the part of those who hear it is that the butler must have gone mad. And as a mad butler is a sight which only the most blasé would ignore, it is not surprising that within a few moments of the commencement of Colonel Tanner's performance the hall had become full of interested spectators.

Mr Chinnery and Mr Waugh-Bonner came from the billiard-room. The drawing-room gave of its plenty in the shape of Mrs Folsom, Mrs Shepley, Mr Profitt and Mr Billing, who had been sitting down to a rubber of bridge.

The discovery of the gongster's identity caused the excitement of the company to turn to bewilderment, tinged a little with disappointment. A mad colonel is always well worth looking at, of course, but he can never have quite the same box-office appeal as a mad butler. And then came the damping revelation that even this poor substitute was perfectly sane. In a few crisp words Colonel Tanner made known the causes that had led up to his apparently eccentric action.

The announcement was variously received by those present.

Mrs Shepley, who was a trifle hard of hearing and understood him to say that he had found a bugler in his bedroom cupboard, was frankly puzzled. Mrs Folsom tottered to a chair. Mr Profitt said, 'What ho!' Mr Billing said, 'What price telephoning to the gendarmes?' Mr Waugh-Bonner, with a spirit that did credit to a man of his advancing years, waved his billiard cue menacingly and stated that the only way of dealing with these chaps was to hit them over the head.

It was while he was beginning to tell a rather intricate story about a Malay servant of his who used to steal his cigarettes at Kuala Lumpur that Mr Chinnery struck an unpleasantly jarring note. He gave it as his opinion that Colonel Tanner must have imagined the whole thing.

'Probably a cat.'

'Cats don't hide in cupboards,' said Colonel Tanner.

'Yes, they do,' said Mr Chinnery.

'Well,' said the colonel, shifting his ground like a good military tactician, 'they aren't nearly six feet tall.'

'How do you mean, six feet tall?'

'That was the height this fellow's face was above the ground. I touched it.'

'You thought you did.'

'Damn it, sir, do you think I don't know a burglar when I see one?'

'Couldn't have been a burglar. Too early.'

The rest of the company murmured approval of this view. Burglars are so essentially creatures of the night watches that there seemed to these well-bred people something indecent in the idea that one could have arrived soon after nine o'clock. There are things that are done and things that are not done, even by burglars. They preferred not to think that a British porch climber could have been guilty of so marked an exhibition of bad form.

'Tell us the story in your own words, colonel,' said Mr Billing.

'Omitting no detail, however slight,' added Mr Profitt who had read a good many detective stories.

'But why would a bugler be in your cupboard?' asked Mrs Shepley, still not quite abreast of the state of affairs.

'What were you doing, groping in cupboards, anyway?'

demanded Mr Chinnery, whose manner now rather offensively resembled that of a heckler at a public meeting.

'I wanted to get some photographs I took in India to show to the Princess. I opened the cupboard door and put my hand in – the album was on the shelf – and I touched a human face.'

'What you thought was a human face.'

'Probably a projecting hook,' said Mr Waugh-Bonner.

'Which you mistook for a nose,' said Mr Billing, who was never very bright during the day, but bucked up amazingly after dinner.

Colonel Tanner drew a deep breath.

'No doubt,' he said. 'Well, the next thing that happened was that the projecting hook came bursting out of the cupboard like billy-be-damned and disappeared.'

The sceptical school of thought headed by Mr Chinnery began to lose disciples. This sounded like the real thing.

'You should have stopped him,' said Mr Profitt.

'Possibly,' said Colonel Tanner. 'But at the moment I was lying in the fireplace. The dashed thing gave me such a shock that I jumped back and tripped over something. And when I got up, the man was half-way down the corridor.'

'Where was he going?' asked Mr Chinnery.

'I didn't ask him,' replied Colonel Tanner shortly. 'But if you are interested,' he continued, 'no doubt he will be able to tell you. Look,' he said, pointing.

Down the stairs a small procession was approaching. It was headed by Adrian Peake and Miss Whittaker, the latter holding the former's left arm in a grip which any student of ju-jitsu would have recognized as the one prescribed for the quelling of footpads. Even seen from a distance, it looked both effective and supremely uncomfortable. Miss Whittaker's face was serene and her demeanour calm and ladylike, but Adrian was not looking his best. The constricted position into which his arm was being twisted had caused his features to twist in sympathy. One of his eyes, moreover, was closed and swelling.

The rear of the procession was brought up by Pollen. Followed by the bulging eyes of the spectators, it turned off at the foot of the stairs and passed down the corridor that led to Sir Buckstone's study.

Sir Buckstone had gone to his study at the conclusion of

dinner to discuss with the Princess Dwornitzchek the details of the purchase of Walsingford Hall, and a man as eager as he was to get those details settled was not to be diverted by gongs, however vigorously beaten. The noise had penetrated to where he sat at his desk and had caused him to shoot an inquiring glance at his companion, but neither had made any move in the direction of an investigation. Sir Buckstone had said 'Hullo, hullo, what's all that?' and the Princess had replied that it sounded like somebody cutting up. Upon which, Sir Buckstone, wrongly attributing what was happening to an outbreak of high spirits on the part of Mr Billing or Mr Profitt, had mumbled something about young idiots, and they had returned to their negotiations.

The entry of Miss Whittaker and her charge occurred just as the Princess Dwornitzchek had begun to talk figures, and the interruption at such a moment caused Sir Buckstone to leap to his feet in justifiable wrath. Then, taking in the details, he changed quickly from anger to amazement.

'What on earth?' he exclaimed. 'Pollen, what's all this, hey?'

The butler was wearing a rather apologetic look, as if he were feeling that it would have been more correct to have brought Adrian in on a salver.

'The burglar, Sir Buckstone,' he announced formally.

And Miss Whittaker had opened her lips to add a few words of explanation when two voices spoke simultaneously.

'Good God! It's Peake!'

'Adrian!'

The Princess was advancing like a tigress about to defend its young.

'Adrian! What has been happening? Let him go, immediately!'

The relaxation of Miss Whittaker's grip enabled Adrian to speak. He indicated Pollen with a shaking finger.

'He hit me in the eye!'

'Is this true?'

'Yes, your highness. I came upon the fellow endeavouring to make good his escape.'

'He was running down the back stayahs,' said Miss Whittaker.

'I ventured in the circumstances to strike him with my fist.'

'And I gripped him and made him prisonah,' said Miss Whittaker, completing the evidence.

The Princess Dwornitzchek's teeth came together with a click.

'Oh?' she said. 'Well, you'd both best be looking out for new jobs. . . . Sir Buckstone, you're going to fire these two.'

'Eh?'

'You heard me. They're fired.'

For a moment Sir Buckstone was too stunned for utterance.

'But they have behaved splendidly. Magnificently, dash it. You don't understand, my dear lady. This is a frightful bounder named Peake. A scoundrel of the worst description.'

'Indeed? Well, may I inform you that he is the man whom I am going to marry?'

'What!'

'Yes.'

'Peake is?'

'Yes.'

'You're going to marry Peake?'

She ignored his babblings.

'Are you hurt, Adrian?'

'Yes, Heloise.'

'Come with me and I will bathe your eye.'

'Thank you, Heloise.'

'But before I do,' said the Princess, ceasing to be the angel of mercy and allowing a familiar note of grimness to creep into her voice, 'you will explain how you come to be here, running about back stairs.'

Adrian Peake had rather anticipated that sooner or later some such statement would be required of him, and he was ready for it.

'I came down here to be near you, Heloise. I knew how much I should miss you. I was going to stay at the inn. I went for a stroll by the river, and I happened to meet Tubby. We thought we would like a bathe, as the afternoon was so warm. So we bathed. And when we came out we found that somebody had stolen our clothes. Tubby suggested that we should wait till everybody was at dinner and creep into the Hall and he would get some more from his room. He told me to wait, and I waited, but he didn't come back, so I went to look for some myself. I went into one of the bedrooms, and put on somebody's suit, and then somebody came and found me, and I lost my head and ran away.'

It was not the sort of story likely to be immediately credible to one of the Princess Dwornitzchek's scepticism. She eyed him narrowly.

'Is this true?'

'Yes, Heloise.'

'It sounds most peculiar to me.'

'You can ask Tubby.'

'Where is he?'

'I don't know.'

'Theodore is in the pantry,' said Miss Whittaker, 'eating ham.'

'Theodore?' The Princess, who had started at this helpful remark, spoke coldly. It is not easy to look at a modern business girl as if she were something slimy that has suddenly manifested itself from under a flat stone, but she was contriving to do so. 'And why, may I ask, do you refer to my stepson as Theodore?'

'He is the man I love,' replied Miss Whittaker simply. 'We are engaged to be marrahed.'

The Princess Dwornitzchek drew in a long, hissing breath, then expelled it more slowly. Her eyes were glittering, as many a head waiter in many a restaurant had seen them glitter when something had gone wrong with the service. As Jane had said, she was not fond of humble working girls. The Cinderella story had never been one of her favourites.

'Indeed?' she said. 'How romantic! You're some sort of damned secretary or something, aren't you?'

It was not precisely the way in which Miss Whittaker would have described herself, but she replied equably:

'Quate.'

The Princess Dwornitzchek turned to Sir Buckstone with a sweeping gesture.

'So!' she said.

There are very few men capable of remaining composed and tranquil when a woman is saying 'So!' at them, especially when a sweeping gesture accompanies the word. Napoleon could have done it, and Henry VIII, and probably Genghiz

Khan, but Sir Buckstone was not of their number. He collapsed abruptly into his chair, as if he had been struck by a thunderbolt.

'So this is how you have looked after my stepson! I leave him in your charge while I go away for a few weeks, and I come back and find him engaged to your secretary! With your complete approval, no doubt.' She turned to Pollen. 'Tell my chauffeur to bring the car round immediately. I am returning to London.'

The butler melted away, glad to go, and she resumed the basilisk stare which she had been directing at Sir Buckstone.

'I have changed my mind,' she said. 'I am not buying the house.' A low moan escaped the stricken man. She swung round menacingly on Miss Whittaker. 'And as for you – '

Into Miss Whittaker's mind there floated an expression which her Theodore had used at the conclusion of that little unpleasantness of theirs over the brown-paper parcel. At the time she had thought it vulgar, and had said so. But now it seemed to her the only possible expression for such an emergency as this. She saw that there were occasions when Kensington could do nothing and only the nervous English of Broadway would serve.

'Ah, nerts! ' she said.

'What? '

'Ah, nerts! ' repeated Miss Whittaker, in a quiet, respectful voice.

There is probably no really good reply to this remark, but the Princess Dwornitzchek made one of the worst ones. She struck Miss Whittaker with her jewelled hand. The next moment, she found herself helpless in the grip designed for the discouragement of footpads, and an irresistible force propelled her to the door.

'Let me go! ' she cried.

'Certainly not,' said Miss Whittaker. 'I am taking you to your room, and they-ah you will remain until the car arrives.'

'Adrian! Help me! '

Adrian Peake wavered. Like some knight of old, he had been offered an opportunity of battling for his lady, but eyeing Prudence Whittaker, he hesitated to avail himself of it, though well aware that if he did not, there would be a bitter reckoning later. Miss Whittaker's face was calm, but there was quiet menace in the sidelong glance which she cast at him. It was the glance of a girl who would require only the slightest provocation to kick a fellow on the shin.

'Well, I – er – ah – ' he said.

He followed his betrothed and her escort from the room. The sound of their passing died away along the corridor.

Sir Buckstone rose slowly from his chair. There was a sort of tentative caution in the way he moved his limbs, as if he had been a corpse rising from the tomb. In his eyes, a spectator, had one been present, would have noted a glassiness. He went to the French window and opened it, and stood there, allowing the night breeze to play upon his forehead – a forehead which had seldom been in greater need of cooling. He passed one hand to the top of his skull, as if he feared lest it might split asunder.

'Gor,' he said in a low voice.

Something glimmered in the darkness outside.

'Buck!'

Jane stood there gazing at him, concerned. She had been on the terrace, looking down on the river, and his figure at the lighted window had drawn her. She was feeling forlorn, and she had hoped to find relief in a chat with a parent whose conversation, though seldom touching heights of brilliance, was always comforting. And it seemed that his need of comfort was greater than hers. She thrust aside the thoughts which had been tearing her like barbed things.

'Good gracious, Buck, what's the matter?'

Sir Buckstone moved heavily from the window.

'Oh, hullo, Jane. Come in, my dear.'

He returned to the desk, and Jane slipped into the room like a white shadow.

'What's happened, Buck?'

Sir Buckstone seated himself at the desk. In this heaving earthquake which was disintegrating his world, the padded chair was agreeably solid.

'She isn't going to buy the house. The Princess. She's called it all off and is going back to London.'

'What? But why?'

Sir Buckstone marshalled his thoughts:

'Well, she thought it was my fault that her stepson got engaged to Miss Whittaker. And then she didn't like Pollen blacking Peake's eye.'

'What?'

'She's going to marry the fellow, you see.'

'What?'

Sir Buckstone quivered slightly.

'Don't keep saying "What?" my dear,' he said, with the manner of one keeping a strong grip on himself. 'If you say "What?" just once more, the top of my head will fly off.'

He had turned away to pick up a pencil which it was his intention to break in half – a poor palliative for the agonies he was suffering, but the best he could think of at the moment – and so did not see the sudden light that came into his daughter's face. It was as if a shutter had been opened in a lighted room.

'The Princess is going to marry Adrian?'

A sudden recollection came to Sir Buckstone. He rose and moved round the desk. He regarded her commiseratingly. It still seemed to him almost incredible that any daughter of his should have fallen in love with Adrian Peake, but Mr Bulpitt had made the announcement authoritatively, as one having inside information, so he supposed it must be true.

'I'm sorry. I hope you're not feeling too bad about it, Jane.'

'I could sing. I will, too, if you'll join in the chorus.'

Sir Buckstone gaped.

'Eh? But aren't you in love with this blighter Peake?'

'Who told you that?'

'That blighter Bulpitt.'

'He got the names mixed. I'm in love with the blighter Joe.'

'Joe Vanringham?'

'That's the one.'

'You don't mean it?'

'I certainly do.'

'Jane! I'm delighted.'

'I thought you would be. You like him, don't you?'

'Took to him at once. Capital chap. Splendid fellow. And – er – rich. Not that that matters, of course.'

'It's lucky it doesn't, because he isn't. He hasn't a bean.'

'What?'

'At least, I don't think he has. But, as you say, what does it matter? Love's the thing, Buck. Makes the world go round.'

The world was going round Sir Buckstone with an unpleasant jerky movement.

'But that play of his – '

'Oh, that's all off.'

'Off?'

'I can't stop to explain now. I've got to telephone him.'

'But, dash it – '

'Out of the way, Buck, or I'll trample you in the dust. Oh, Joe, Joe, Joe! For the last time, Buck, will you get back to your basket and stop twining yourself round my feet? ... Thank you. That's better. ... Oh, sorry, Mr Chinnery.'

She rushed from the room, and Mr Chinnery, who had been entering and had received the impact of her weight on his protruding waistcoat, stood for a moment panting like a dog. Then he recovered himself. He had news to impart which made collisions with stampeding girls relatively unimportant.

'Abbott!'

'Well?'

'Abbott, that man Bulpitt is in the house! I've seen him.'

'So have I.'

'But jiminy Christmas!'

Sir Buckstone, who, in the excitement of listening to his daughter's revelations had forgotten to break his pencil, now did so.

'I wish you wouldn't come charging into my study like this, Chinnery,' he said. 'I know Bulpitt is in the house. And it doesn't matter a damn. Not now. That breach-of-promise business is off. They've made it up.'

'They have?'

'Yes.'

'That girl and young Vanringham?'

'Yes.'

'And the Princess hasn't found out that young Vanringham was being sued?'

'No.'

Mr Chinnery subsided into a chair.

'Phew! What a relief! When I saw Bulpitt coming down

those stairs a moment ago, I near swooned. Then everything's fine.'

'Splendid.'

'There's nothing now to stop the Princess buying the house.'

'Nothing. By the way,' said Sir Buckstone, glad at the prospect of having a companion in misfortune, 'she has decided not to.'

'What?'

'Everybody says "What?"' grumbled Sir Buckstone.

Mr Chinnery was heaving like a stage sea.

'She isn't going to buy the house?'

'No.'

'And you won't be getting any money?'

'Not a penny.'

'Then how about my five hundred pounds?'

'Ah,' said Sir Buckstone buoyantly. 'That's what we'd all like to know, wouldn't we?'

In the silence which followed, Lady Abbott entered the room. Behind her, neatly dressed in one of Tubby's suits came Mr Bulpitt.

Sir Buckstone and Mr Chinnery, perhaps naturally in the circumstances, were not in that serene frame of mind which enables a man to be a close observer, but if they had been they would have noted that, since they had seen her last, a subtle change had taken place in Lady Abbott's demeanour. She had lost to quite a perceptible extent that statuesque calm which gave people meeting her for the first time the sensation of being introduced to some national monument. If such an idea had not been so absurd, one would have said that she was excited.

'Sam wants to talk to you, Buck,' she said.

The momentary exhilaration which had come to Sir Buckstone as the result of the shattering of Mr Chinnery's daydreams had already ebbed. He looked at his brother-in-law bleakly. The man was no longer a force for evil, but he did not find himself liking him any the more for that. He resented particularly the disgusting grin which was distorting his face. That anyone should be grinning at a moment when he had failed to sell the home of his ancestors and had been informed by his daughter that she was marrying a man without a bean seemed, to Sir Buckstone, intolerable.

'I don't want to talk to him! ' he cried passionately. 'I don't want to talk to anyone but you! Get him out of here, and get Chinnery out of here, and let's relax! Toots, that damned woman isn't going to buy the house! '

'No, but Sam is.'

'Eh? '

'That's what he wants to talk to you about.'

It was twenty-five years since Lady Abbott had danced – if that word can legitimately be used to describe the languid stirrings of the lower limbs which used to afflict the personnel of the ensembles of musical comedies at the conclusion of a number in the days when she had earned her living on the stage – but she seemed to Sir Buckstone to be dancing now.

'He wants to turn it into a country club.'

'That's my line now, you see, Lord Abbott. Night clubs and country clubs. I took over the holdings of the late Elmer Zagorin.'

'He was a millionaire – '

'Multimillionaire,' corrected Mr Bulpitt, who liked exactness of speech. 'I'll tell you about him and the way he got mixed up with me. Quite a romance. He was the only guy I ever set out to plaster that I didn't plaster, and at the time I first started out to plaster him, he was suffering from onwee. Couldn't seem to get no enjoyment out of his riches. And then I started after him with the papers in connexion with this suit for forty dollars for hair restorer, and it kind of gave him a new grip on things. He didn't have it long, poor stiff, because he croaked suddenly while in the act of laughing his head off at the way he'd fooled me. Heart failure. But he was grateful to me to the last.'

'And when his will came to be read, it was found that he had left everything to Sam.'

'On account I'd done him this kindness of making him get a kick out of things. Well, sir, I took the fifty million dollars and I came over to Europe and started living the life of Riley. And what do you know? First crack out of the box, I found I'd gotten onwee too. I bummed around in the south of France for a while, trying to take an interest. No good. I put in a couple of weeks in Paris. No good again. Onwee. I missed the old zestful life. So when I come to London and hear of this job of plastering young Vanringham, it was like the answer to prayer.'

'Tell him how you got the idea about the house, Sam.'

'I'm coming to that. Just a short while back, this Miss Prudence Whittaker brings me clothes, and after I'd put them on, we got chatting, and she tells me the heart-balm suit is off, on account she's become reconciled to her loved one whom she thought faithless – which he wasn't really; just one of those tiffs – and what she wants is a job for her sweetie, because she has an idea his stepmother is going to cast him off like a soiled glove. And then she tells me that the deal for the house has fallen through, and I say to myself, "Why not?" It would make a sweet country club, Lord Abbott. Just the right distance from London. Plenty of room. Spacious grounds. Picturesque outlook. The boys and girls would come out in their cars in thousands. So, if you're prepared to talk turkey, I'm in the market. I'm planning to put Miss Whittaker in to run it. Got a lot of sense, that girl. Oh, and I almost forgot to mention it, I'm going to settle half a million dollars on that niece of mine the day she marries. I was trying to tell you that up in the bedroom, but you wouldn't wait.'

'I think it's a good idea, don't you, Buck?' said Lady Abbott.

Sir Buckstone made no immediate reply. He was gazing at his brother-in-law, torn with remorse that he should have been so blind to his sterling qualities. What had ever given him the idea that he disliked Samuel Bulpitt, he could not imagine. Samuel Bulpitt, standing there with that delightful smile on his face – the one he had mistaken for a disgusting grin – and scratching his head with the hand which could at will write a cheque for millions seemed to him the ideal man, the sort of chap he had been hoping to meet all his life.

'Well, I'll be damned!' he said, at length.

Nor was the ecstasy of Mr Chinnery greatly inferior to his own. Five hundred pounds might not seem much to one of the ex-Mrs Chinnerys, who took the large view about money, but it meant much to him. All these weary months, he had been thinking of that five hundred pounds as a loving father might have thought of a prodigal son who had gone for ever. And now it was going to return to the fold. He removed his horn-rimmed spectacles and wiped them in a sort of trance.

236

'Gosh!' he murmured.

'Well, I'll be damned!' repeated Sir Buckstone.

'I told you everything would be all right,' said Lady Abbott.

Forty miles away, in his London flat, Joe Vanringham heaved himself out of the chair in which he had been sitting. It seemed to him that a ten-mile walk through the streets might do something to help him pass the leaden hours. He went out and banged the door behind him.

He paused and stood listening. Then he opened the door again and went back.

The telephone was ringing.

MORE ABOUT PENGUINS, PELICANS
AND PUFFINS

For further information about books available from Penguins please write to Dept EP, Penguin Books Ltd, Harmondsworth, Middlesex UB7 0DA.

In the U.S.A.: For a complete list of books available from Penguins in the United States write to Dept DG, Penguin Books, 299 Murray Hill Parkway, East Rutherford, New Jersey 07073.

In Canada: For a complete list of books available from Penguins in Canada write to Penguin Books Canada Limited, 2801 John Street, Markham, Ontario L3R 1B4.

In Australia: For a complete list of books available from Penguins in Australia write to the Marketing Department, Penguin Books Australia Ltd, P.O. Box 257, Ringwood, Victoria 3134.

In New Zealand: For a complete list of books available from Penguins in New Zealand write to the Marketing Department, Penguin Books (N.Z.) Ltd, Private Bag, Takapuna, Auckland 9.

In India: For a complete list of books available from Penguins in India write to Penguin Overseas Ltd, 706 Eros Apartments, 56 Nehru Place, New Delhi 110019.